Roger A. Price is a retired detective inspector who had been in charge of a covert unit, which received national acclaim for its successes in engaging those who openly sold Class A drugs.

Prior to this, he'd been in charge of the C.I.D. at Preston, having first led a dedicated informant unit.

He also worked on murders, drugs squads, and the regional and national crime squads, often in covert roles across the UK, Europe and the Far East, receiving several commendations.

Now writing crime thrillers, he uses his previous professional experiences to add gritty realism.

Visit the author's website at www.rogerapriceauthor.com

By Their Rules

Roger A. Price

By Their Rules

Vanguard Press

VANGUARD PAPERBACK

© Copyright 2013
Roger A. Price

A CIP catalogue record for this title is
available from the British Library.

ISBN 978 1 84386 754 8

Vanguard Press is an imprint of
Pegasus Elliot MacKenzie Publishers Ltd.
www.pegasuspublishers.com

First Published in 2013

Vanguard Press
Sheraton House Castle Park
Cambridge England

Printed & Bound in Great Britain

Dedication

For Monica, John and Barry. I miss you all in equal measures.

Acknowledgments

To my son David for his help and structural advice on the early draft, and his feedback on the latter version. Also, to my friend Chris for his pointers and help on some of the procedural matters. Without either, the book would have been all the poorer.

You can visit my website at *www.rogerapriceauthor.com* for which I thank my friend Ivor for a professional job and his patience in dealing with me.

I welcome any feedback readers are kind enough to give, which can be emailed to me at *bytheirrules@aol.com*

Thanks to Adele, Chris, Martin, other family, and friends for their support and interest, though my biggest thanks goes to my wife Candace for putting up with my daily wittering about all things relating to this book over the last two years.

Finally, many thanks to my publisher, Pegasus Elliot MacKenzie, for all their professional work and guidance, from editorial, production, publication and marketing. The book could not have been in better hands.

Prologue

The look of terror on the man's face was a sight to stretch the imagination. A look few will have seen before, but for those watching, John Burrows knew most would never forget it. He wouldn't.

He saw the man's blank eyes stare back at his tormentor, the faintest glimmer of hope flashed across them, but in an instance faded, as they lost all colour once more.

Transfixed, he watched as the man he knew as Billy, pleaded in his thick Mancunian accent, "Please Boss, I don't know who's telling you this," adding. "I've not spoken to no one."

Blood and sweat combined on Billy's forehead, he blinked as the pink mixture ran onto his cheek in a stream of bloodied teardrops. The fluid oozing from a wound that didn't appear too severe, but for the fact it was now where his severed left ear was stapled to the top of his brow.

John Burrows had to look away for a moment's respite. Billy was only a small man of slight build, but he appeared gaunter than usual, and looked older than his thirty years. Burrows could see the light reflecting off his perspiration covered head, accentuating his baldness, and his complexion, which was turning grey. His breathing now coming in short rasps.

Ropes bound Billy securely to a wooden kitchen chair, which was screwed to the concrete floor with angled hinges of some kind. The room was obviously no kitchen. The only illumination came from a single low-wattage electric lamp overhead. No natural light was apparent, and the wall visible behind Billy was of plain brick, an old warehouse of some kind. Only Billy was clearly visible. His tormentor stood in front of him, in his personal space, at an ever-threatening proximity.

"I'm going to take a leak now," the tormentor said. "And when I come back, I'm going to ask you one more time, one last time, the name of the filth you've been talking to. If you don't tell me, I'm going to start cutting off other bits, until you do."

"No, please no."

The tormentor, who appeared to be in his late thirties, was a colossus of intimidating proportions. He turned and walked away, still holding in his huge, gloved hand, the bloodied staple-gun he'd used on Billy.

John Burrows stayed in the room to witness the one and only glimpse of the tormentor's face. He knew it didn't actually matter that he saw it, but it was vital that everyone else in the room did.

He looked back towards Billy on hearing him shout, "Ok, ok Boss, it was John Burrows, but honestly, he made me talk to him. I was going to tell you, straight up. But in any case, I only fed him shit."

Billy then looked down as if to avoid his tormentor's attention, should he turn back towards him. He appeared to know how shallow his excuse sounded. A dark wet patch visibly spread across his trousers. He sighed, and seemed resigned as to his fate. He appeared feeble. He looked spent.

Burrows turned to watch the remaining people in the room, as they all gasped, whilst viewing the video footage. He hoped it was the last time he'd have to watch those scenes replayed, unless they visited him in his dreams. They hadn't until now, but who knew what the future held?

Billy's admission had gone unanswered, the film continued, showing Billy tied to the chair, alone and unmoving, with his head down, his breathing heavy.

A few minutes later, came the sound of a door bursting open, followed by the sight of several uniformed police officers rushing into the room, and onto the images.

"Don't worry mate, you're safe now," the lead officer said to Billy. "You're safe now," he repeated.

"Thank God," he replied, "but be careful, Shonbo is still here, he just went for a leak."

"Don't worry, this place is now swarming with police, we'll get him if we haven't already."

However, Burrows knew they hadn't caught him, not until days later. How he slipped the police cordon remained unresolved. The loss of forensic evidence caused by the delay in his arrest had been significant. This had always troubled him.

The video ended, and the lights in the room came back on. He heard sighs of relief from the two rows of jurors who'd been watching the grisly show.

His Honour, the Judge, turned to face them. "You have endured an extremely unpleasant few minutes watching that police video evidence, for which the court is grateful to you, and also, for your rapt attention. I feel that before we continue with this case, now may be a suitable time to break for lunch."

And with that, a voice bellowed from the back of the room, "All rise in Her Majesty's Crown Court, and provide your attendance at two-fifteen."

As all who were in attendance slowly made their way out of the room, Burrows kept his gaze on Shonbo Cabilla; the man in the dock. He stood there grinning—as if to himself, rather than anyone else. Prison officers led him, handcuffed, still smiling, down the stairs to the court cells. Several of the jury members glanced at him as they shuffled their way out of court, and back towards the jury room.

Burrows could see that the grinning Cabilla in the dock looked different to the tormentor on the film. He had dyed his hair blonde, grown a black moustache and beard, and was wearing spectacles. The tormentor on the video had been clean-shaven, bald, and with no glasses. But the huge bulk and ethnicity were the same; he couldn't hide that.

Burrows hadn't wanted to remain in the courtroom to hear his name called out by Billy on the video footage, but he knew he was an experienced detective sergeant, and no one in the courtroom knew who he was. He also knew, he wouldn't have shown a reaction to hearing his name; he was confident in his training and expertise, to know how not to react. But he also knew he'd taken a huge risk sidling into the rear of the court in the first place. He couldn't stop his name being bandied about, not that anyone in the courtroom knew what Burrows looked like. He had just wanted to see Cabilla in the dock, and note the jury's reaction to the video. Surprised, at how he'd altered his appearance, Cabilla in the dock and the tormentor on the film, were obviously the same as far as Burrows was concerned. He just hoped the jury saw that too.

Burrows was an informant handler, amongst other skills, and Billy, or Billy the Kid as he knew him, had been the informant, or Covert Human Intelligence Source to give him his official title—CHIS for short—in Cabilla's case. Normally, he used an alias when handling an informant, but that was pointless in Billy's case, as they knew each other well. He had nicked Billy several times in the past, before he'd moved to a different covert role. Normal operating procedure would not have recommended he take the role of lead informant handler in Billy's case, but these had not been normal circumstances; he knew Billy well, and Billy trusted him, a relationship his bosses wanted to exploit for the greater good, anything to bring Cabilla down.

Burrows liked Minshull Street Crown Court for its charm; it was the oldest of the crown courts in Manchester, built in the late 1800s.

Consequently, it was ornate with dark wood panels and hand-carved adornments, relating back to when it had been an Assizes court, used for the quarterly sessions, which had been the forerunner to the modern day crown courts. It retained that charisma from those early days with its décor more than paying respect to Italian gothic architecture—a character which the newer purpose-built crown courts lacked. But he knew it was built in a different age, and was a small building compared to the main Crown Square court building, which was located just over a mile away. He had read up on the Minshull street building's history, the intricacies of design fascinated him when compared to modern architecture.

However, as soon as Burrows walked out of court number one, he felt the confines of the building, and knew he could not hang about without drawing unwanted attention to himself.

Once outside, he turned his mobile telephone back on, and rang his Boss Detective Chief Inspector Frank Briers, who picked up on the third ring.

"Are you out, John?"

"Yes, I didn't stay long, just watched the video, and then the Judge adjourned for lunch."

"Good, I was never that happy with you showing your face in there in the first place," Briers said.

"Is there any news on Billy the Kid?" Burrows asked, more in hope than in expectation.

"Sorry John, we've been searching everywhere but to no avail," Briers said, adding. "As to how he got out of the safe house in the first place? Well, that's a question we'll have to deal with later, and more worryingly, whether he had help. If he did, we've no idea how they knew where to find him. Billy himself didn't even know which town he was being housed in, let alone the address."

"I think he had help getting away all right, if help is the right word—and if it is Cabilla's men who have him—then both he, and the trial are probably sunk," Burrows said.

He felt an uncomfortable pause before Briers spoke again; they agreed to meet for lunch at a nearby bistro café. Burrows cut the connection and headed down Minshull Street, generally towards Piccadilly Gardens and the city centre.

As he headed off on foot to meet his boss, he couldn't help musing over how the trial was progressing, or not, as the case may be. He knew without Billy giving 'live' evidence to validate what appeared on the film, the video evidence on its own was of limited value, and challengeable by Cabilla's defence team.

It had taken him eighteen months to get Shonbo Cabilla to trial, and that was further than any other law enforcement agency had managed. He knew how far Shonbo Cabilla's reach could be, though until now he had prided himself on being a member of the Serious and Organised Crime Agency, the modern day 'untouchables' in his mind. But after Billy the Kid's disappearance, he was no longer so sure. He was getting a bad feeling about things.

Then he felt spots of rain on his face as the Manchester weather closed in.

Chapter One

Twelve Months Later

Shonbo Cabilla sat in the back of the black BMW saloon. Den Mackey, his right hand man, was on the front passenger seat next to the driver, who was hired help. Although, Mackey weighed around eighteen stone and was over six feet tall, Cabilla was slightly taller and larger than he was. He was also a year older at thirty-one. It added to his feeling of superiority over Mackey, he enjoyed that.

They'd been in the car parked up for over an hour, hidden in the shadows on the industrial estate with a view of the entrance to it. Cabilla had to agree to himself that Mackey had picked the venue well. The estate was located off a major urban thoroughfare in north London, adjacent to a large retail park. It was dark, and all the units within it were closed, probably had been for hours. Weak street lighting, sporadically spaced, only partly lit the empty parking area; ideal, he thought.

"You did remember to change the number plates didn't you dickhead?" Mackey asked the driver. Cabilla knew he was asking the question more out of something to say, rather than really expecting that the driver hadn't changed the plates.

"Of course I have, what you take me for?" the driver replied.

Mackey just grunted. Cabilla knew Mackey liked harassing the hired help, especially in front of him. He also knew the registration plates on their car related to the exact same model, age, and colour, as a different BMW parked up on a driveway at its owner's address in east London, whereas the BMW they were in, was stolen from south of the river Thames.

"That wagon is half an hour late and it'll be light in an hour—I'm beginning to wonder if someone is dicking with us," Cabilla said, before adding. "You set this up Den, you vouched for these Turkish bastards, this had better not be a rip?"

Cabilla noticed how Mackey's face abruptly lost some of its swagger, and he started to look pressured.

"Honest Boss, this firm comes highly recommended. Don't forget, our man rang us from Dover, so we know the wagon has cleared customs, there must be a hold up on the way into London," Mackey said.

"Perhaps," he answered, without looking at Mackey. If this was a rip-off, he would make someone pay dearly.

Ten minutes later, Cabilla heard the articulated wagon before he saw it. It drove past their secreted BMW, and onto the deserted industrial estate. The BMW driver was about to start the car engine when Cabilla put his huge hand on the man's shoulder, stopping him.

"Wait until I tell you, idiot; the wagon driver was told to park the wagon in the centre of the car park, and then to walk around the lorry a full circle, as if he's checking it, just to show us everything's all right."

"Sorry Boss, I didn't know," the BMW driver said.

"You weren't supposed to, you're just hired help," Mackey added.

Cabilla watched as a full five minutes passed. The wagon driver seemed motionless in the cab of the vehicle. Engine and lights turned off. Just sat there doing nothing.

"I don't like this; something's wrong, we need to make a call," Cabilla said. He told the BMW driver to start the engine, but keep the lights turned off. Then slowly drive out of the exit from the industrial estate, and down the urban dual carriageway for about half a mile, to where he knew a public telephone box was. He wouldn't risk using his mobile; when they got to a telephone box, he'd get Mackey to ring his contact to see what the hell was going on.

The BMW crawled a few feet within its secluded space, towards the exit road, when Cabilla heard the sound of revving car engines approaching fast from both sides out of the shadows. The first car braked hard to a halt, right in front of them, blocking their forward path, forming a letter T out of both their vehicles. An instant later, a second car approached from their right, from within the industrial estate, braking hard as its driver spun the steering wheel and forced the car into a J turn. It came to a stop next to the BMW, side on. Their car was blocked; a wall behind and to the left, and one car alongside them, with the other across their front.

Cabilla paused for a moment to think, and then shouted at the BMW driver. "Backwards, then ram the bastards."

The BMW only had a few feet of reversing room before the rear wall, but Cabilla hoped it would give them enough momentum for going forward again.

As the BMW driver slammed the gear into reverse, the drivers from both blocking vehicles were out of their cars and leaning over the roofs, pointing towards the BMW.

"Armed police, stay where you are," they shouted in unison.

Cabilla realised it wasn't their fingers they were pointing. He fell back into his seat as his driver started to accelerate, his foot clearly flooring the pedal.

"Ram the bastards, quickly," he shouted.

The BMW shot forward, and smashed into the front blocking car's passenger side with such force, that the officer who'd been leaning over the roof from the drivers' side, was knocked from view by his own car. The impact rocked Cabilla sideways, bashing the side of his head against the grab-handle above his door.

He swore as the BMW forced its way through the gap it had created, and as soon as it was clear onto the exit road, Cabilla told the driver to stop. The rear of the BMW was now facing back towards the two plain police cars. He looked out of the rear window to see officers clambering out of their vehicles. Some were running to help their stricken colleague, and some were turning their attention towards the idling BMW.

"I'll draw their attention, and you open up," Cabilla said to Mackey as he turned forward again. He then opened the car door, and slowly got out. Standing up square, he cautiously walked towards the two police cars, his hands above his head as he shouted, "Don't shoot, I'm unarmed."

Cabilla knew all the attention would be on him; as he walked towards the officers he veered wide to his left—away from the BMW. He'd effectively told Mackey, back in the car, to get out of the BMW quietly, whilst he drew the cops' focus.

He reckoned they were each approximately forty-five degrees to the police vehicles, when he heard Mackey open fire from the passenger side of the BMW. In the split-second that followed, all attention was now drawn from Cabilla towards Mackey—the hitherto unseen assailant now shooting at them with automatic fire.

During that moment, Cabilla drew his own MAC 10 machine pistol, and opened fire on the outmanoeuvred cops.

He knew the MAC 10 was a crude and inaccurate weapon at anything other than close distance, but it was able to 'spray' 1000 rounds a minute on fully automatic—'Spray and Pray'—as it had been nicknamed by various criminal gangs.

Seconds later, it was all over. Eight cops lay dead. It took less time than Cabilla would have expected. Not that he'd killed eight cops before, and all slaughtered without firing a single shot in reply.

The night air was thick with the smell of cordite and muzzle gases, which he watched rise and swirl into the downward gaze from the lamp standards. It left an eerie yellow hue, which Cabilla thought had a Jack the Ripper quality in the absolute silence that followed. Both men stood for a moment; Cabilla looked down on their handiwork as he inhaled the acrid aroma. Mackey moved forward, saying he'd check that no one was moving; nobody was. Cabilla returned to the BMW and Mackey followed, both throwing their weapons into the boot. He knew the barrels would be too hot to put back into their coats.

He then watched Mackey turn around to glance at the lorry, before looking at Cabilla, who understood the unspoken question.

"We haven't got time," Cabilla said. "We'll have to leave the gear. By the time we get the heroin out of the concealments, this place will be full of more filth. But don't worry Den, some fucker is gonna pay for this."

As they both climbed aboard the BMW, Cabilla could see the searching look in the driver's eyes in the rear view mirror. He broke the temporary silence. "We don't like witnesses. Do we Den?"

"No Boss, we don't."

"But they barely got a glimpse of us," the BMW driver said.

"A glimpse is all it takes to put you on trial, as I know to my cost, so shut the fuck up and get us out of here."

***

The undercover officer was in the wagon's driving seat when the shooting started. Though, the entrance to the estate was a hundred metres away, the continuous muzzle flashes were plain to see in the door mirrors. He could clearly see what was happening, and knew it wasn't part of the script. He was unarmed, and knew there was nothing he could realistically do to help. He decided it was plainly unwise to hang around in the wagon, in case the shooting headed his way. So he climbed out of the cab, and ran to a privet-hedge that boarded the tarmac parking area. No sooner had he buried himself into the hedge, the shooting stopped, and was shortly followed by the sound of a car being driven away at speed with tyres screeching. The undercover officer slowly emerged from the hedge, thereafter the full horror of what had happened extended before him. There were bodies and blood

22

everywhere. He rushed over to the men, his finger pushing number 999 on his mobile as he ran.

Arriving, it was all too obvious they appeared beyond help. He wasn't medically trained, but that didn't matter; it wouldn't have been of any use. Then he heard a muffled sound. He looked down towards the noise and by the driver's door of one of the cars—the one that had been rammed from the other side—there was a man about his age, no more than thirty. A fellow officer, lying on his back, clearly badly injured. The man was holding his left side, and blood was coming from numerous wounds to his legs, oozing from him at a steady pace. The current pulsed, at a slowing, rhythmic speed. It throbbed like a heartbeat. As he took in the horror of all that was apparent, mixed with the smell of cordite that caught the back of his throat, he vomited.

The stricken man looked up at him from where he lay. His lips were moving but his voice was weak, the man kept mouthing the same shape repeatedly, but with little audible sound. The undercover officer wiped his mouth, and then lent over the man, turning his head to one side so that his ear was close to the man's face. With what was clearly a huge effort, the weakened officer raised up a little to meet him, and said one word loud enough for him to distinguish, "Cabilla."

And after that ultimate exertion, he fell back onto the tarmac, and the undercover officer could only watch as the blackness consumed him.

Chapter Two

Three Months Later

John Burrows was dozing in his armchair, bathed by shards of afternoon sun as the rays sliced their way through the semi-closed venetian blind covering his front room window. He succumbed, and was drifting into the haze-like state that was neither fully asleep, nor fully awake. Then abrupt banging on his front door brought him around with a jolt. Now that he had the time to take a siesta, he rarely managed it, he thought to himself as he climbed to his feet, and the mists in his head cleared.

Bang, bang, bang. The pounding resounded in rapid time.

Burrows shouted, "Alright, you impatient sod, I'm coming." When he reached the door, he opened it, and continued. "With a knock like that you should apply to join the cops."

"Hello John," the male caller replied as he came into view. "I see retirement hasn't done anything to improve your temperament."

"Well bugger me, if it isn't Frank Briers, the best governor I ever worked for. I didn't think I'd see you again Frank, you must really be in the soft stuff to come and dig me out," he said.

"Firstly, I'll decline your kind offer of sodomy, if it's all the same. Secondly, I'm not in the soft stuff as you put it, and thirdly, you can cut the fake platitudes. I'm here to make you an offer, though I'm not sure I could put up with your cheek again."

Burrows clasped Briers's outstretched hand with both of his, and shook it warmly, having enjoyed their opening banter. He invited Briers inside, and made some tea after Briers turned down the offer of anything stronger. He led the way into the living room, and noticed Briers seemingly take in the room as he entered. It was average size, with a three-piece suite and a 1980's retro glass coffee table he'd bought from a local charity shop. It was mostly clean and tidy though he knew it could do with a wipe down. The sun streaming through the blinds bringing the floating dust into sharp focus, only emphasised the point.

He had not seen Briers since the trial of Shonbo Cabilla at Manchester Crown Court some fifteen months ago. After the disappearance of the witness Billy the Kid, defending counsel had argued that the man in the video was not Shonbo. Without a 'live' witness to give evidence, and identify Cabilla as his attacker, the case was doomed. He knew it was generally a fundamental right in English Law that an accused person had the right to face his or her accuser. Cabilla's barrister had all the ammunition he needed to cast doubt in the jury's minds, and that was all he had to do, job done. Cabilla had been acquitted. These events flooded his mind on seeing his old boss again.

Neither he, nor Briers had returned to court to watch the collapse of the case, and the following day Briers had disappeared from the squad office. Having been seconded down to London on some assignment, as he recalled. Burrows had taken the collapse of the case personally. A thing he knew he should never do, but it was difficult not to, he had put all his energies into the investigation, and it was a hard knock for even a case-hardened veteran like himself to take. It wasn't long afterwards that he decided to retire, or 'put his ticket in' as it was known in police circles. He'd done his thirty years and had had some great times, especially latterly with the Serious and Organised Crime Agency. He'd been with SOCA since its inception in 2006, having transferred directly from the National Crime Squad, which it replaced. It was now being reconstituted into the National Crime Agency. Similar thing, but with a new name, though many said it would be comparable to the old national crime squad, but only time would tell. He didn't have the energy to be part of another political re-shuffle. Having made his decision, he left a month later, and his only regret was that Briers couldn't make his retirement do. They spoke on the phone but Briers had been stuck in London, the job getting in the way again. So after all that, it was nice to see Briers once more.

Pleasantries and small talk out of the way, he asked Briers what his 'offer' entailed.

"I'm not sure where to start, but since I last saw you I have been working on a prototype, working deep inside the Home Office, and answering only to the Home Secretary Bill Dwyers. I've been promoted to detective superintendent for my troubles, and the prototype has been put into place for an operational trial," Briers said.

"Has this prototype got a name?" Burrows asked.

"Yes," Briers replied. "The special projects unit or SPU for short."

"So how does this affect me, a retired detective sergeant?"

"There is only so much I can tell you before you decide to hear more, and you'll have to re-sign the Official Secrets Act to hear what I have to say, but basically John, I'm offering you a job. But a very different job to anything you've done before."

Briers told him that when he had first been seconded to the Home Office, after the collapse of the Manchester trial, it had been swift and with no notice. This was why he had been there one moment, and then gone the next. He explained that he had no choice in the matter, and the speed was for operational security reasons. The pre-arranged cover story being that he was doing some crime-related policy study for the Home Office. But the truth was far more solemn.

"You've got my full attention Frank."

"That'll be a first."

Burrows listened, as Briers went on to explain how the whole concept of the SPU was something the Prime Minister David Greg, and the Home Secretary had been considering in private for some time. Apparently, they were only too aware that a certain number of criminals were becoming too hard to deal with. This was notwithstanding SOCA, MI5, and all the other law enforcement agencies working flat out within the rules, to bring the worst of the worst to justice. But, it was working within those rules that had become the problem. Briers carried on, saying that they'd realised things had only got worse since the Human Rights Act, which as he reminded Burrows, had banned most of the covert measures used by the police. Although, to redress the balance Government had brought out the Regulation of Investigatory Powers Act, which made it lawful again to conduct covert tactics such as surveillance, and planting listening devices, but Parliament had added very strict caveats into the law, which had not been present in the mere guidelines they had used to work by. Briers continued, highlighting the unfairness of the balance, and how the scales of justice were permanently tipped towards the bad guys.

"Frank, I know all this. Will you get to the point mate?"Burrows said, noticing that Briers had not lost his ability to drag a sentence out. Even if he had put on a few pounds, and gained more grey hair since last they'd met.

Appearing undeterred, Briers continued, explaining how the PM had reacted when briefed about the collapse of the Cabilla trial in Manchester. It was after that, that the executive was brought into being, or commissioned, as Briers put it. He explained that the prototype involved an executive committee of three people; the home secretary, the director of public prosecutions and the head of the serious and organised crime agency—which had become the national crime agency. Their job was to sit in committee ad hoc when required, and evaluate the greatest threats to communities by

26

criminals who continue to escape justice. He added, the executive had no chairperson, but all three had to agree on the level of threat, and that 'executive' action should be taken. Then the home secretary would report back to the prime minister for final approval.

"If I understand you correctly Frank, what you're saying is when the bad guys are above the law, then the law goes out the window?"

"That sort of sums it up, though I wouldn't quite put it like that."

Briers then got up out of his chair bringing about a natural break in the briefing as he walked over to the window and put two fingers between the slats of the blind, widening them to provide a view into the garden.

Briers now had his back to Burrows who was still in his armchair. He watched Briers as he walked to the window, his back straight, immaculately turned out in his dark blue light wool suit. The sun was still shining through the blinds and to some degree hid Briers by his own silhouette. It seemed to add to his presence. Burrows broke the silence, "Ok Frank, I'm getting the picture, and I'm comfortable with it, so let's move on."

Briers walked back to the sofa, and opened his briefcase, he sat down as he passed Burrows a piece of paper. Briers explained to him that this was a copy of the official secrets act, to cover the outline he had received so far. Burrows signed it, and handed it back to Briers who continued; going on to explain that over the last few months the executive had been receiving trial intelligence assessments, which amounted to pretend reports, containing pretend threats. They practised their decision-making, and the projected outcomes from those decisions.

"What are the criteria which the executive run by?" Burrows asked.

"The threat has to be one that endangers the interests of the UK, its citizens and community cohesion. Normal investigative techniques within the law, either have failed, or are extremely unlikely to succeed. That established; the executive has to answer yes to two questions."

Briers paused, apparently in thought, before continuing, "First, is it in the public interest to take executive action? And if they all answer yes to that, then they ask themselves, is it against the public interest *not* to take executive action?"

Burrows raised his eyebrows, but before he could speak, Briers continued. "The difference between the two may sound too subtle, or even daft. But the test in that subtlety is to ensure we don't leave more damage behind *after* the action we take, weighed against the harm removed."

"Ok, I've got all that, so what's the upshot? And where do I fit in?"

Before Briers answered, he offered him a second piece of paper, similar to the first but entitled, 'Briefing Part Two'. He took it, read and signed it, and Briers continued.

"Something happened recently, something really bad. The PM went ballistic, and using some hitherto virtually unknown constitutional process, he has activated the executive, and they have considered their first real threat."

Burrows sat up straighter, his interest further heightened. "Don't tell me, I'm guessing they have given it two yesses?"

"They have indeed, or a Yankee, Yankee as it's known as. The PM has already technically agreed the decision, and will ratify it shortly, so the job is now ready to be operationalized. We're looking to recruit a two person team John, and we want you to be the lead operative, what do you say?"

He didn't reply straight away, he was slightly taken aback; he wasn't expecting to be offered an operational role. He could see where the conversation was going, sure enough, but he just assumed they wanted him for some sort of backroom advisory position.

"Who's the target? And what are the objectives?"

"Sorry John," replied Briers, shaking his head, "you've got all you're getting unless you sign up. But if you do join us, it will be on a contract by contract basis, job by job, so to speak."

Briers then gathered his papers together into his case, and stood up to leave.

"When do you need an answer by?" Burrows asked.

"I'm afraid, I can only give you forty-eight hours, things are progressing and becoming time-urgent."

Burrows just nodded, and then showed Briers out of his house and they said their goodbyes. He watched him drive off, and then went to the drinks cabinet in the dining room, grabbed a bottle of Scotch whiskey, and headed back to the lounge. He collapsed into his armchair. He had some serious thinking to do.

Chapter Three

Burrows woke the following morning with a bad headache, and an arid mouth, which made his tongue feel twice its normal size. His bedroom faced west so didn't get the morning sun, which always made getting up that bit harder. He'd bought the cottage ten years ago after his divorce. When they first parted, he decided he needed a new direction, and transferred from Manchester CID to the National Crime Squad at their Lancashire Branch Office. The divorce became Absolute a couple of months later, and whilst he was looking around for a house to buy, he had been approached by Briers for the first time. Frank Briers was a detective inspector who was clearly going places, whilst Burrows was a crusty old career detective sergeant, and proud of it, but both seemed to get along ok.

Because of his array of covert skills, Briers suggested he buy a house in the Home Counties near to London. He said that the 'firm' – their name for the national crime squad – would pay for a rented flat in the north west of England and he could use both addresses depending where in the country he was deployed. It was clear the bosses wanted him to remain as part of the Lancashire Branch Office due to his knowledge and experience of the worst that the North West had to offer – criminal-wise. However, as he was a fully trained undercover officer amongst his many covert skills, and as importantly, not known in London, he knew he would be an excellent asset at the crime squad's disposal. Briers explained to him at the time, being unknown in London wasn't just about not being recognised by the bad guys, but by the good guys as well. Some of the good guys weren't all that good.

So for the last ten years he had divided his time between Manchester and the North West, and London and the South East. But since he had bought his two-bedroomed cottage in Thame in Oxfordshire, he had settled there and it seemed like a good place to retire. He was divorced, and he and Kath had never had children, which had been one of the many causes of friction between them. Both his parents had passed away, and he had as many friends in Oxfordshire as he did in the North West, probably more.

He walked into the bathroom for a drink of water, and took stock of himself in the mirror over the washbasin. Apart from the hung-over look, he was still in pretty good shape, save for a couple of inches around his waist. But at fifty years of age, he guessed he was allowed that. In fact, only a few weeks before he left the cops he had passed a physical and his handgun requalification. Maybe that's why Briers had offered him the job; he had only been gone a few months so was still fairly current and fresh, yet as far as anyone in the job was concerned, he was history. He could see the sense in the cover his situation provided.

By early afternoon, he was still undecided what to do, sure, he fancied the job; sure, he liked the idea of really sticking it to the real bad guys, but did he need all the renewed hassle once again. He decided to go for a walk as it might help him think. He headed down East Street towards Kingsey Road and the outskirts of Thame. As pretty as this historic market town was, he wanted some open spaces to help him ponder.

***

Cabilla looked at the screen on his mobile phone to see who was calling him, even though he was careful who had this particular mobile phone number, he always checked nonetheless. If he didn't know the caller, he didn't answer. He pressed the green icon to accept the call, and put the phone to his ear without speaking.

"It's me," the caller said.

Cabilla recognised the male caller's cockney accent, so he responded. "Go on."

"It's still well hot down here, and they're still digging around; but before you go off on one, there's no problem. Suspecting and knowing are two different things, and they can't prove shit."

"And it better stay that way, all the money I'm paying you," Cabilla said.

"For which I'm truly grateful," the caller replied.

"Just ring me if there are any developments, yeah?"

"Yeah, will do."

And with that, Cabilla ended the call, and turned on his bar stool to face Mackey before speaking. "The Runt says they're still pissing blind."

"That's good news Boss," Mackey answered.

Cabilla drained the remains of his pint glass before adding. "I can't stand that Runt, the moment we don't need him anymore I'm going to 'off' the bastard."

Cabilla stood and laughed, as did Mackey, before following him out of the pub. He squinted as they entered the bright spring Manchester sunshine.

**

Burrows was deep in thought as he crossed over the roundabout and headed up the A4129. Even though it was an A road, it was narrow with no footpaths so he decided to get off it before he got himself knocked down. To his right as he headed out of town was a thick scrubland with trees next to open fields. It reminded him of a landscape painting by Constable he had once seen. An opening from the road led between the two, so he opted for it. Walking away from the road with trees to his right, and open fields to his left. It hadn't rained for some time and the ground was firm underfoot.

All of a sudden, he heard a woman scream from deep within the woodland. He froze on the spot and listened as intently as he could, closing his eyes to add to his auditory abilities. Seconds passed, and then he heard muffled noises. He headed into the bush towards them when after only a few metres; the sound of an enraged male voice brought him to a standstill again. He listened, and heard the man speak.

"Right bitch, if you make another noise I'm gonna break your neck, do you understand?"

He then heard a muffled "Yes," spoken in reply.

It was a woman's voice, and it sounded as if her mouth was bound or covered.

"You have to understand that I can do what I want to you, I got off the attempted rape charge, so I can do what I like, and no one's gonna believe a word you say. But you gotta pay for going to the cops in the first place, so I reckon if you're real nice to me with that big mouth of yours then we'll be quits," the male voice said.

Burrows had heard enough, but just as he started to run towards the voices, he heard the man screech in pain followed by the sound of branches rustling and heavy footfalls. As he continued towards the noise, he saw the flash of white clothing heading the other way through the trees to his right, heading towards the road. It was clearly a woman. And it was clear she hadn't seen him.

He carried on, and after a few more metres, broke through into a small clearing measuring only three metre square at most. He slid to a halt in front of a man in his thirties, who was stooped over himself, holding his left

31

hand. Blood was pumping through his right fingers as he held the damaged hand.

"Who the fuck are you?" The man asked, looking at Burrows with a surprised expression.

"Never mind about who I am pal, what the hell do you think you were doing?"

"None of your business, just a quarrel with my girlfriend, so why don't you mind your own, and fuck off back up north or wherever you and your dumb accent are from."

Burrows stood up square; his legs shoulder width apart, one foot slightly behind the other to give him balance. He kept his gaze fixed on the other man's eyes, not flinching for a second. He lent slightly forward.

"I'm not going to debate this with you," he said. "But you've got to understand, you're coming with me."

The man then spoke with a slight hint of hesitation in his voice. "Who do you think you are? Some kind of cop or something?"

"I used to be, but that doesn't matter, I'm making a citizen's arrest."

"Oh, so you used to be a cop did you northern boy? You were obviously shit at it."

As the man spoke, he pulled an object from his coat pocket, and brandished it towards Burrows in his out stretched arm.

Burrows knew he had to concentrate on keeping eye contact with the man. He ignored the powerful urge to look at the outstretched arm in front of him. Knowing that any slight deviation of his attention would be all the man needed to gain an advantage, and initiate an attack. He relied instead on his peripheral vision. A skill honed after years of surveillance; the art of seeing something but without directly looking at it. He could walk past a target in the street, never turning his head towards them, but still be able to describe everything about them. Peripheral observations were extremely tiring to maintain for long, but he could plainly see the knife in the man's right hand. Black handled with a narrow six-inch blade sharpened on one side. The sharp side was on top as the man held it. His mind was racing, evaluating the threat. This was no professional knife man, but dangerous nonetheless. A professional would attack with an upward lunging motion. Morons like this would usually attack with a downward stroke. His initial defence would be similar either way, but a downward attack would be easier to deal with.

"Look, this isn't worth this. Put the knife down," he said.

But as the words left his mouth he saw the man's eyes widen slightly just before, he lunged at him, raising the knife above his own head, and then he started to swing it down towards Burrows.

The split second warning of attack he had perceived in the man's eyes was all the head start he needed. He stepped forward towards the danger, which could only serve to confuse his assailant. As he did this, he threw his own arms up in the air, and crossed them mid-forearms. This gave him a raised V shape between his hands, and he aimed the V at the man's outstretched arm as it headed towards him. The knife was already on too high a trajectory thanks to him making forward ground at the point of attack. The armed forearm of the man crashed into the V of his open crossed forearms with spectacular result. Though the attacker managed to hang onto the knife handle, he looked momentarily stunned by the pain that Burrows knew would now be shooting up and down his right arm.

Burrows kept his forward momentum, grabbing the man's right wrist with his left hand, and putting his right hand across the man's hand as it remained clenched around the weapon's handle. His right fingers now took a firm hold on the assailant's right little finger, and with as much force as he could muster, he pulled the little finger backwards effectively peeling the man's hand from the knife. As he pulled, the knife fell to ground, and he kicked it into the undergrowth. He felt the little finger break the moment after the man dropped the knife.

He was now stood behind the man, his right hand still squeezing the broken finger, whilst his left hand had a firm hold of the man's triceps, keeping the assailant's right arm straight and under pressure. He then kicked the man's legs from under him and put him on the ground face down. He continued the pressure on the man's right hand in a twisting motion until he felt the wrist bone snap. He then let go and stood back.

He hadn't meant to break the man's wrist, but he hadn't wanted to let go of his only tactical advantage until he was certain the man was compliant, and posed no further threat. Once he'd let go, he knew his only hold over the man would be a psychological one.

"Oops," he had said, unwittingly, as he felt the bone fracture.

The man screamed in pain before gathering his injured arm into himself. He sat up and cradled his hand.

"Oops. Fucking oops," the man said. He paused and breathed hard before continuing. "You're no fucking ex-cop. Cops don't do shit like this. Look man, whoever you are, just leave me alone."

Burrows could see the sweat on the man's forehead and watched his complexion turn sallow. He guessed the man was in shock. Not enough to kill him, he was sure of that, but in shock nonetheless. He, on the other hand was buzzing with the adrenalin rush that comes after combat. His hands were shaking slightly, so he put them in his pockets to hide them. He didn't want the man to see them, and misread the situation.

But now he faced a dilemma; his use of force had probably been justified, and lawful, given the threat from a knife attack. But did he want to put it to the test by bringing the man in. He needed to ask the man some questions, firstly, where did he come from. He hoped he wasn't local.

Five minutes later, he had all the information he needed. The man called himself 'Zingo'. He came from Watford northwest of London, and he'd kidnapped the girl Burrows saw running away, in retribution for reporting an earlier attack. The man had tried to rape her, got arrested, been put on trial and was acquitted; she apparently hadn't gone to the police quick enough, and without DNA or other supporting evidence, it had been her word against Zingo's. He'd also paid a mate to give evidence, saying he'd seen Zingo and the girl on the night of the attack together as an item and all 'lovey-dovey'. It had been enough to cast doubt in the jury's mind. But obviously not satisfied with defeating justice, Zingo had wanted payback. He really was a piece of work.

By the time the five minutes was over Zingo was on his feet, and though in no position to fight, he appeared to be getting his confidence back. Burrows realised that after Zingo had blurted out the answers to his questions, an uneasy calm had prevailed; time was growing since the attack, and during which he hadn't done any more harm to Zingo. If he was going to do worst, Zingo probably thought he'd have already dished it out.

"You're full of shite, you ain't gonna do no more, I can see it in your eyes. Defending yourself, is one thing with all your fancy dancing; but starting it? No, I don't think so," he continued, with an unearthly grin on his face. "I'm off now, but when my hand's better I'm gonna find you, and hurt you. But before I do, I'm gonna hurt another bitch, any bitch, and I'll do it just because of you."

Burrows came to a decision. And he thought that Zingo had probably just made the biggest mistake of his life. By the time Burrows finished with Zingo, he wasn't able to attack another women, not now, or ever again. Burrows hadn't killed him, just rearranged him for the better. In the public interest, he'd thought to himself. He also realised it would have been against the public interest *not* to have rearranged Zingo's anatomy. He walked away towards home and used the first telephone box he passed to call for an ambulance, anonymously. As he continued, he had expected to feel bad about himself; he knew he had just crossed a line. But he didn't, he actually felt elated. He had spent a lifetime working with the heavy weights of morality around his neck, whilst the bad guys laughed and spat in his face, sometimes literally. A few months earlier, he'd have locked Zingo up only to watch him get off with a non-custodial sentence at best, acquitted again at worst. Free to carry out whatever retribution his twisted logic demanded. But not this time. Perhaps sometimes the ends do justify the means. This had been a sort of 'Yankee, Yankee' he told himself.

Chapter Four

The Runt eventually approached the table where the big oaf was waiting. He knew Cabilla didn't like meeting him face-to-face, not just, because they may be seen together, but he knew what Cabilla really thought of him. Cabilla had been sat with his pint at the small round wrought iron table on the front of the pub for about twenty minutes. Slumped forward, his huge forearms covered most of the table. It was a quiet pub in a sleepy suburb thirty miles north of London's M25 motorway, which is why the Runt had suggested it. His shadow cast across the table as he joined Cabilla and sat down.

"You're late," Cabilla said.

"I'm not; I've been here for an hour."

Cabilla looked about to admonish him, but before he could, the Runt continued. "I came early to make sure this place wasn't being staked out. I then took up a covert position and watched you arrive to make sure you hadn't been followed here, and when I was sure it was safe to approach, I did. You're got to start trusting me; I know what I'm doing."

"Ok," Cabilla replied, adding, "look I've been up north out the way like you suggested, for three months now, but I've got to get back to London to continue my business. I lost a lot of money on that last job—100 grand to be fucking precise—and I need to get things sorted. I want your guarantee I'm not going to get lifted the second I hit Soho?"

He'd tried to explain the situation on the phone to Cabilla, but a mixture of not being able to talk too freely, and the fact that Cabilla was as thick as he was brutal had made it difficult. That was why he had insisted on a face-to-face meeting. Notwithstanding that, such a meet came with its own risks. He had also demanded that they meet outside the pub where they would be surrounded by ambient noise from other tables and passing traffic, making it virtually impossible to be eavesdropped on. He knew he was taking a huge risk meeting Cabilla, but even if he was seen – which he thought impossible after his counter-surveillance moves – he could claim he was trying to recruit Cabilla as a source, or 'snout' as he preferred to think of him, not least because of his huge nose.

He went on to explain that the undercover side to any investigation is kept totally separate to the evidence gathering side. The main reason being to protect the sources of information; be they physical as with a snout or a surveillance team, or technical as with eavesdropping equipment. Sometimes information gathered covertly was actually used in evidence, but the preferred option was to use it as intelligence only.

"So when that dying pig – no offence – blurted out my name to the lorry driver, what happened to that info?" Cabilla said, before adding. "And what the fuck happened to the lorry driver?"

"I don't know how they got the info; either the lorry driver is a snout, or they had some recording equipment somewhere, possibly on the dying cop," the Runt replied.

"The lorry driver is no grass. Mackey met him personally and checked him out, so I know he's OK. Mackey can smell 'em a mile away."

"Well, it must have been the other way then," the Runt said, before continuing, "As for where he is now? I've no idea; he probably fucked off back to Turkey as quick as he could after the show you put on."

"Anyway fuck all this, what's happened to the info with my name on it?" Cabilla asked again.

"Well firstly, if SOCA or the National Crime Agency had you as their original target I think you'd have known about it by now, so the covert operation had probably been focused on the Turkish end," the Runt answered, paused and added."They probably couldn't believe their luck when you showed up on the plot. Anyway, the info with your name on it was passed to our office, and it was my job to make sure it was disseminated to the Senior Investigating Officer running the murder enquiry side of things. Because of the ultra-sensitivity of the info, it was passed verbally to me from outside the Met, no paper trail."

"So the trail came to you, and then stopped with you?" Cabilla asked.

"You've got it in one, no one in the Met knows about it. Sure, you're a suspect, but only because you're one of only a handful of people who fit the profile of someone capable of doing it. A complete 'fishing expedition', no actual intelligence or evidence points to you. As far as the murder enquiry team are aware anyway," explained the Runt.

He could see Cabilla was starting to feel better, but then his face darkened again.

"Well if someone has recorded that dying pig saying my name, then won't someone want to know why the info has not been acted on? You know once it was given to you," Cabilla asked.

The Runt couldn't answer that. He was slightly taken aback by Cabilla asking it. A more informed question than he would have expected. So he just said, that eventually that would happen, as he couldn't suppress it forever, but if they came for him, they still had no evidence, so he would walk away without a charge.

Cabilla looked calmer again, appeared placated by everything he had told him. Cabilla said ten grand would appear in his bank account the following day, and to keep him informed of any developments. They parted company and went their separate ways.

On the journey back to London, the Runt was happy he had pacified Cabilla. But he couldn't work it all out. If the naming of Cabilla had come by way of a recording device at the scene, be it hidden somewhere, or on one of the dead cops, he couldn't understand why that hadn't been put into the 'evidence chain'. It was far better to use it openly as evidence, due to the serious nature of the offences, than to keep it under wraps as intelligence. His conclusion being, it could only have come from the lorry driver. This, in his mind meant he must be someone's snout. But whose? And why hadn't they followed up on their initial report?

It was generally an unbroken rule that any information passed by an authorised informant— or CHIS—was only ever used as intelligence. This was to protect the identity of the informant as the source of the information, and not to put off future would-be CHIS's from coming forward.

However, this was a multiple cop killing, and if the senior investigating officer had any inkling that the information had come from a 'live' source, rather than a technical one, he would be bringing a lot of pressure to try to get the informant in the witness box. That's what really bothered him. He knew he could only suppress the information for so long, before the author of the intelligence report that contained Cabilla's name would start asking questions. And when the senior investigating officer finally became aware of it, it could be very serious for Cabilla, and him. He had to make sure that didn't happen. He had to find out who the lorry driver really was.

***

Cabilla watched the Runt walk away before he went to his car and drove off in the opposite direction. The Runt was dressed in his usual scruffy casual clothes with a shirt that was too big for him, accentuating his scrawny neck. Cabilla knew he was about thirty years of age, but looked nearer forty. He despised having to use him. He drove back onto the motorway and settled into his journey north. He was beginning to wonder whether after the next job was done, if he shouldn't disappear properly. Maybe head back to The Congo. But then he bethought himself. That wasn't really such a good idea, not even in the short term. Easy to forget the past, but foolish to do so, he told himself. His mind wandered over the conversations he'd had with the Runt. Irrespective of what he'd said to him about Mackey's adeptness at smelling out potential grasses, he needed to know more. He rang Mackey, and arranged to meet him in three hours or sooner if he made good progress back to Manchester.

He had made good time, and when he walked into the pub Mackey had a pint at the bar waiting for him.

"I'm telling you Boss, the guy's sound. He was just a driver anyway. He didn't know who he was really working for, or who he was collecting from," Mackey said to Cabilla as they both sat down in the corner of the pub.

They used the same small old-world pub on a side street off Deansgate—one of the main streets in the centre of Manchester. Full of dark alcoves, discreet lighting and plenty of dark wood everywhere. It was an old Victorian style pub that had yet to yield itself into a modern wine bar. Cabilla picked it because the same people seemed to come in day-after-day. Strangers were easier to spot. It took nearly a month before eyebrows stayed down when they walked in. Now no one seemed to notice them. It was never too busy either, another plus.

Cabilla made Mackey account for his enquiries into the driver. He explained how he'd been recommended by someone that they and the Turks knew and trusted well. Cabilla was happy with the credentials of the middleman, but as he explained to Mackey, if the driver had gone over to the other side, how would anyone know?

"Fair point Boss, but the Turks said the guy had done several runs for them prior to ours with no problems," Mackey said.

"Ok, so he's not a cop, but it doesn't mean he's not a stinking rotten grass," Cabilla continued, "and where is he now?"

"I don't know, and neither do the Turks."

"Well, I want him found and spoken to, to satisfy myself, and I want you to do it Den. And I don't want you speaking to the Runt about this either. I don't like that shit knowing everything we do, so start with the Turks and work backwards. Ok?"

"Sure thing Boss, I'll find him."

**

The Runt arrived back at his office mid-afternoon after his lunchtime meeting with Cabilla. He walked past his boss's open office door, heading for his own desk. He noticed his boss was in, with his head down, looking deep in thought. The Runt thought he had slipped by unnoticed.

"I can see you sneaking back in. In here now."

The Runt caught his breath for a second. What if he had been seen meeting Cabilla? He had his cover story ready; he just didn't want to put it to the test. He turned around, and walked into the boss's office, trying his best to look calm, and making a conscious effort to slow his breathing down, and thereby reduce his heart rate.

The DI looked hot and troubled the Runt thought, but then again he always looked sweaty, probably due to his excessive weight. He seemed clammy whatever the weather. But never more so, than when he was under pressure. He could see the boss in his chair, pivoted on its back legs rather than sat square, leaning on his desk. A good sign, he thought. He had learnt to recognise that one pose meant his boss was calm, and the other meant he was not. He relaxed as he sat down on the other side of the desk.

"Listen, I don't mind you being out of touch if you come back in with something. Have you come back with something?" The DI asked.

"Sorry Boss, I've been trying to recruit a new source but got the knock back," the Runt lied.

"Never mind recruiting new sources, we need to put some pressure on the CHISs we already have. Have you any idea how much burden I'm under from the Murder Investigation Team, to come up with some intelligence on the multiple cop killing job?"

The Runt didn't answer. He knew the question was rhetorical. At least he knew his meeting with Cabilla had gone unnoticed, and that told him no one had followed Cabilla, and if no one was following Cabilla, then no one was 'looking at him'. Cabilla was not being actively investigated. But how long it would remain like that, he wasn't sure. He pushed the thought from his head.

Chapter Five

Burrows arrived home after his interesting wander through the lanes, and although he was certain Zingo wouldn't be giving him any more problems—he'd made it quite clear what round two would involve if there was ever the need—he still took precautions. He showered and changed, and then put the clothes he'd been wearing in a bag with his old trainers, took them to the nearest council tip, and threw them into the non-recyclable household waste skip.

It was early evening when he returned home and he decided to ring Briers before he ate. He rang the mobile telephone number that Briers had left after his visit, and Briers picked up on the third ring.

"Hi, Frank it's me," Burrows said, before continuing, "I'm ringing a day early I know, but I thought you'd like to know I'm ready for the third part of the briefing."

"That's excellent news," said Briers, sounding genuinely pleased, though Burrows thought he heard a hint of relief in his voice as well.

"What decided it for you?"

"Nothing much Frank, I just tripped over a pile of dung whilst out for a walk. I'll tell you about it when I see you."

"Well, I'm really glad you're in John, and thanks for letting me know early. You won't believe how fast things are moving down here; in fact can you come to see me tomorrow, at say, twelve noon?"

"Sure, but where do I come to? Whitehall?"

"I can't tell you over the phone, but do you remember the offices the national crime squad and SOCA used to have in Pimlico, Central London?"

"Sure, I remember."

"Well, I'll see you at the reception there, at noon."

Burrows acknowledged and hung up.

He arrived in Pimlico early the following morning, and went to find a café until nearer midday. He sat on a busy side street wondering what the future held as he sipped his espresso. He watched the constant stream of commuters sidle past, each inside their own world unaware of anyone else's,

41

and especially oblivious to Burrows and his thoughts, he knew one thing though; it felt good to be operational again. It felt good to be of value.

Overnight, he'd rationalised that what he'd done to Zingo was brutal, but deserved. After all, he was a rapist, and he had attacked him with a knife. And if that wasn't enough, he had made it plain he had no intention of stopping his monstrous assaults on women—or whoever else got in his way—and the next person he attacked with a knife might not come out of it as fortunately as he had.

Burrows had spent thirty years working as a policeman in an eclectic array of specialisms, and all of that time he'd had to play by the rules. He'd always had to do the right thing within the law, whilst the law-breakers just did as they pleased.

In truth, he had found retirement frustrating, not that he had given it long, he knew, but he was too young to retire from purposeful work. What had happened in Thame the other day had released Burrows from his thirty-year straitjacket. And it felt liberating.

He finished his coffee and found his way to the old national crime squad headquarters. He was buzzed in after announcing himself via the intercom on the plain featureless door. On arrival at the reception, a tall slim man met him; he was in his thirties dressed in a smart lounge suit.

"Follow me John," he said, and then set off towards the entrance before Burrows could answer.

Burrows was led to an idling Range Rover waiting at the kerb. He hadn't noticed it there on his way in. The windows were blacked out so he couldn't see inside. Mr Lounge suit opened the rear door for him to get in, which he did. Lounge suit got into the front passenger seat, and it was clear that neither lounge suit, nor the driver, were in the mood for conversation. So he didn't try. Ten minutes later, he was led from an underground car park to a subterranean floor where he was told to wait outside a steel door. His escorts then left.

After a few minutes, the steel door was opened from within, and Frank Briers greeted him.

"Hi John, sorry for all the subterfuge, but we had to ensure you weren't followed to Pimlico, operational security and all that," he explained.

"No worries Frank."

Burrows knew about operational security or 'Op-sec' as it was called, and appreciated the need for it. He entered the room, and could see it had few features. In the centre was a large round table with wooden upholstered chairs around it. Seated at the table was a woman he hadn't seen before, he was sure of that. She was athletic-looking, tall, in her forties and attractive with it. Her brown hair cut into a bob. She smiled at him as he entered the room, a salutation he eagerly returned.

"I'll formerly introduce you to Jane, in a moment John," Briers said. He turned away from Burrows to face the coffee table in the corner before he continued. "But first let me introduce the Home Secretary, the Right Honourable Bill Dwyers MP."

Burrows jolted around in surprise, to face Dwyers, feeling more than a little embarrassed.

"Sorry sir, I didn't see you over there," Burrows said.

"Don't worry about it John, Jane is far better looking than I am, but please grab yourself a coffee and take a seat; we have a lot to get through."

Burrows did as he was asked, and when he sat down Dwyers continued."Firstly, my thanks to both of you for taking up Frank's offer. Shortly he will give you an operational briefing and I'm afraid you will only have a couple of days to prepare yourselves before we will need you both in the field. From now on, it will be exceptional if we meet again, for security reasons as I'm sure you will understand."

Both Burrows and Jane nodded.

"I realise that you do not know each other, but with your varied skill bases I am told that you will complement each other excellently," Dwyers continued. "This is the first live operation that the SPU has undertaken, as you are no doubt aware. I just want you both to know that the instructions you are to receive have not been compiled lightly, and a great deal of thought and soul-searching has gone into the decision making process."

More nods.

"At the risk at starting to sound like the politician that I am, I'm going to finish now, and hand you over to Frank, who will no doubt answer any questions you have. Thank you."

Without pause, Dwyers spun round on his feet and headed for the door.

Briers then approached the table and sat down between Burrows and Lee.

"Jane, this is John Burrows, retired detective sergeant of thirty years' standing. He's only recently retired, so shouldn't be too rusty. He's served in a variety of covert roles including Level 1 undercover ops. Firearms trained, surveillance trained etc. Though I want you two to work closely together, John will be the lead operative. His designated call sign is 'Alpha'. I am 'Zulu', and you Jane, are 'Bravo.'"He continued before he was interrupted. "John, Jane Lee is a seasoned spook of nearly twenty years' experience.

Though most of her work has been with MI5 she has been on several overseas secondments with 'six' in a variety of operational and undercover roles in the field. She is certainly no Intel desk-jockey."

"Are you still with Five?" Burrows asked Lee.

"Like you John, I recently left the service," Lee replied, without further explanation.

Burrows took the hint and didn't press her further.

"Suffice to say, you are both off the books, no longer work for HMG and don't appear on anyone's HR systems irrespective of their access levels," Briers said.

Briers then gave both of them a further document under the Official Secrets Act to sign, and a 'Need to Know' policy, which listed the only people who were briefed, and with whom they could speak to. As Burrows expected, the list of names was the Executive, the PM, Briers and themselves only.

Briers said he would now give them their operation briefing, and instructions. Adding, that they would only have two days to get to know each other, and collect their kit before getting started.

Chapter Six

Burrows listened intently as Briers brought them up to date on the mornings' happenings. How the executive of the Special Projects Unit had met only an hour earlier in this very room. That the executive consisting of— the Home Secretary Bill Dwyers together with George Reed, the Director General of the National Crime agency, and Susan Jones the DPP—had all been present when the PM David Grey had addressed them for the very first time.

How the PM had sought confirmation that, having assessed their first ever threat for real, they were all agreed. Briers explained this was the reason why the table they were sat at, was round in shape, to emphasise that each member of the executive had an equal voice. There was to be no chairperson.

Briers further said that the PM had backed the executive's decision, and agreed on the operational response. In future, he would only meet the executive in order to agree or refuse a proposal. He had apparently said that such decisions were too important to be misheard in a phone call.

Briers paused for breath and took a sip of his coffee before continuing."The Executive have been evaluating this individual, and his close associates for some time, but before I bring you right up to date, I want you both to read his history."

He then gave each person an 'Eyes Only' marked document binder with the words 'Top Secret' stamped on its header.

Burrows picked up his bundle and started to read the file as Briers left the room. Even though the documents within the binder were all marked 'Top Secret' he noticed that the papers had been redacted, and the subject's name omitted or blanked out. He glanced at Lee but she appeared already engrossed in her copy.

Burrows read that their subject had been born in the Belgian Congo, which was now the Democratic Republic of the Congo or DRC, in Africa. Not that democracy was overtly evident there. It always amused Burrows at the number of countries around the world that misused the word 'Democratic' within their respective titles. Nevertheless, the DRC government, apparently, was trying to sort out the corruption and tribal conflicts that had blighted the region over the last twenty years. He read on. The capital of the North Kivu Province of the Congo was Goma, which is near to the Rwandan border. Rwanda itself had seen some brutal in-fighting but was now relatively calm. Once peace had broken out, many of the tribal fighters crossed into the Congo. One of the most brutal of the tribal militias apparently was the Hutu. A lot of them were located in the Walikale jungle region of the Congo and they seemed to be in constant conflict with the Congolese Army. Other militias such as the Tutsi, to name but one, had joined forces with the Congolese Army in an effort to face down their common enemy; the Hutu.

Briers re-entered the room but Burrows only glanced up before turning back to the brief. He read on. Their subject had been a member of the Hutu since he was a child, and had grown up with brutality as the norm.

"Oh my God," exclaimed Lee.

"What?" Burrows asked as he turned to face her.

Her face twisted. "Read the top of page five."

Burrows finished page four and turned over. He read on. Apparently, the Hutu were well known for their brutal ways, and regularly used rape as a weapon. Not just against the individuals concerned, but in order to terrorise whole communities. One intelligence report said that their subject had a particular hatred of informers, and he was often the first choice by militia leaders to vent dreadful retribution against those suspected of complicity: either with the Army or the UN peacekeepers who worked the region.

On one occasion, a local family man was accused of such collaboration, and their subject was sent after him. Together with his henchmen, they burst into the local man's home where they found him together with his wife and daughter. They raped and killed the man's wife in front of him and his daughter. Then they gave him a choice; rape his own daughter, or they would. When he refused, they cut off his ears and scooped his eyes out. As he lay there in agony, the subject and his thugs raped the daughter. The man couldn't see, but heard everything that was going on. Then they shot him dead in front of his daughter.

They let the girl go, only so she could report the horror to the rest of her village. The subject told her to make sure everyone knew what would happen to anyone else thought to be a collaborator. She was eleven years old.

Having finished page five Burrows put the binder down for a break. Nobody spoke for a few moments.

Then Lee said, "You're not telling us this monster is now on the loose in the UK?"

"I'm afraid so Jane," Briers said.

Lee shook her head in obvious despair, and turned back to the binder, the reluctance on her face obvious to Burrows. It mirrored how he felt as he read on.

Apparently, their subject had made his money in the illegal production of Colton Ore, which was mined all over the Congo, and indeed other parts of Africa for use in electrical capacitors. All sorts of electronics required Colton Ore in their production, mobile telephone circuitry for one. There were legalised Colton Ore mines in the Congo, but there was a lot of illegal production as well; workers at the latter were over-laboured, and paid a pittance. But no one dared stand up to the Hutu, too afraid of the terrible consequences.

The Congolese Army did have some successes, and in one such raid, they closed down an illegal production site and rounded up the criminals running it. Unfortunately, their subject, who was there, managed to evade capture. This was five years ago. Since then, he had slipped into Belgium, obtained a Belgian passport in a false name, and crossed the Channel into the UK. He had now set up a large scale 'Organised Crime Group' based in London and Manchester.

Burrows finished reading as Lee looked up and closed her folder, he sat back in his chair, and she leaned on the table. Mentally drained, he was sure Lee felt the same.

Briers took the binders from them and promptly put them through a crosscut paper shredder located under the coffee-machine table. Then he returned to the round table and sat down.

"All that remains now is to briefly bring you up to date on this man's current activities within the UK," Briers said.

"Before you do Frank, isn't it time we both found out who we are up against?" Burrows asked.

"Yeah, I need a name to hang my growing hatred on. The term 'subject' is far too impersonal," Lee added.

Briers glanced at them both, before seeming to settle his gaze at Burrows. "Well it doesn't really matter what his real name is. But for our purposes, we know him as Shonbo Cabilla."

Chapter Seven

Detective Sergeant Steele was glad his Unit detective inspector had called a meeting. He had a few questions of his own. He was with his 'cover officer' Johnny, whose job it was to look after his welfare. Even though every undercover operative—or U/C for short—had a 'cover officer' as their welfare support, Steele had particular faith in Johnny to ensure any operation's objectives were not unwarrantedly dangerous. He was a seasoned U/C Officer too, and knew which risks were manageable and which were not. However, as regard to the 'lorry driving job' the intelligence gaps in that case were big enough to drive a convoy of juggernauts through. He did not blame Johnny though; risks can only be assessed based on the available information, which sometimes meant you were unaware of some of the pitfalls. That was the nature of undercover work, and he knew and accepted that.

Even so, he still had nightmares about what he saw that night, and they all ended with the face of the dying cop looking up at him. Instead of uttering Cabilla's name in his death throes, it was Steele's. As if it was his fault, the slaughter took place, as if he was to blame for making the rendezvous on that desolate industrial estate. That was the part when he always woke up. He knew what happened wasn't his doing, and his psychologist repeatedly told him so, but it didn't make the nights any easier. It was over three months since the job went down and Steele had only resumed work a few days ago. He hadn't wanted to go on sick leave—didn't want it on his record—so the DI agreed to put him on 'gardening leave' and Johnny his cover officer keep in constant touch whilst he was off.

He had to think seriously if he wanted to return to the unit, but as the weeks spun out he realised that the alternative; normal CID duties would 'do his head in'. Not that there was anything wrong with the day-to-day detective work his colleagues did so well; it was just that once you've been a U/C there's no going back. Not for Steele anyway. The last job being an exception, but normally the adrenalin rush was just too much. Not that he would ever say as much, especially to his psychologist; if there was any hint of him having the 'James Bond Syndrome' he would lose his authority to act as a U/C quicker that it would take him to tell his next lie. Once gone, it would be gone forever.

James Bond Syndrome, he knew, was when an individual became too hooked into the whole persona of being an undercover officer. The buzz of the role became the main driver and that was a dangerous thing to happen. Not only could a U/C start breaking all the rules of engagement in his or her thirst for the buzz, they could put others at risk of compromise, not to mention turn all the jobs to rat shit. Steele knew he wasn't that bad. But he'd yet to meet a U/C who didn't occasionally get a hard on doing the job—or whatever the female equivalent was for the lady operatives. Anyway, he'd passed a psychometric evaluation and been cleared fit to resume undercover duties. That was all that mattered to him.

Johnny parked their car outside a non-distinctive office building in Manchester city centre and they headed into the reception of WD Holding Co. Ltd. Steele was aware that the company was a 'cover', it was owned and run by the National Crime Agency to provide logistical support for the undercover unit, and it was a great place to meet covertly away from prying eyes.

Steele and his partner were shown into a conference room behind the main reception. A coffee pot was already placed in the centre of the light-coloured wood veneered office table. They were the first to arrive and they both sat down and poured themselves a drink. Steele looked at the coffee table and recognised it as the same make of cheap quality office furniture he had seen in many police stations. He considered saying something. Did the choice of furniture; make their fake company look a bit policey? On the other hand, was he being a bit paranoid? He decided it was the latter, an easy thing to do in the U/C game. Whoever supplied the table no doubt supplied many other types of office space as well.

Johnny had told him that the unit DI had called the meeting, as he wanted to look at how they should proceed after the cop slaughter. Had the job gone to plan, he knew that everyone who turned up at the lorry park would have been arrested, including him, and taken to the nearest Police Custody Office. As with all covert operations, they had an exit strategy; for Steele, that would be to get him out of custody without being charged with importation of Class A drugs, and in a way that would not compromise his cover as a 'bent' lorry driver. One of the reasons he'd been picked for this particular job was his ethnicity. Although his father was a white British man born and bred in Lancashire, his mother was Turkish. So not only did he look the part, he could speak the part too. His Turkish wasn't perfect, but he knew

49

it was good enough to support his back-story that he had been brought up in England from an early age. He remembered as a young child in Preston, watching his mates play outside whilst he was taught Turkish by his mother. She had told him he should cherish both his parents' heritages. Steele knew that with his personal profile as it was; it made him a very valuable asset as an undercover officer.

His 'get out of jail card', as his cover officer liked to refer to exit strategies, was due to his ethnicity. Once arrested with the lorry, it would soon become apparent that he was 'wanted' by the Turks for very serious offences over there. The plan had been not to release which 'offences' he was actually wanted for, just to say that it was so serious that it took primacy over the drugs bust. That gave the good guys the excuse to release him from custody into the hands of Immigration officials so he could be extradited to Turkey. Or so it would appear. But after what had happened, he had been pulled straight out and taken back to Manchester for his own protection.

The DI walked into the room, a middle-aged man with greying hair and the result of too many lunches around his midriff, though he did look a little slimmer than when Steele had last seen him. The DI greeted them both and poured a coffee before settling down at the table.

"Thanks to you both for coming, but before we start I just want to check on how you're doing?" the DI said aiming his remark at Steele.

"I'm fine Boss, I've been cleared by the—" Steele started to reply before the DI waved his hand in the air.

"Never mind the shrink; are you sure you're OK? I understand you've had the odd bad dream, which is entirely understandable given the circumstances," the DI said.

"Yeah I'm sure Boss, but thanks for asking."

The DI then looked at the cover officer.

"What about you Johnny? Have you got any concerns?"

"No, not at all. In fact even if he was never to go undercover again," Johnny said, and then added quickly, "which I know is not the case," he said just before Steele was about to interject, before further adding, "I think it would add to his safety."

"Sorry Johnny, I don't follow?" the DI said.

"Well, what I mean is that, instead using our plan A exit strategy; where-by our lorry driver Mr Steele here would have been taken away by some nice pretend-immigration officials in the middle of the custody suite, in front of all the other bad guys; we had to knee jerk, and pick him up close to the lorry park and the get the hell out of there."

"I know that Johnny, but spell it out will you?" the DI asked.

"Well I think that we can still use part of the original story to explain why our 'lorry driver' disappeared all of a sudden. I was thinking if we put Steeley back in to the bad guys with a script saying he legged it after the slaughter before the regular cops arrived, and went to ground not only in case he was fingered for being the driver, but also because he is using a fake ID as he is wanted in Turkey."

"I see, so it explains my extended absence and the reason why I've been out of contact," Steele said.

"Exactly, you can say you ditched your phone and legged it across the channel until things calmed down a bit. That way, not only do you explain your absence, you reinforce your legend as a bent half-Turkish lorry driver who's wanted back in the motherland. Further protecting your real identity as a U/C in the process," Johnny said.

"So if you did decide to hang up your undercover mask, you could just disappear again, and no one would think anything amiss?" the DI added.

"Or, as is the case with me, having further enhanced my legend, I can be available to be re-deployed in my role as a bent lorry driver," Steele said, stressing the word 'or'.

"I like it," the DI said, "and I'm sure I can get your authorisation for this job renewed accordingly. However, I think to be on the safe side, your re-immergence in London should be subtle, and just long enough to support your position before we consider re-deploying you any deeper. Let's just see how it goes, and review things as we go along," he concluded.

The meeting then drew to a natural conclusion and the DI said his goodbyes before heading off, saying he would sort the paperwork out relating to their decisions straight away. Steele and Johnny headed out to where they had parked the car to drive back to their other office across the city. As they drove through the heavy Manchester traffic they further discussed a plan of how they would re-introduce 'Larry the lorry driver' from a tactical point of view, so when the authorisation was renewed in a day or so, they would be ready to go.

"I'm buzzing Johnny, It's nice to be back operational," Steele said.

"It's nice to have you back Steeley, but remember you will get some scrutiny and questions will be asked, so we need to be ready."

"Oh bollocks," Steele exclaimed before continuing, "I meant to ask the DI what had happened with the murder investigation side of things down in London? Whether or not they have got hold of this Cabilla bloke yet?"

"I'm sure if there had been any developments he would have told us," Johnny said in reply.

Steele had no idea who Cabilla really was; he just assumed he was some 'nutter' hired by Mackey. As part of his infiltration, he had met Mackey on many occasions, and as big a thug as he was, he didn't think he was capable of the slaughter that had taken place. In fact, he'd gotten on very well with Mackey and was confident he could again. No, he was more than happy that Mackey would be pleased to hear from him again, and that he would buy the story he would give him. He might even be able to find out a bit more about this 'nutter' Cabilla; thought he was in no doubt that Mackey would have sacked him and distanced himself from him. Even among thugs, there was a code of conduct and this Cabilla guy had obviously overstepped the mark by a long way.

***

A few miles away on the other side of Manchester Cabilla and Mackey walked into Piccadilly railway station. Cabilla was happy to be heading back south. Half an hour later, they were on the train for Euston.

"When we get back to London, I want you straight on this Den, no pissing about until he's found," Cabilla said.

"No problem. I've already spoken to the Turks who haven't seen or heard from him, so he's probably keeping his head down in the East End somewhere," Mackey replied.

"How long did you say you'd known him for again?" Cabilla asked.

"Years, Boss. We go way back," Mackey replied.

Cabilla wasn't sure if he detected a hint of something in Mackey's voice. He decided not to push it, probably just a few nerves on Mackey's part at being questioned. He'd hold off until they found this Larry bloke; then he could judge things for himself.

Chapter Eight

Burrows couldn't believe he'd heard Frank Briers say Cabilla's name. He'd certainly kept it hidden until the punch line. It was typical of Frank to build things up to a grand finale, he thought to himself. But that had always been Briers's way; it's how he motivated people, not that he needed to encourage Burrows, or Lee from what he'd seen of her so far, but it had always been his way of doing things. That said; he'd certainly got the result he was looking for. Well, out of Burrows anyway.

"You kept that little gem until the end Frank," Burrows observed.

"I'd say by the look on your face, you hadn't seen it coming either," Briers said.

"No I hadn't. And what's more, I'd no idea about his Congo past."

"Will one of you two tell me what's going on here? I take it you've both met this slime ball in a previous life?" Lee interjected, her eyes flicking between both of them.

Burrows turned to Lee and apologised, as did Briers, and then Burrows spent the next twenty minutes giving Jane Lee a run down on the previous investigations into Cabilla and his organised crime group, culminating in the collapse of the trial in Manchester after Billy the Kid's disappearance.

"What happened to this Billy the Kid character? And did you ever find out how the safe house was blown?" Lee asked.

"Well, the Kid just 'did one' and we haven't seen him since. He didn't have any family that we were aware of, and all of his so-called friends were really no more than criminal associates," Burrows answered.

"So he could be dead?" She asked.

"He could be," Briers said, "but we don't think so. If Cabilla had got him out of the safe house, or indeed got to him afterwards, or at any time, I'm sure we would have heard about it. Cabilla wouldn't have been able to keep his mouth shut; he'd have wanted it known within the criminal circles as a deterrent to others."

"The safe house part is more worrying. Billy, either bottled it and then ran, or he was taken. If it was the latter, then we have a problem. One we never solved," Burrows said.

"We know Cabilla must have someone on the payroll; he always seems to be one step ahead. That's partly why he's come up before the Executive of the SPU," Briers added.

"Well it sounds like it's time he got his arse kicked then," Lee said.

"I think you and I are going to get along just fine," Burrows said with a big smile across his face.

Pretty and with attitude, he mused to himself. What a delightful mix.

Burrows and Lee were then taken to the underground car park where Briers bid them farewell, for the next two days at least. They were then driven out of London into the countryside somewhere in the middle of rural Essex; Burrows couldn't work out exactly where. They arrived at what appeared from a distance to be an old farm, situated at the end of a long woodland driveway. They had driven through miles of tree-lined country roads before turning off down a private lane, the entrance of which was heavily obscured by overgrown vegetation. After about a quarter of a mile down an uneven rough track, they came to a steel five-bar gate, which turned out to be a covertly manned checkpoint. Once past that, Burrows realised they were obviously on government, probably military land.

Once inside the 'farm buildings' they were introduced to a man who Burrows guessed to be in his thirties, dressed in plain clothes and who identified himself only as 'Ian'. It was obvious to Burrows that Ian—if that was indeed his real name—was military in civilian clothes. Burrows smiled inwardly. It was like putting a traffic patrol officer in plain clothes, or dressing up a farm hand in a city suit. It just didn't work. Burrows was going to ask Ian if he had left his uniform at home, but thought better of it. He'd no idea what training Ian had lined up for them over the next forty-eight hours, so best not to wind him up too much at the outset. He looked at Lee and saw a small smirk on her face as she turned to face him.

"I know what you're thinking," she said, "he's definitely no spook. He couldn't walk any straighter if he tried."

"And he's no detective either," Burrows whispered back at her through his grin.

"If you two schoolgirls have finished gossiping, I'll show you to your rooms. Everything you need including clothing is in there. I'll see you outside in ten minutes with your tracksuits on. Let's see how fit you two desk jockey types are. We'll start off with a nice five mile run as an aperitif," Ian said.

Lee and Burrows glanced at each other, their grins gone. Burrows realised that the next forty-eight hours was not going to be a vacation, and by the look on Lee's face, she thought the same.

Forty-five minutes later, it was Ian who was smiling, stood erect and hardly out of breath outside the main building. Both he and Lee had struggled to keep up, but both had just about managed it. Either that, or Ian had slowed to let them catch him. They were both now stood in a similar stance, legs apart with their hands on their knees, bent double getting their breath back. Burrows kept his head up so he could see ahead, rather than looking at the ground.

"Not too bad," Ian said.

He moved to face Burrows as he spoke. Lee had stood to one side and looked as if her breathing was returning to normal quicker than his was.

"You could be fitter, but you'll do," Ian said.

Burrows dropped his gaze slightly to give his neck a rest, but then glanced back upwards just in time to see Ian launch at him from about three feet away. Ian's right hand was raised with his fist clenched and he was swinging it towards Burrows in a downwards motion aimed at the top of Burrows's head. It was as if Ian had an imaginary knife or other similar weapon in his clenched fist. It took a split second for Burrows to register what was happening; he decided to react as he'd done with Zingo back in Thame. He pulled himself upwards, straightened his back and raised his arms above his head in a crossed forearms formation in order to defend against the fast approaching arm. He was confident he had managed to raise his defence in time. Then he received his second surprise.

Moments before Ian's arm was due to crash into Burrows's defensive V, the attacker abruptly shot off to Burrows's right, he crumpled towards the ground as he went. This was because Lee was now horizontal, having flown through the air feet first; both of which had just made a sickening, crunching noise as they connected to the outside of Ian's right knee. Lee broke her fall with her forearms as she hit the ground. Ian did not. Neither Burrows nor Lee rushed to further restrain Ian, there was no need; he was rolling around the ground instinctively holding his right knee with both hands.

"Hey, thanks for that," Burrows said to her. "They were pretty smart moves," he added.

"Don't even think about saying, 'for a girl,' or you'll be joining Ian on the floor."

"Alpha and Bravo stand down," Ian shouted, and paused before adding. "And get me a fucking medic; I think you've broken my fucking knee."

Burrows looked at Lee and could see the same surprise on her face that he was feeling. Before they had arrived at the camp, they had been warned to expect surprises. Burrows thought the five-mile run was surprise enough. However, they were also told that if clarity was needed, they would be addressed by their call signs. They were also told that if they were ever told to stand down, then that is what they had to do; immediately cease whatever it was they were doing.

"Sorry about that Ian, but it was just instinctive. I hope your knee's not really broken. I didn't realise your attack was part of the script. But not too bad for a desk jockey was it?" Lee said.

Ian now sat up, rocking to and fro and holding his knee tightly. He glanced up at Lee. "It's not a crash course you two need, but a fucking restraining order each. God help whoever they're training you to go after."

Burrows decided to head back to the main building in search of some help whilst Lee stayed with Ian.

Fortunately, as it transpired, Ian's knee wasn't broken, though by the way it had swelled up, Burrows was surprised. The ligaments however, were bruised—according to one of the other trainers who attended to Ian—along with his self-respect. Both he and Lee went out of their way to make it up to him. After a shower and change of clothes, he joined Lee and Ian for supper in the mess room; which was no more than a front room knocked through into a kitchen. The other two trainers at the site—including the one who had treated Ian—also joined them for the evening. They were both so obsequious towards Ian that Burrows couldn't contain his laughter. However, several beers later he noticed that the fraught atmosphere had lifted. Helped by Lee's numerous apologies and the other two trainers eventually getting bored with taking the piss out of Ian by feigning their servitude.

The following day involved much of the same, though they were both clearly told that there would be no more surprise attacks. Burrows was glad to hear it, since it meant they had clearly passed that test. Apart from physical training, they were both taken to a closed firing range deep in the forest where they were put through their weapons' handling and shooting ability tests. Burrows enjoyed this until he realised that Lee had achieved a higher score— she was certainly full of surprises. The other two trainers were Ian clones; they even called themselves Ian-2 and Ian-3. But Burrows realised they were all okay guys. It was obvious after the incident with Ian-1, Lee and he had earned their respect. Lee had certainly earned his own respect. He was enjoying Lee's company both professionally and personally. Helped along by a similar sharp sense of black-humour that he thought was only the domain of detectives. It seemed that the traditional attitude of understatement was common to both departments. He'd explained to Lee that, when a detective was faced with the most heinous of crime scenes, then understatement and dark sarcasm were the norm. He'd always thought this was just a police thing but Lee had explained it was just the same in the security service; apparently, section heads would telephone the director general with some urgent intelligence update on a serious national threat with all the aplomb of someone ordering a pizza. This amazed him; he'd always held the stereotyped view of MI5 staff being no more than politically correct, secret civil servants. They certainly had a lot more in common than he'd expected, and he was sure Lee felt the same by her reactions to what he'd said. He could see that she had achieved a high level of success in her field—as he had too—though he'd added respect for Lee knowing all too well how much harder it can sometimes be for a woman in such occupations; not that sexism was anything like what it had once been, but they were both still macho organisations irrespective of how hard they'd tried not to be. Burrows didn't voice this added respect he'd found for Lee, the last thing he wanted to do was sound patronising in any way.

By the third day, he noticed Ian-1 was hobbling around with increasing deftness. They finished their final assessment; a paper fed analytical exercise, which Lee completed in half the time it took him. Then the three Ians each congratulated them, and with mutual salutations over, the 4 x 4 that had brought them there, arrived to take them back to London.

Chapter Nine

By the time they arrived at Euston railway station in London Cabilla had told Mackey to go on alone after Larry. He'd said that he had some business to sort out and headed off to where a car was waiting. He had told Mackey to keep him informed of any developments, but otherwise they would meet up for a drink in a couple of days. Mackey made his way to the taxi rank that he knew was situated in an underpass at the side of the railway station. He'd muttered under his breath, "Thanks for the lift," as the pair had parted company on the large concourse at the front of the station.

He made sure he was already walking away from Cabilla so his boss couldn't hear him. But he was starting to wonder if the lack of a lift was a sign that Cabilla was a little pissed off with him. Or was he just being a little paranoid. He wasn't sure which. But he knew, as he pushed himself to the front of the taxi queue, he had to find Larry the lorry driver, and fast.

Mackey's first stop was the small rented flat in Fulham he used when in town. He showered, changed and grabbed something to eat from one of the many fast food outlets nearby, before heading out to trawl around all the east end boozers where Larry used to frequent. He'd been to six of them when he decided to call it a night and head back to the flat. No one had seen or heard of Larry for months. Mackey put the word out that he wanted to see him to offer him some work; another driving job.

The last thing he wanted to do was scare him off by giving anyone the impression that Larry was in the shit. In fact he wasn't sure that he was in the shit, he really hoped he wasn't as he quite liked him; they'd had a few good nights on the piss and he had always found him a good laugh. Larry was definitely good company, but he didn't want to have his own reputation ruined if he turned out to be a grass. He knew that Cabilla had reservations about Larry, but that was because he hadn't met him. He'd left Mackey to find a reliable and trustworthy driver. Mackey just hoped, for both Larry's and his sake, that he had.

***

The day after their meeting with the DI in Manchester, Steele was happy with the tactics he'd agreed with Johnny for getting back out as Larry the bent lorry driver. The timing had turned out to be critical too, but for different reasons. That morning he had taken a call from the DI who first told him that his authority to resume and re-engage with Mackey had been granted. Secondly, he told him that once he'd done that, he was needed for a second deployment whilst he was in London. It was to do with a firm of villains from Essex he had previously been involved with, who had been touting around for a driver for a 'job' they were planning. Steele had been introduced to them from one of his east end drinking buddies but they never got back to him. They seemed happy enough with him, but just never got back in touch. Maybe they had changed their minds about doing the job—whatever it was— or they had just sacked it for any number of reasons.

The Metropolitan Police unit that had been running the investigation had identified the team as well-known active criminals, who were all part of the same organised crime group. But it seemed for whatever reason the job was off. That was a couple of weeks before he'd met Mackey, and thereafter got involved in his job. He'd always wondered if the initial inquiry from the Essex villains had helped establish his credentials as a bent lorry driver, and was possibly why Mackey had made his approach.

Anyway, the Met intelligence suggested that the job was back on, and the guy who'd initially introduced him to the Essex lot had been back round the east end asking after him. The Met had asked for Steele to put himself about and meet up with his 'buddy' to see what was happening. They'd renewed his separate authorities for this job, so all he had to do once back in London was meet the DI who was running that job to get his briefing and he could service both enquiries at the same time. He'd catch up with Mackey to explain why he'd been off the radar and try to find out what was going on since the cop slaughter, and put himself forward for the Essex team, if he could find the go-between.

Johnny had offered to come to London with him, but he said it wasn't necessary. Just so long as he was on the end of his mobile phone. He knew the Met DI well enough, and their undercover unit would provide a local cover officer should he need anything. In any case, he only expected to be down there for a couple of days at most. Therefore, Steele packed a small holdall and Johnny dropped him at Piccadilly railway station the following morning.

The journey had only taken two hours and had been a good run with few stops. At Euston, he was picked up and taken to a hotel well away from the east end and, after booking in he was further driven to a covert address to meet the operational team's DI, a man called Mike Jones. He was offered a full surveillance team but told the DI that until he had met his buddy and established exactly what the Essex mob wanted him for; i.e. if the job was back on or not, he thought the use of a full surveillance team a waste of resources. But it was the DI's call. The DI agreed but said he wanted a local cover officer to be contactable on the phone with a motor and be no more than half an hour away if needed. After that was all agreed, he rang Johnny back in Manchester who concurred. All that remained now was for the London DI to give him his formal briefing where his objectives for the evening's deployment would be formally recorded together with a list of what is, and is not acceptable.

Once that was over, the local cover officer, a DS called Bill Jones – no relation to the DI – had asked Steele if he wanted to wear a wire. He declined. Always better to leave the wearing of technical equipment until things were clearer and he was accepted by the bad guys. He always thought it a schoolboy error to wear a wire too soon on any job. If anyone he met for the first time had any concerns about him, the first thing they would do would be to search him. And not always when they had concerns, sometimes it was just seen as good practice as far as the bad guys were concerned; they would often go through the motions of searching someone just to show their professionalism, without really expecting to find a wire. He'd nearly been caught out like that once before; lesson learned, it wasn't going to happen again.

He hitched a lift back to his hotel to grab something to eat before changing his clothes. He then set off towards the East End to start putting himself about around his old drinking dens. He got on the tube at Oxford Circus and took the Central Line to Mile End where he started off down the Mile End Road towards Bow. He liked this end of town; it was earthy and real. It felt good to be back.

He didn't have any contact telephone numbers for his drinking buddy; he just knew him as John and usually found him in any one of three or four pubs off the Mile End Road. He thought he would try to find him first before he looked for Mackey. He was more likely to come across John playing pool in any of the local pubs rather than Mackey. He would probably ring Mackey's mobile telephone from a pay phone in one of the pubs; it would look better that way. He'd told the London DI that he would try and establish contact with John as his first priority—he hadn't explained exactly what his second priority was—they didn't really need to know, though he had mentioned Mackey to Bill Jones the local cover officer.

There was no sign of John in the first three pubs Steele went into. He'd given it half an hour in each, and got one or two nods of recognition from punters. He'd spoken to each barman who served him, the last one he recognised though he couldn't remember his name.

"Haven't seen you in here for a couple of months or more mate, not got yourself locked up have you?" asked the barman.

Brilliant, he thought that was a great feeder-line from the barman, it gave him the chance to put in some of his exit strategy story. This way he wasn't pushing it, and there was a good chance it would get around to the right ears.

"No mate, but I had to do one over the channel for a while or I might have been," Steele replied.

"Well nice to see you back in the manor, me old son, my takings dropped when you fucked off," the barman said, and then guffawed at his own joke.

Steele smiled, and after a short pause tentatively asked. "You haven't seen John around have you?" Steele noted the unsure look on the barman's face.

"You know John," he pressed, "the scrawny git who cheats like fuck on the pool table."

"I know who you mean," the barman answered slowly, "no he got into a bit of bother over a pool game with some eastern European a couple of weeks back. The Slovak—or whatever he was—gave him a slap and he ain't been back since. But if you give it half an hour or so, the Slovak is usually in by nine, he may know where to find him. Why do you want him? Does he owe you?"

"Naw, it's just about a bit of graft. But I'll hang on a bit like you suggest. Let me know when the Slovak turns up," Steele asked.

"Sure thing," the barman replied, adding, "If you'll excuse me I've got to ring the old lady." Steele nodded and watched the barman as he walked to the opposite end of the horseshoe shaped bar, his shoes echoing on the bare boards taking Steele's attention with him. He saw the barman pull his mobile phone from his pocket as he went.

Twenty-five minutes later, Steele gazed through the pub windows and saw that the weather had turned to drizzle. He noticed a black ford transit van pull up outside the pub. It drew past the window out of his view except for the last couple of feet of side panel. Seconds later, he heard the spring-loaded pub door swing open and shut behind him, and he glanced towards the entrance.

His eyes widened with surprise on seeing Den Mackey walking straight towards him.

"Bloody hell Den, this is spooky. I was just about to ring you," Steele said.

"I thought you had been nicked or summat Larry," Mackey said. "Your phone's been off since I last saw you," he continued, "where the fuck 'ave you been?" he spoke with a fixed grin on his face.

Steele, or Larry, as Mackey knew him, felt uneasy. Mackey's grin looked false, though he thought that was probably to be expected. "Can I get you a beer Den?" he asked, without answering Mackey's questions. He didn't want to push his excuses too readily.

"No, I'll tell you what. I only popped in to pay the bloke behind the bar some money I owe him," Mackey said as he handed what looked like a twenty pound note over to the barman. "Then I was going to go up west on the piss. You come with me and we can have chat over a drink."

Steele smiled and relaxed a little. He'd got over the initial surprise of seeing Mackey.

"Yeah, good idea," he replied before draining his glass.

He followed Mackey to the exit, who opened the door for him; he walked out onto the pavement with Mackey directly behind him. He saw the driver in the idling van in front of him nod towards him, but realised he must have been nodding at Mackey behind him. A second later a sliding side door of the van opened, and he felt Mackey push him hard from behind in the centre of his back, propelling him towards it. He could only grunt in shock before he'd been bundled fully into the back of the van, grabbed and held in place by an unknown pair of hands. Mackey slammed the sliding door shut before jumping into the front passenger seat and turning backwards towards him.

"What the fuck's going on Den? He said, as Mackey turned to face him, trying to make sense of what had just happened.

"You'll find out soon enough. Now shut the fuck up and sit quiet or your new best mate sat next to you will shut you up," Mackey said before turning to face the driver. "Take us to the warehouse," he ordered, and the driver just nodded and pulled away from the kerb.

The man sat next to Steele just looked at him with an unhinged sickly grin on his face. He realised he was in a whole load of trouble.

Chapter Ten

It was mid-evening by the time Lee and Burrows arrived back at Pimlico. Lee noticed the late spring; early summer sun was setting over west London. As she got out of the 4 x 4, she inhaled the familiar warm city aromas. Over the last couple of days, she had got to know Burrows quite a lot. She knew he lived on his own in Thame and that he was in his early fifties—though he didn't look it—was six feet two inches tall, and weighed around fifteen stone. She had told him all about her one-bedroomed flat in Millbank situated off Vauxhall Bridge Road. How she had picked it, as it was handy for both MI5 offices at Thames House, north of the river as well as MI6's impressive headquarters on the south bank.

"You look as knackered as I'm starting to feel," Lee said to Burrows as he slammed the 4 x 4's passenger door.

"Yeah, I think the last two days have started to catch up during the journey back from Essex."

They had initially agreed to have a nightcap in the pub opposite, before heading off in their respective directions, but Lee was glad when Burrows suggested they leave it until next time as he still had a journey ahead of him.

They said their goodbyes and she watched Burrows head off towards the tube station, before she walked away in the opposite direction to look for a cab. Twenty minutes later, she was back in her small flat, it was nice to see some familiar surroundings. She put the kettle on, sat in her favourite armchair, and mulled over events of the last few days. They had both signed up for something that was pretty unique. She decided to have a brew before heading back out to the 24-hour supermarket around the corner. She put her feet up on the coffee table and then next thing she knew, it was morning.

***

Steele had no idea where they were taking him. He had a canvas bag put over his head soon after he'd been lifted. From the sounds of traffic and the length of the journey, which he guessed was no more than twenty minutes, he was sure they were still in central London. In fact, he thought he heard the driver use the word Dulwich more than once. Dulwich he knew was in south London. The last few minutes of the journey sounded like they had turned off a busy main road down a side street and then he reckoned they had entered a compound at the end of it as the road noise turned from tarmac to gravel without a change of direction.

He had then been led across the gravel into a building, which echoed his captives' voices and smelled musty. A disused commercial building of some kind, he guessed. They led him down some stairs and then made him stand still whilst his bag was removed.

When he'd been lifted he tried to remonstrate with Mackey—once he'd caught his breath—trying to sound as shocked and angry as he himself would have expected Larry the bent lorry driver to sound. But it had fallen on deaf ears. As soon as he'd tried talking to Mackey, the sickly smiler sat next to him and put gaffer tape over his mouth and the bag over his head. Nothing much more had been said to him or between the others. It was Sickly who had taken the bag off his head and was alone when he did so. Sickly then cuffed his hands behind his back and chained the handcuffs to a steel ring fastened into the brick wall about twelve inches from the ground. As he tried to get comfortable seated on the stone floor Sickly had slammed and bolted shut a thick wooden door on his way out. He then heard the sound of a chair being pulled along the floor outside followed by a grunt, and knew that Sickly was obviously sitting guard outside his room. He tried to slow his breathing in a vain attempt to control the rising fear within him. Looking around the room there were no windows, just a single light bulb overhead and a kitchen chair in the centre of the room. He noticed that the chair was screwed to the floor and his fear turned to dread.

He'd no idea what the issues were going to be with Mackey; after all, he hadn't had the chance yet to explain where he had been these last three months. Surely once he had done that Mackey could be reassured of whatever it was that was bothering him. Steele just prayed that they didn't suspect him of being a cop. That was every U/C's worst nightmare. Though they were trained to deal with challenges, often these were half-hearted, as if the villains went through a mental checklist when getting to know a new associate. It was custom, the done thing. It would be suspicious if they didn't challenge someone new. But Steele certainly wasn't expecting a challenge on this level. If indeed, that was what this was all about. He had to keep his mind active and to calm himself. It would not be natural if he was not scared, but he had to show some mettle when he was interrogated by Mackey, which would undoubtedly happen, probably sooner than later. He first started going over his 'back story', his legend of exactly who it was he was purporting to be. Checking for mistakes, though he was sure there were none. He also went over and over his exit strategy as formulated by Johnny and himself back in Manchester, so he was as prepared as he could be.

It was amazing what a calmative effect of doing something positive with his mind was beginning to have. He was starting to ease a little, his confidence returning.

Then he noted a strong smell of disinfectant in the room, a fact he didn't want to think about.

***

At 9 a.m. the following morning, Burrows arrived back at Pimlico a few minutes after Lee. He felt rested after a good night's sleep. Lee had just poured them each a coffee from the machine in the downstairs briefing room when Briers entered with his usual brisk and business-like manner.

Salutations over, he started. "Firstly, you two, well done on your crash course over the last two days. You can both collect your kit after this briefing, which will include your weapons of choice. I'll need your house keys so the technicians can visit your homes today and install the latest floor safes for you. Weapons must be locked up when not being carried on the person. OK?"

Both Burrows and Lee nodded and handed over their respective door keys.

"I'm confident from what the Ians tell me that you are both fully cognisant of the standing operating procedures, so I won't labour on about the admin. I just wanted to reinforce it about the weapons," Briers said before continuing. "Anyway, your final instructions are quite clear, but before we get into that I want you both to read the Intel updates on Cabilla. Who incidentally, will henceforth be referred to only as 'The Subject'. It's time to sharpen our tradecraft now that we are going operational."

Briers then handed them each a binder marked 'Top Secret' and then passed their keys over to a man in overalls who appeared at the door. Briers poured a coffee whilst giving them time to read the binders. Burrows sat quietly at the round table and shook his head as he read. When he'd finished he looked up to see Lee drop her hand from over her mouth as she put her copy of the file down.

"I remember reading about this awful incident. It was like reading something from a novel. How come the investigation team haven't nicked the bastard?" Lee asked.

"Because they don't know it was our Subject," Briers replied.

"I'm sorry Frank, I don't get it either," Burrows said.

Briers went on to explain all about the ill-fated Turkish importation job; how they were well ahead of the game for a change because the Lorry driver was an undercover police officer called Steele. How, because of this they were confident that this time they were going to catch their man red-handed. Have him absolutely caught with nowhere to go.

"What actually went wrong?" Burrows asked.

"Well, the plan was as soon as the U/C had driven the wagon onto the industrial estate, we were going to strike. We had it fully plotted off with armed officers and we'd seen the bad guys seated in a car parked covertly on the plot. We didn't know who was in it though. It may have been our man, or it might have been hired help paid to collect the wagon and take it somewhere else. There was a lot of debate going on in the incident room in the final few minutes. No matter how our staff tried to position themselves, they couldn't get a decent view inside the parked BMW that the bad guys were in. If they were just gofers, we didn't want to strike too soon and miss out on the big boys. If we could have confirmed the main targets were *not* in the BMW then we would have given the order to just sit tight; watch the exchange and then follow both the BMW and the wagon as they were taken away to the next point on their journeys," Briers said.

Burrows and Lee sat up staring at Briers as he continued. "The problem was the lorry driver had been instructed by the bad guys to park the wagon up in the centre of the car park and then walk around it to signify all was well. However, it was thought too dangerous in case things got out of hand and guns were drawn, so the U/C, or Larry as he was known as, was told to just stay put in the parked up wagon."

"Who was the U/C's contact on the firm?" Burrows asked.

"Mackey, who as you know is our Subject's right hand man. Larry had rung Mackey once he'd cleared Dover to let him know he was safe and sound back on UK soil. But we still didn't know whether Mackey or indeed our Subject were in that car or not," Briers added.

"So what happened?" Lee asked.

"A decision was made to strike the BMW. That way we could lift the U/C at the same time—which was part of his exit strategy. It was thought that whoever was in that car would probably be armed and we simply couldn't let armed villains drive off even under surveillance. Where the BMW was parked it was already hemmed in on two sides, it was on an industrial estate well away from the public so the call to 'strike' went in. What we couldn't have anticipated in our worst nightmares was what happened next," Briers said.

He went on to explain the dying declaration made by one of the cops and the fact that they couldn't—as of yet—even consider using the undercover officer Larry as a witness, as he had been off work and had only come back a few days ago and had already been operationally deployed, on some other job.

"I understand that last bit Frank, but surely with a job as serious as this you could break all the usual rules and get the U/C to give evidence behind closed doors. It's not like it hasn't been done before, when needs must and all that," Burrows said.

"That was still an option. In fact, the intelligence naming our Subject as one of the killers had been fed into an intelligence unit linked to the murder investigation team. But guess what? It never got disseminated to the investigation team. The senior investigating officer was never told. We suspect one of our Subject's rotten apples is somehow involved. This meant keeping the fact there was a U/C, and his details protected, became paramount in our organisational duty of care towards him. We could pass the info on, but we would just be giving them a name with no supporting evidence as to where it came from and in what context," Briers explained.

"I'm getting the picture. The cops could drag our Subject in, but end up kicking him back out a few days later with no charges to show for their efforts," Lee said.

"Yes, and the only person any the wiser for it, would be the Subject himself. Not forgetting that the U/C's evidence, though admissible, would be open to a lot of examination in court; after all it wasn't he who saw our subject committing the atrocious acts, but the dying cop. So with all that in mind, exacerbated by the threat from an unknown bent cop or cops, the Executive of the Special Projects Unit considered the threat and came up with two yesses," Briers finished.

"A 'Yankee, Yankee,'" Burrows said.

"Exactly," Briers said before adding, "plus, we know the Subject is planning something else. Something bigger and worse, but we don't know what. The bastard never stops. So, your instructions are simply this. Trace and identify the Subject and eliminate his threat to the United Kingdom. By all means necessary. And just so we are clear; collateral damage within the

Subject's organisation is permitted if you deem it appropriate due to operational contingencies."

Burrows and Lee nodded before heading to the shredder with the intelligence files. They were then taken to collect their stuff; weapons, Kevlar vests, Timberland boots and other pieces of kit, Burrows was impressed. They were also given the keys to a nearly new grey Ford Mondeo with a two litre turbo-charged engine. A technician showed them the vehicle and some of its extras. In the boot was a safe so they could store weapons and ammunition. Burrows was happy with it, and he could see that Lee also approved. It was non-descript; the sort of vehicle that any number of sales representatives would be using up and down the country every day. It wouldn't draw second glances, so would be good for surveillance, the engine was a two litre, so it had some oomph.

Burrows suggested that as he lived the farthest away, he would take the vehicle home at night and collect Lee in the mornings. She nodded her agreement and then the technician gave them both a requisition form of some kind to sign. That done, they packed all their respective kit into the car. Burrows looked at his watch; it was 10.30 a.m. time to get started.

Chapter Eleven

Back in the warehouse basement during the previous evening, Steele spent at least two hours going over things in his mind, trying to work out what the problem was. He was also starting to focus on how uncomfortable he was when he heard a chair outside the door move, followed by the sound of bolts being withdrawn. Sickly walked in and placed a bucket with a lid on it on the floor. He quickly returned with a thin mattress and coarse blanket and laid them on the floor too. Steele was under the distinct impression that these items had been outside in the corridor all along, but he chose not to ask Sickly and give him the pleasure of confirming this. Next in, was a wooden tray with a large plastic cup of water and a pre-packed sandwich—the sort you get from petrol station shops.

As Sickly walked towards Steele, he instinctively tensed and brought his knees up so the flat of his feet were on the floor, protecting himself as best he could.

Appearing to sense his unease, Sickly smiled. "Don't worry I'm not going to hurt you, unless you give me cause. Don't get me wrong, I'd love to hurt you. I don't like you, and I do like to hurt things, but I'm under instructions not to touch you unless you give me cause. I'm going to unfasten you now so you can eat, piss and sleep. If you try anything then it's fun time; for me anyway."

"Look, I'm grateful for you unlocking these cuffs, but when do I get to speak to Den? Then I can straighten up whatever's wrong," Steele asked.

"Probably in the morning now, Mr Mackey is a very busy man."

Steele felt flattened, realising he was being kept all night. Sickly just looked back at him with a widening grimace.

***

Burrows and Lee had finished storing their kit in the Mondeo and were about to go when a call came through from Briers.

"Before you two set off on your mission, there's something else you need to know."

Sardonically Burrows said. "What, you've doubled our contract fee?"

"This is serious John. The undercover officer who acted as the lorry driver on the Turkish importation job has gone missing," Briers explained.

"Shit, sorry Frank. When did this happen?"Burrows asked, as Lee was getting into the front passenger seat. He mouthed the word 'Frank' as he continued to listen.

Briers went on to explain what had happened, "Steele the U/C, or Larry the lorry driver as we should refer to him as, has been sent back down to London."

"What for?"

"Well, his DI in Manchester wants him to try and reconnect with Mackey to try and find out what's going on."

"Sounds a bit iffy Frank."

"Well, they have a good cover story for why he's been away, and it's only supposed to be a quick look and see, sort of deployment."

"Still sounds risky."

"The point is that you may come across him at some stage, so you'll have to be extra careful if you do. The last thing we want is him sussing you two in any way, and of course you'll have to be very wary of what you do in front of him."

"How deep is he being put back in? Do we know?"

"That's the good news, as far as I can tell, he's only supposed to make informal contact with Mackey and then report back before he goes any further. At this stage we may be able to get him pulled out somehow."

"Sounds like a plan Frank."

The problem is that he was deployed last night in the east end, and he had a secondary objective, to try to find some link to an Essex team that's being looked at down here by the Met. And as of this morning, he is nowhere to be seen."

"How come you know all this so soon?" Burrows asked.

Briers explained they had telephone intercepts on the U/C's phone, his DI's and his cover officer's, which was how they'd got the early heads up.

"Bloody hell, I didn't realise we could put phone taps on our own people," Burrows said.

He knew all about the strict rules and law governing the obtaining of telephone interceptions—or lines as they were known as—which were nowhere near as common as people imagined. How each phone tap required a warrant of interception signed by the Home Secretary and was subject to regular and rigorous reviews. He also knew how high the justification case for each interception had to be due to the level of intrusion into a person's private life.

"There's a lot we can do John that would surprise you. You'll soon learn that's what the special projects unit is all about. Anyway, this Intel is only thirty minutes old and I wanted you both to know it before you set off on your travels."

"Thanks."

Briers continued, "There is nothing yet to confirm that the U/C's disappearance is anything to do with our job, but we can't discount it. It may well be he's got involved in this Essex team and not had chance to call in yet. I'll keep you informed, but for now I'll send you both an encrypted text to your mobile phones with his details and photo." Briers then said his goodbyes and cut the connection.

Burrows turned to Lee and filled in the blanks.

"If his disappearance is Cabilla related, then it might mean Cabilla is in London," Lee suggested.

"It could be, but Cabilla is just as likely to have him taken elsewhere. But what it does means is, if Cabilla has lifted him, then we'll have to work fast," he answered.

***

Cabilla wiped the grease from his mouth as he and Mackey finished a mid-morning fry-up at a small side street bistro. It was the one British meal he really enjoyed. Mackey stood up to leave and said he was heading straight to Dulwich. Cabilla told Mackey he wanted him to speak to Larry the lorry driver first, and then report back. He was confident Mackey would get the truth out of him.

"Look Den, if Larry turns out to be a grass, then we'll sort it. Don't worry about it. I won't come down all heavy on you. Even the best of us can be shafted from time to time. Go and have a nice chat and then give me a bell."

He watched Mackey as he walked away from the table looking a little more reassured, as he headed into the midmorning sunshine. He'd got the reaction he had wanted from Mackey, but in truth, he hadn't decided what he'd do if Larry did turn out to be a grass.

Then Cabilla's phone rang interrupting his thoughts. "Yeah," he answered.

"Shonbo, it's me," the caller said before continuing. "The boat has just left Ostend and cleared the harbour no worries."

"Any problems with the bitches?"

"No probs. They all swallowed the story. And to think they've paid for the privilege," the man replied.

Cabilla laughed, as did his man. "Good, let me know when you've landed in the UK and cleared customs," he added before cutting the connection.

He smiled inwardly as he leaned back into his chair; things were starting to come together. Moreover, the women had paid a handsome fee when they had been approached back in his native Congo. All had readily accepted the offer of a new life as models in the UK. He was confident that they wouldn't be discovered, the hide that had been constructed in the articulated wagon sounded good. The lorry didn't have a false bottom but it did have a false length. The last eight feet behind the cab was a compartment with the women in it. Even if customs did randomly search that particular trailer it was filled with heavy machine parts to put them off, they'd soon get bored.

And in any event, he had his secret weapon—Amber Kimba—she was the only one of the six women who spoke English. She would keep them all calm until they landed at Ramsgate.

Chapter Twelve

Steele jolted on hearing the bolts being drawn back from the cellar door. He'd been awake for hours seated on his mattress with his back against the wall. The lack of any activity during the morning had started to eat away at his resolve. But now there was activity, or about to be, signified by the door being opened, he felt worse. It was the fear of the unknown.

In walked Sickly, with his trademark grimace. "Someone's coming to speak to you. I do hope you don't tell them what they want to know," he said as he walked towards Steele with a purposeful stride.

Steele was up on his feet before Sickly reached him. Always better to face a possible attack stood up, than to assume there wouldn't be one, and stay down. Sickly grabbed his arm, but instead of leading him out of the room, as he'd expected, he was led to the centre and plonked down on the kitchen chair. Sickly told him to put his hands behind the chair back, and Steele realised he'd be fastened with his arms behind the chair, and thereafter, would be well and truly stuffed. He put his arms behind him as instructed so he would appear compliant. Sickly pulled a pair of plastic cuffs from his jeans back pocket and looked about to make his way to the rear of the chair in order to fasten his wrists. He knew that this was his one chance. The door was still open behind Sickly, and he had never heard any noises other the ones he presumed Sickly had made whilst sat guard. He was as sure as he could be that they were alone. Sickly stood up, and his concentration was clearly diverted preparing the plastic cuffs for use.

Steele gripped the chair-back to give himself added leverage, as he knew the chair was fixed to the floor, and hopefully wouldn't move. He then launched his right foot forward with all the power he could muster. Pushing back hard with his arms as he did. A fraction of a second later, Steele's right foot made a stomach-turning contact with Sickly's crutch. Instinctively, Sickly bent double and yowled in pain as he dropped the cuffs and his hands went straight to his injured genitals. His eyes appeared wide with surprise, as much as with the pain.

Steele bolted. He was out the door before Sickly could react. He hadn't a clue which way to run as his head had been covered when they'd brought him in. He chose left. It was a long bare-brick walled corridor with a concrete floor. He could see a further door ahead of him; it looked ajar, so he ran for it as fast as he could. He heard heavy footfalls behind him as he did.

He threw the door open and was faced with a set of stairs. He ran up them two at time. At the top was another door. It looked shut and he prayed it was unlocked, as the last had been. The foot falls behind him sounded closer. He dared not glance. This door was also ajar. He was through it quicker than the last, and as he swung it to behind him, he noticed a large steel bolt at the top. On seeing this, he could also glimpse Sickly powering down the corridor towards him with a look of hatred in his eyes. He was only a few metres away but Steele had made a decision. It was going to be close. He stopped, turned, and pushed the swing door until it shut. He hoped the bolt wasn't fast through lack of use, but it wasn't. It slid neatly into its slot, a moment before Sickly hit the door from the other side, the handle turning vainly as he did. Steele took a second to catch his breath.

"There's no way out of here dickhead. The building is totally secure, and when I get my hands on you, I'm going to hurt you. Hurt you real bad," Sickly shouted.

Steele was sure the latter part of what Sickly said was certainly true. But as he took in his surroundings he was starting to worry that the former part was also so. He found himself in a large ground level empty space. The size suggested it had once contained a large workshop of some kind. All the windows were high up off the floor and were covered on the outside by large steel shutters. He could hear Sickly running back the way they had come, and he had to admit to himself that he had no idea what was at the other end of the basement corridor. But the fact that Sickly was running that way didn't bode well. Steele could see a large double-door at the other end of the workshop and sprinted over to it. It was locked shut with a large mortice lock, for which Sickly no doubt had a key. Steele was beginning to believe what Sickly had said. There had been a certain confidence in his voice.

He looked up, and then got his break. He could see that the ceiling was high and full of steel girders with lighting rigs from which hung large industrial size florescent lights suspended on chains. At the side by the wall was a rope ladder, which hung down at least twenty-five feet from the girders to the floor. If he couldn't escape straight away then he would have to hide. He ran back to the bolted door and listening intently before slowly, and quietly, sliding back the bolt. He waited for a second and closed his eyes in an effort to enhance his hearing even further. Ready to re-shut the bolt at a moment's notice, but he heard nothing. His heart raced, as he slowly, and gently opened the door. He knew he was risking everything by doing so. If Sickly was behind the door then he was surely done for. He wasn't. There was just an empty staircase. Steele had no idea how big this building was, or how many floors it had, but if he just hid in the rafters, even Sickly would work it out. He pulled the door fully open before returning into the large room.

Five minutes later, he was up amid the girders with the ladder pulled up. He had managed to find a recess at the gable end that he was comfortable in. He was out of sight and had a great view of the entire room. He also realised that as he was now above the florescent lights, he was totally obscured from anyone on the ground looking up. He got his breath back and further took in his environment. He couldn't see any further egress from the room. As scared, as he was, the fact that he was doing something positive, taking some control over his own destiny gave him a huge psychological lift. He just hoped he had done enough.

Minutes later, Sickly appeared from the opposite end of the room, from somewhere near the main door, but he hadn't come through it. Steele had heard him running down stairs before he'd appeared. He was puzzled, as he hadn't seen any other way out the room when he ran to check the main door. That said, he had been focused on the door and getting out of the building. He had obviously missed a staircase, door, or both, but hopefully that would only add to Sickly's confusion, and it did increase Steele's options.

Sickly came to halt in the centre on the room on seeing the open door that Steele had come through, and since left unlocked and ajar.

"Fuck. The little shit," he said as he exhaled hard.

As Sickly's breathing started to return to normal the big man walked over to the door, re-shut and bolted it. He then walked back the way he'd come into the room and disappeared from Steele's view. It went quiet but Steele could still hear Sickly's breathing, which hadn't quite fully calmed. He realised Sickly was waiting; presumably for Steele to suddenly appear into the room the way Sickly had.

Several minutes passed, and then Steele was shocked by the sound of the big mortised door being unlocked from the outside. He struggled to try and see around the corner of the recess but couldn't.

"What the fuck are you doing stood there? Why aren't you guarding Larry?" A voice said.

Steele recognised it straight away. It belonged to Den Mackey who walked into view with two of his thugs following on behind. Steele's heart sank as he heard the door being relocked. Sickly stared to reply. His speech nervous and his diction had lost all of the menace Steele had become used to hearing. But before he had finished speaking Mackey's bellow exploded at Sickly.

"You stupid bastard, you're given the simplest of jobs and you always manage to fuck it up. The Boss is coming over here in a few hours and he wants answers before then. What do you want me to tell him? Sorry, we seem to have misplaced Larry."

"Honest Den, the little shit can't have got out. He'll be hiding somewhere. Give me five minutes and I'll find him," Sickly said.

But his entreaty appeared unheard as Mackey turned to the two men stood behind him. He addressed the one on his left.

"You find Larry," Mackey commanded. The man nodded, turned and was gone.

He turned to the other man. "And you get rid of the body."

But before the man could reply, Sickly interjected.

"I thought you only wanted to interrogate Larry? Do you know for sure now that he's the grass?"

"I'm not talking about his body. Well, not yet. I haven't spoken to him. I'm talking about your body knob head. You're fucked up once too often."

As the words left his mouth, Steele saw that Mackey was already pulling a large pistol from his inside pocket. If Sickly needed a moment for Mackey's words to make sense: there was no doubting the sight of the handgun now pointing straight at him. His hands came up in front of him, as if they would be any defence, an instinctive move Steele thought.

Sickly slowly started to back away from Mackey. "Look Den, you're scaring the shit out of me now. I've learnt my lesson. I'll make it up to you, please put the damn gun down?" He begged.

"You're right," Mackey replied before pulling the trigger."I am scaring the shit out of you."

The round hit Sickly in the centre of his forehead. Brain and bone fragments sprayed across the floor behind him, and he was no doubt dead before he hit the ground. The echo of the shot resounded around the room, accentuated by the enclosed space being empty. Steele couldn't believe how loud the sound was. He also couldn't believe what he'd seen. Mackey calmly bent down and collected the spent shell casing before turning to the shocked thug behind him.

"Well? What are you waiting for? Get rid of the body."

Chapter Thirteen

John Burrows had always appreciated how much damage organised crime groups did to society. It was society that didn't always realise the threat. Criminals like Cabilla would operate in a seedy underclass whose activities went unnoticed by the general public. That in itself wasn't a bad thing, he always thought, as it helped to reduce people's fear of crime; what they didn't see they didn't know about. Reactive crimes, like armed robbery or murder are what people were scared of, these and other reactive crimes are visible and in your face. They caught the media attention, and were over-publicised. Consequently, they attracted a lot of resources in policing and investigation terms and rightly so. But Burrows had always understood the true threats to society by people like Cabilla. He had always appreciated how difficult these people were to deal with.

He'd explained this to Lee over the last two days and she'd asked him if that was why he'd preferred covert squad work when he had been in the cops.

"Pretty much," he'd answered as he'd gone on to explain. "Firstly, you are investigating the individuals and their networks, as much as their crimes—many of which went unseen by the public—and that was always harder to do," he'd said. "Not to underestimate how difficult investigating reactive crimes are, but you have a trail of clues to follow. The skill was finding those clues, so it was far from easy. But trying to infiltrate the private lives of active criminals? That was a different thing altogether. And as for recruiting informants: grasses, snouts, assets, covert human intelligence sources—CHIS—or whatever names you gave them, that was always very hard. The risks were high, and the rewards were never enough."

He now knew just how true this was with Cabilla, given the man's pathological hatred of informants. Now made all the clearer since reading the historical brief on what he had done to collaborators back in the Congo.

Burrows had told Lee how hard it had been to recruit Billy the Kid to inform on Cabilla in the first place, which had only led to his kidnap, torture and potential death. Though, after the collapse of the trial in Manchester they were never able to establish what had gone wrong. One hypothesis was that

Cabilla had identified the 'safe house' where Billy the Kid was staying, and had lifted him from under the noses of his handlers. Another theory being, that Billy had simply bottled it, and run off before he was required to give evidence. The majority view was that Cabilla had located the safe house, and waited until Billy went for a stroll in the garden or similar, and then lifted him before anyone could have known.

He'd always had his suspicions about this premise. He understood why the powers that be choose it; if Cabilla had taken him then, he could very well be dead. And if Cabilla had killed him, they wouldn't expect to find a body. Cabilla would have made sure of that. And with no body, there was no murder to investigate. That's the way the reactive bosses would think, as far as Burrows was concerned, but he'd always thought that a bit of an easy way out. Billy the Kid was a loner. He had no family, and few friends. No one was going to ask too many questions about his disappearance.

"It still bothers you, doesn't it?" Lee had asked.

"Yes," he'd answered. "It does."

***

After Burrows and Lee had taken Briers's phone call about the missing undercover officer Steele, Lee had suggested they go for coffee at a local Costa, to talk through what to do next. Burrows finished off explaining his previous days' thoughts about Billy, and paused to drink some cold coffee.

"So you're saying if Cabilla had killed Billy, he may not have carelessly left a body lying about, but he would have made sure people knew about it; as a deterrent?"

"I reckon so, yeah."

"And you didn't pick up any chatter at all after Cabilla's trial collapsed?" Lee asked.

"Only that Cabilla was looking for Billy the Kid, and that he didn't know where he'd gone. We got that from his telephone interception. It was picked up in a call he made as soon as he got outside the court buildings. Unfortunately, that's all we got. As soon as word of his acquittal reached London, they switched off the intercept."

"Bloody Hell, they didn't hang about did they?" Lee said.

"As soon as he was acquitted, the justification to intercept his phone ceased in their eyes. They actually turned it off whilst he was in mid-sentence," Burrows went on to explain.

"The bastards could have at least let him finish his call first," Lee sympathised.

Burrows went on to explain that the consensus at the time was that Cabilla had made the comment on purpose in case the cops were listening. And that subsequent enquires showed that after the call ended, his phone was switched off and never turned back on. He had probably ditched it, and no doubt had other phones they didn't know about. He concluded that their first line of enquiry should be to go to Manchester, and find out for sure what happened to Billy the kid.

"You really think he's still alive?" Lee asked.

"I'm really hoping so. I mean, apart from for the obvious reasons, it would be handy in using his historical knowledge to give us a lead on tracking down Cabilla," Burrows answered.

"What makes you think he'll talk to us, assuming of course that he's still with us?"

"That'll be the tricky bit. But regardless of whether he talks to us or not, it'll give me the chance to make things right with him."

"One last question before we pack our overnight bags and head up the motorway. Why do they call him Billy the Kid?" Lee asked.

"That's an easy one," Burrows answered.

"His real name is Henry McCarty, as in Billy the Kid fame, Henry McCarty. His parents obviously had a sense of humour, not to mention an obvious love of the Wild West. And also because both Henry McCartys allegedly committed their first murders at the age of fifteen," Burrows finished.

***

Steele was starting to assimilate what he'd just witnessed. Not that he'd anything other than disgust for Sickly, but had he really deserved to die? That wasn't a matter for Steele, not now anyway. Nor did the fact he was dead particularly bother him in principle. But to witness the shocking callousness of his demise made Steele feel sick. He was also starting to shake which he guessed was the shock kicking in. Mackey's thug dragged the lifeless form out of the building and out of Steele's sight, which in itself was a small relief. The noise it made gave him the cover to rearrange his legs a little to stave off the onset of cramp, which was hovering around threatening to take hold at any time.

Then he got his second shock.

Mackey was still holding his gun down by his side. He turned towards the inner-room, his back facing the main doors. Then he started to raise his arm.

"Time to come down now Larry or I'll shoot you out the rafters," Mackey stated.

The first thug that Mackey had sent to find Steele now walked into view.

"He ain't anywhere Den," he said.

Steele froze. Could Mackey really see him or was he bluffing. Mackey told the thug to turn the lights off, which he did, and Steele realised it was no bluff. He was sure he would be very visible now the room was returned to semi-darkness, the only natural light coming by way of the reopened main door and cracks around the window shutters.

"Ok Den, don't shoot I'm coming down," he answered.

Two minutes later he was frog-marched back to the cellar room. He tried to explain to Mackey that he was only trying to hide from Sickly, as he was a psycho who had obviously taken a dislike to him. Mackey didn't answer or show any sign that he was even listening. Steele tried to reassure himself that if Mackey was going to kill him, then he would have done it in the large room as soon as Steele had come down from the rafters. A further two minutes later, and he was on the kitchen chair, his legs and arms firmly secured: his ankles to the chair legs, and his arms behind his, and the chair's back. Mackey stood back a couple of paces with his thug stood behind him.

"Right Larry, from what you have just seen you know I'm not in the mood to be fucked about. So first question: Where the fuck have, you been? And why has your phone been off?"

Steele took a deep breath without being obvious about it, and started to recite his well-prepared back-story of how he had legged it from the Industrial estate. He made sure to add inflections into his voice, so as not to sound like he was reading from a script, which of course he was. When he'd finished, Mackey didn't say anything, he just walked around the room obviously considering something whilst the thug kept a close eye on Steele. Not that he was going anywhere. When Mackey broke the silence, it wasn't with what Steele expected to hear.

"You're not stupid Larry that much I know about you. So I'm going to give you the chance to save yourself some serious pain."

Steele felt a primeval dread within himself at the mention of the word 'pain'.

"I like you, I really do. We had some good nights on the piss together, and I really don't want to believe you're a grass. Apart from anything else, if you are, it makes me look a right twat. And the last person to do that was about fifteen minutes ago, and we both know how that ended," Mackey said before continuing. "So I'm going to give you the chance to admit that you've betrayed me to the filth, rather than me have to beat it out of you."

"Look Den, for God's sake I've just told you I'm wanted by the Turks and—" Steele started to say until Mackey silenced him with the wave of his hand.

"Look, we are pretty busy at the moment, and I don't really have the time to spend days torturing you. You probably think, that if you fess up, you'll be signing your own death warrant. Well I have a proposition for you; rather than killing you for being a grass, I can use you, but this time you'll be grassing on the filth, *not* for the filth."

Steele was reeling at what he had just heard; it confirmed what Sickly had said just before his demise. There was only one thing worse than being found out to be an undercover cop, and that was to be thought of as a grass. It was one thing to kill a cop; with all the grief and attention such an act would naturally bring, but to kill a snout, a grass, that was easy. A dead grass was just another dead criminal, killed by another criminal, or that was the way most villains saw it. But to kill an undercover cop would bring about a whole lot of extra-unwanted attention that most criminals didn't need. So contrary to popular belief promulgated by TV and movies, Steele knew that villains generally didn't kill those they suspected to be undercover cops. Even the absolute nutters had to think twice. So, having got over the shock of being thought of as a grass, he now faced a moral dilemma; did he out himself as a cop, and hope Mackey wasn't a nutter? Or did he stick to his script? It was clear to Steele what Mackey was suggesting, but only a cop or a grass would have grasped that straight away, so to buy himself some thinking time he 'stayed in character'. "I'm no grass Den, and I don't understand what it is you're suggesting to me," he said, trying to look confused.

"What I'm saying grass, is if I have to beat it out of you then you're no use to me. If however you come clean and fess to being a grass—I mean for all I know the cops may have had you by the balls, and given you no choice but to grass—then I can use you. I can put you back into the cops but this time you'll be working for me and not them. You'll feed them what I tell you to feed them, just enough shit to keep them satisfied in you. But really, you'll be informing on them, what they know about us, and what they think we are doing. That way, we stay one-step ahead of them.

"But to do that, I have to be able to trust you Larry. Jim here will put you up as his long lost cousin and you'll wear one of our wires when you see your handlers, so we know you are not fucking us over again," Mackey said as he pointed towards the thug stood behind him.

"You've got five minutes to think about it before the pain starts," Mackey added, before he and the thug Jim, left the room, locking the door behind them.

Mackey was being very clever. He had obviously played this card before Steele thought. He was clearly not as thick as he was vicious, which in Steele's experience was uncommon, as the two facets usually went together. It appeared Mackey and Cabilla, and whoever else was involved, didn't suspect Steele of being an undercover cop. He wasn't sure why, perhaps they had done their own background checks and his legend had held firm. This perversely, might turn out to be his downfall, now they thought he was a grass, the lowest of the low in their eyes. He had to think fast, he knew he only had minutes to consider all the options. Does he take his chances and tell them whom he really is? Does he take Mackey's offer at face value and claim to be a grass? Or does he stick to his original script?

He discounted the first option; there were no guarantees they would play by the rules, even if Mackey wasn't a nutter, his boss might be. He didn't believe the second option as genuine, as clever as it was. He was sure that if he had been a real informant, then Mackey's offer would have been hard to resist. It had probably worked for him in the past. Steele made his decision as he heard the keys being put back into the door lock. He was going to 'neck' it out as his old undercover trainer used to say, 'Never be swayed from your legend, no matter how tempting. Always neck it out unless you are in fear of imminent and serious harm' he used to say. So that's what he'd do, but if Mackey started to beat a confession out of him for being a grass, he'd own up to being a cop and take his chances.

"Well grass, is it to be the easy way or the hard way?" asked Mackey as he swung back into the room with Sickly mark 2 grinning behind him. Steele knew he had to put on the performance of his life.

Chapter Fourteen

It was early afternoon when Burrows and Lee arrived on the outskirts of south Manchester. Burrows had forgotten how tedious the journey could be. However, they'd made good time on the trip up with no real traffic problems. They had split the driving, stopping for an early lunch at a motorway service station on the M6. Lee drove first so that he could drive when they arrived, as he knew Manchester better. Lee said she had been to the city before in her previous role in MI5; once spending a week working out of the Manchester field office in the wake of 9/11 and London's 7/7 terrorist attacks. The north was known as a hotbed for Islamic fundamentalists within some quarters of the Muslim communities and she told him how she and others had been dispatched to assist the Manchester office in a recruitment drive, for CHIS— or agents as the security service called them—within those communities. She'd explained all this to Burrows on the journey up as they'd chatted to pass time, and continued to get to know each other a little more.

It was true that they were getting on well, Burrows thought, and even though Lee was a strong character, she was easy to get on with nonetheless. After she'd explained the reason for her last visit, he asked how successful she'd been.

"We were able to recruit some really good sources," she said, unconvincingly.

"So that means it was a wasted trip," Burrows replied with a grin on his face.

They both burst out laughing. It was very difficult to recruit Muslim agents to inform within their own communities; he had faced these difficulties in his previous employment, and could see that Lee had faced similar problems too.

"Maybe I should not have added a plural," Lee said.

"Recruiting one human source or agent as you call them, in that sort of environment would be pretty good," he offered, before refocusing on his driving.

The area of south Manchester they were headed to was Wythenshawe, and as he'd told Lee, it was not far from Manchester's Ringway International Airport. Whilst Lee had taken the first stint at driving, Burrows had rang ahead and made a reservation for a twin room in the Britannia Airport Hotel. They wanted to give the façade of being a married couple, but in order to maintain some privacy, Burrows had asked for a room with twin beds citing his 'wife's bad back. The hotel itself wasn't on the airport site as its name implied, but it was nearby and obviously wanted to cash in on the airport trade by having the word airport in its title. But the main reason he had picked it, was its closeness to Wythenshawe, which was Billy the Kid country; not so much the 'wild west', but more like the 'wild south', well south of Manchester anyway.

After they had checked in and freshened up, they both headed out again. One of the main pubs where Burrows used to meet Billy was on an estate in Wythenshawe. It was a post-war drab looking pub, with the uncreative name of 'The Workers' Retreat'. In truth, Burrows didn't really know where to start looking. It was true that after Billy's disappearance during Cabilla's trial they had looked everywhere for him, but that was different; he either hadn't wanted to be found, or was being kept away by Cabilla's men. But there was a truism that Burrows believed in; villains can't stay away from their tribal habitats for too long. No matter what the reason for an absence, the majority will always naturally drift back to their own 'back yards'. Or so Burrows hoped in this case, as long as Billy was still alive that is.

They arrived at the pub car park late afternoon and Lee suggested it was a good time to try. It shouldn't be too busy at that time of day, and whoever was in there at that time obviously wasn't working, which meant at least some of them were villains. Or so she had speculated. Burrows agreed; it was as good a theory as any. He was also conscious that there might be one or two people in there that would recognise him, and even though they didn't know him as a cop, he suggested they entered separately.

"It might look better if I go in on my own, as I always used to. But if you follow me in a few minutes later, and sit apart from me, you can watch my back without being connected to me."

He'd noticed that Lee had changed at the hotel from tight fitting jeans and 'T' shirt into an old pair of jeans with a baggy sweatshirt on top, with her hair tied back through a baseball cap. She had dressed down appropriately; he was impressed. Burrows realised Lee had noticed him looking, as she next spoke in a ridiculous northern accent.

"Aye lad. That sounds 'bout right, I'll make sure them naughty men don't ge ya a slap."

"I'm impressed Jane, you clearly are a woman of many talents, though accents clearly aren't one of them." And with that, Burrows smiled, got out of the car, and headed into the pub.

As expected, the pub was fairly quiet. A few old boys sat in the corner with half pints of ale and playing cards, and a few 'jack-the-lads' at the end of the bar drinking, and seemingly showing off amongst themselves about something or other. Burrows recognised the barman straight away. He was an Irishman in his thirties, well-built and tall, similar in stature to himself. Burrows ordered a pint of a local bitter and if the barman recognised Burrows, he didn't show it. As he was taking the head off his drink, he noticed Lee enter the pub, and go to the other end of the bar and order a drink. As the barman was serving her, one of the 'wide' boys must have made some sort of remark to her, as she responded with a single finger gesture before walking to a table in the corner. The three men burst out laughing. Burrows noticed that the barman was watching her walk to her table, his gaze lasting a little too long for Burrows's comfort, and not in a leering way. It was time to break the barman's thoughts. "You got a minute pal?" Burrows asked.

The barman duly looked towards Burrows and walked over to him. "What?"

"I used to meet a mate of mine in here, a while back. I've sort of been away," Burrows paused on purpose.

The barman nodded before Burrows continued.

"I'm trying to hook back up with him but I don't know where he's living now, wondered if you could help."

By the barman's nod, Burrows hoped he had taken the inference that 'being away' really meant, 'being locked up'.

"Yeah I remember you, vaguely. Who're looking for?"The barman asked.

"Billy. Billy the kid."

There was a slight hesitation before the barman spoke again, and Burrows saw a reaction to the name register in the Irishman's eyes. It seemed a little more than just recognition.

"I can ask around. Haven't seen Billy myself in a while. Who shall I say is asking?" The barman replied.

" Burrows didn't want to scare Billy away with his name, so he wrote one of his mobile telephone numbers on the back of a beer mat and handed it to the bar man, wrapped in a twenty pound note.

"Just say it's an old cell mate who wants to pay him some money I owe him. My number's on the mat, and please have a drink on me for your trouble," Burrows eventually replied.

"It's no trouble, and thanks, I'll be sure and have that drink," the barman said.

Burrows emptied his glass, before nodding at the barman and walking out.

As agreed beforehand, Lee stayed in the pub for a full five minutes before she followed Burrows out.

As arranged, Burrows had driven off before Lee left the pub, just in case they were watched leaving. He'd waited around the corner and Lee joined him a few minutes later. As they drove back to the hotel, Burrows filled Lee in with the conversation he'd had with the barman.

"He knows where Billy is, I'm sure of it. Or at the very least, he knows how to contact him," Burrows offered.

"I'll go with that John. He was on his phone as soon as you walked out the pub."

"Brilliant," Burrows exclaimed.

"What do we do now then?" Lee asked.

"Just sit back and wait," Burrows answered as he pulled a silver pay-as-you-go mobile phone out of his pocket.

"This one's the Billy phone," he explained.

Twenty minutes later, they were both back in the hotel room when the Billy phone rang. Burrows picked it up off the coffee table and pressed the green button. "Hello."

"Who's this?" The caller asked.

Burrows recognised Billy's nasally tones. "Don't put the phone down Billy, but it's John Burrows here. I want to make things up to you."Burrows had noticed as he answered the call that the caller's number wasn't displayed. If Billy hung up, he had no way of calling him back.

After what seemed like an age, Billy spoke again."Have you any idea what those animals did to me? Have you? No, of course you fucking haven't. They lifted me from right under your stupid fucking noses and kept hold of me until the trial was over. Then, with no help from you, I managed to get away and hide for a while, until they found me again. Then they gave me 'a little incentive' not to ever talk to you bastards again. And some fucking incentive it was. Look the only reason I'm even ringing you is that you said you owed me money. Well, I reckon you do, big time. So I'll take one last risk so you can pay me what I'm owed, then I never want to see or hear from you again. And paying me what you owe me, better be the only reason for your little social call, 'cause you're getting fuck all else from me John."

As soon as Billy started his rant Burrows was happy just to listen, at least he hadn't hung up. And one thing he knew about Billy, was that he never turned down money. He was like most petty criminals: greedy. But Burrows knew in this case, that Billy was owed. They had let him down after the collapse of the Cabilla trial in Manchester, a fact that had always troubled him. Prior to leaving London, Burrows had made a call to Frank Briers who arranged for them to collect a holdall of operation funds before they hit the motorway. Burrows just hoped they had enough to sate Billy. Only then, did they have any chance of trying to get further information from him, and Burrows knew this was very much a one-off opportunity.

As soon as Billy had vented his initial anger at Burrows, he asked the question Burrows had been waiting for.

"How much John? And I warn you, if it's not enough, I'll not even risk meeting you. Cabilla still has loads of goons working for him up here; I'll just put the phone down, and disappear."

"Twenty five grand in used notes, and trust me that's as much as I could get," Burrows answered.

Another pause, and then Billy replied."Ok, but the quicker the better. It's safer that way."

They made their arrangements to meet 'in the country', and then ended the call. Burrows turned to Lee and blew out a lungful of air before filling her in on the bits of the conversation she couldn't have heard.

"So we are heading out of town into the sticks for the meet are we?" Lee asked after Burrows had finished.

"Oh no Jane, 'in the country' was code for one of our meeting places," he said, as he grinned at her, "ten o'clock in the morning, we are heading to Blackley cemetery."

Chapter Fifteen

Steele took a deep breath as his two captors entered the room and closed the door behind them. Sickly-2 stood with his back to the door, legs apart, wearing a similar ghoulish grimace that Sickly mark one had been such an exponent of.

Den Mackey stood in front of Steele, also with legs apart, and his hands on his hips. His facet wisted into a snarl. "I'm waiting for an answer grass, easy or hard, it's all the same to me," he said.

"Look Den, you can think what you want, but if you think I'm a grass then perhaps you are a twat," Steele said. He knew his comments would enrage Mackey; and no doubt provoke a violent response, but he had to show the right amount of indignation at the suggestion that he was one of the lowest of the low. He didn't have to wait long.

Mackey swung his right fist in a roundhouse punch connecting with the side of Steele's head. He saw it coming so had a split-second to tense himself. Nevertheless, the force would have knocked him and the chair over, had it not been fastened to the floor. He did not see the second blow. It was a short left-handed jab that hit his stomach with such force he projectile vomited down his front and onto the floor. Mackey sprung back to avoid the noxious fluid, giving Steele a few moments of reprieve.

"If that shit splashes on my shoes I'll make you lick it up," Mackey said.

Steele spat on the floor and looked up as the next blow landed from Mackey's right. It missed the side of Steele's head but connected with his nose. He cried out, as he felt the cartilage snap, and warm blood flow into his open mouth. The pain was worse than he would have expected, and he was trying his best not to heave again. He knew he couldn't put up with much more. He was a cop, not a soldier. He was on the verge of putting his hands up—metaphorically—to stop the onslaught, and to out himself as a cop, when he passed out.

A bucket of cold water woke him with a shiver. He opened his eyes and came to his senses as he felt Sickly-2 unfastening him from the chair. Steele was struggling to digest what was happening when Mackey spoke.

"Ok Larry, I reckon I owe you an apology. Grasses are weak, and if you were a grass, I reckon you'd have fessed up by now. But just for the record, if you had, then I wouldn't have turned you into a double agent like I was suggesting. I'd have turned you into fish food."

Steele couldn't believe his plan had worked, and he was right; he'd seen Mackey's offer for what it really was; bullshit. Elation coursed through him, numbing the pain.

"Ok, Den what happens now?" He asked.

Mackey explained about what had happened at the Lorry Park, and how his boss's name had been mentioned. How they thought, that either Steele was a grass, or one of the dead cops had a recording device. It was clear to Steele that Mackey was now happy it was the latter. He also realised that Mackey's boss was someone he was wary of. It also dawned on him that they had an 'in' on the Police side which wasn't exactly what he wanted to think, but forewarned and all that.

Mackey then went on to explain that they had another driving job for him to do, and that they would pay him well at the end of it, to make up for the 'misunderstanding' as he put it. He said they had to go to Ramsgate the following day to collect a cargo but didn't elaborate. He also told him that Sickly-2—or Jim—as Mackey called him, was to be his new best mate until the job was done. Not that they didn't trust him now, or anything, it was just safer that way, apparently.

"Jim will take you back to his gaff, get you fixed up and sort you out with some clean clobber. Then you're on the road early doors tomorrow," Mackey finished.

Steele looked across at Sickly-2 who had dropped the grim grin act.

"No offence Larry," he said, as he stuck his hand out.

Steele took it, and shook it, as he knew he had to and then followed Sickly-2 out of the room. He followed him out into the warehouse where he had previously hidden, and noticed the floor was wet with water where someone had cleaned up the mess left by Sickly-1. Steele shuddered as he walked through the room, and was glad to get back outside and breathe in some fresh air. He was put into the back seat of a large 4 x 4that had darkened windows, it was parked side-on across the front doors of the building so he didn't get chance to take in his surroundings. Mackey got in the front passenger seat and threw a black cloth bag at Steele telling him to put it on. Steele did as he was told and then they headed off. The brief glimpse he did get was of a large red brick building set in its own grounds.

Sickly-2 dropped Mackey off somewhere in the West End, apparently, and then drove to his flat on the outskirts somewhere. Sickly-2 wasn't one to make much small talk and after Steele had eaten, he showered and settled down in a spare room. As he was preparing to get into bed, he heard the click of a lock being turned in the bedroom door. He also noticed that the one window in the small single room had locks on it. He was pretty sure they did trust him now, but they were clearly not taking any chances yet. But he was just glad to have come through Mackey's interrogation with his legend intact. He lay down on the bed and was asleep as soon as he shut his eyes.

***

Burrows and Lee were out of their hotel before 7.30 a.m. the following day. The journey to Blackley Cemetery and Crematorium would normally only take about thirty minutes Burrows reckoned. They were close to the M60 ring road and the cemetery was close to junction 19 near Heaton Park in the north east of the city. Rush hour traffic would double the journey time but he wanted to get there early, well ahead of the 10 o'clock meeting he had arranged with Billy.

The cemetery, as he recalled, was in its own massive grounds, and was close to Heaton Park, which in itself was a considerable area of city parkland. When he had handled Billy, as an informant, it was considered one of the safer places to meet, without having to travel too far out of the city. He'd agreed to meet Billy by the crematorium where they could wander discretely down one of the many pathways.

Lee had suggested Burrows didn't introduce her to Billy; it would only complicate things and may even spook him. She suggested that she would stay hidden, but watch them from cover. Burrows knew that the area was far too big and rural to carry out any meaningful reconnaissance, but he wanted to give them at least an hour to do what they could. Especially for Lee, who had never been there before.

The journey took just over an hour and they both voiced gratitude on arrival that the weather was fine and dry. Burrows drove around the perimeter roads before entering the site and parking up on the crematorium car park. Nothing looked out of the ordinary and there were no signs of anyone. He agreed with Lee, which path he would walk with Billy on, and she disappeared to identify her own parallel route. She reappeared about twenty minutes later and re-joined him in the car. There was still no one around, so each checked the weapons they had drawn from the car's boot safe. They both had a SIG Sauer P226 semi-automatic service pistol. Each had a magazine of 19 x 9 mm Parabellum rounds. Lee pushed hers into the rear of her waistband under her baggy sweatshirt, and Burrows put his into a shoulder holster under his bomber jacket. The time was approaching a quarter to ten, so Lee got out the car and vanished into the undergrowth.

Ten minutes later, Burrows heard Billy before he saw him. He had been expecting a car to approach but he heard a humming noise. Then he saw it. A motorised disability scooter rode into the car park and stopped by the entrance to the crematorium. Burrows recognised its driver straight away. He got out of the car, and slung the holdall over his shoulder to make it look less suspicious, rather than carrying it by the handles. Billy turned to face Burrows as he approached, but didn't acknowledge him.

Once Burrows was nearer, Billy spoke. "Bit of a shock eh? Seeing me in this."

"Sorry Billy, I truly am. When you said they gave you an incentive, I didn't think it meant anything like this."

"Yeah well it did. The bastards cut the tendons at the back of my knees, and then shot me through the kneecaps just for good measure."

"How did you manage to get here?" Burrows asked, regretting the question as soon as the words had left his lips. He was still getting over the shock of seeing Billy in a wheelchair.

"Mate of mine is a taxi driver, and he's got one of those wheelchair hydraulic lift things attached to his van. He's just dropped me at the entrance. I'll ring him when we're done. Anyway, that's my problem not yours, all I want to know is, is that the money in there?" Billy said pointing at the bag.

"Yeah, but let's go for a wander down the path, somewhere out of sight should anyone drive up."

Billy nodded, and they both headed off down one of the access paths. Billy vented a bit more angst before he started to calm down. Burrows didn't want to patronise Billy, but he did tell him he wasn't done with Cabilla and that when he was, he would make sure Billy got some more support. Billy said that he would believe it when it happened. He also told Burrows to have no further contact with him until Cabilla was well and truly locked away for life. After a few minutes, Billy was clearly starting to relax, after all Burrows and he had always got on well in the past. They stopped at a 'T' junction of paths as they continued to chat. Burrows put the holdall in a basket at the front of Billy's scooter.

"It's all there Billy. Twenty-five large ones, and there will be more once I've sorted Cabilla out. Just so I know though, Billy, who actually did the damage to you?"

"It was Cabilla, along with that Mackey. Both the bastards enjoyed every second of it. Said the only reason they didn't kill me was they wanted others to see their handiwork, as a deterrent to talking. They also said if I ever spoke to you again they would finish me off, so no offence John, but I'm going to head off now. And remember, don't even think about coming near me again, well not until both of those bastards are properly banged up," Billy said, as he started to manoeuvre his scooter.

He stopped to add. "Good luck John, but remember one thing."

"What's that Billy?"

"Tread carefully, 'cause if Cabilla ever got the chance of taking you out, he'd 'off' you without a second thought."

Burrows was about to respond, when he saw Billy's head explode. A cascade of pink mist flew from the back of his skull. It all happened in a split-second of silence, closely followed by the sound of rifle shot that resounded all around. A migration of birds lifted in unison from the treetops and scattered. It seemed like an age, but it only took a microsecond for Burrows's brain to assimilate what his eyes were reporting. He threw himself into the undergrowth that bordered the path. He drew his weapon as he rolled onto his front, trying to get a view of the direction of the shot. As he hit the ground, a second bullet ricocheted off the path, where a moment earlier he had been stood. This time Burrows was able to get a clearer view of the area where the sniper lay. It was in the middle of a thicket, approximately 150 metres away.

Burrows didn't return fire; his weapon was almost useless at that distance. He would only have given away his exact position if he had. All he could do was wriggle more into the undergrowth, and wait for his assailant to break cover, to come looking for him. He glanced across at Billy, who was now lying lifeless on his back behind the scooter. The force of the contact had flung him out onto the path.

Then Burrows heard the distinctive sound of a double tap from a small calibre weapon. A few seconds later, his mobile phone rang; he looked at the screen before answering it.

"It's me, Jane. The gunman's eliminated, I'm coming out now, so don't shoot me."

Moments later, Lee appeared from the same thicket the gunman's shots had come from. Burrows rolled out from his makeshift hide and got to his feet. He looked around as Lee approached, fortunately, there was still no sign of anyone, but he knew that wouldn't last too long.

"I owe you, and some," Burrows said as Lee arrived.

"No worries, but let's talk later, for now let's just get the hell out of here before your old firm turn up," Lee said.

Chapter Sixteen

An hour later, Burrows had just come off the phone to Frank Briers. He turned towards Lee who was on the other twin bed facing him.

"Frank agrees there was nothing else we could have done. We didn't have time to search the gunman, but he had all the hallmarks of a professional, so I'm sure there was nothing to find on him. Thing is, was I identified and therefore a target? Or, did the gunman just not want any loose ends, once he had taken Billy down?"

"I reckon it's a bit of both," Lee said.

"Well, there is only one person who could have blown Billy out, and that's the Irish barman at the pub," he added.

"Either that, or Billy told someone about the meet. Obviously, someone he trusted. Maybe it was his taxi driver mate?" Lee suggested.

"Yeah, it's a pity we couldn't hang around. But all we've got at the moment is the barman, so let's go and have a little word with him shall we?"

It was just before noon before he and Lee had recced the Workers' Retreat pub. It was locked up, and didn't appear as if anyone lived on the premises. No punters were queuing up for it to open, and they both said they hoped the opening time would be midday, and their talkative barman would be the man doing the opening. Burrows parked their motor on the car park facing away from the pub to give them both a bit more cover; they were hiding behind their seat backs effectively, and using the door mirrors to see. At ten past twelve, he saw the Irish barman appear at the front doors alone, he tapped Lee to warn her, and they slid down in their seats as the barman unlocked and entered.

Two minutes later, he and Lee entered the pub, Lee closing the front door behind them. The barman was already behind the bar with his back to the door.

"You'll have to give me a few minutes, I've only just opened up," he said before turning to face the doorway.

He stopped in his tracks, and his mouth hung open. Burrows wasn't sure whether the obvious shock on his face, was from seeing Burrows, or from the Sig Sauer handgun he was pointing at him. He guessed it was a bit of both.

"Hands on your head, then come around this side of the bar and kneel down in front of me," Burrows instructed.

"Look man, there's no cash in here so there isn't, just the float in the till," the barman said in a stutter.

"Don't insult me you piece of shit, or I'll pop you right here. The bloke, I came in here looking for yesterday, is now dead. And that can only be thanks to you, so unless you want to join him, you'd better start talking."

The barman came around from the other side of the bar and knelt as instructed. Then, much to Burrows's relief, he started talking.

The barman told them that over a year ago, around the time Billy and Burrows stopped coming into the pub, he received a visit from a cockney villain who said he was a mate of Billy's, and that he was trying to find him. The bloke had given the barman £500, and said that there was another 'monkey' in it, if he could turn Billy up. The barman pocketed the money and said that he would. But what he really did was ring Billy to warn him that some cockney bloke was looking for him. He didn't see or hear of Billy again, until he surfaced a couple of weeks later in intensive care. The barman never 'ratted' Billy out, as he put it, he was just happy to pocket the original £500. That was until yesterday. He'd rung Billy as soon as Burrows left the pub. He passed the message, which Burrows left, and asked Billy for some cash for passing the info on to him. When Billy told him to 'go fuck a leprechaun', he became angry, so he rang the number he still had for the cockney guy, told him about Burrows looking for Billy hoping to cash in that way. The cockney also told him to get lost, but only after he had asked the barman for Burrows's description. Burrows asked for the cockney's telephone number, and then told the barman what he thought of him. It was clear from his reactions that the barman thought Burrows and Lee were villains, and it was safer for them that he thought that. Just before they left, he warned the barman that if he ever spoke of their visit, they would make sure everyone in Wythenshawe knew he was the snout that grassed Billy up, and caused his death. That would be a death warrant in this part of Manchester. Then Burrows knocked him out, partly to reinforce their cover story, and partly because he thought it was the least the slimy barman deserved.

An hour later, they were both heading southbound on the M6 back towards London. Lee was driving and Burrows had just come off the phone to Briers.

"What did Frank say?"

"He's going to do some work on the mobile phone number the barman gave us, and he's also going to make discreet enquires with Greater Manchester Police, to see if they come up with anything on the sniper. Poor sods, they're going to be chasing their tales on this job; one dead disabled ex-criminal, and one dead assassin, it's going to keep them busy for a while."

"Well, there's no way we can be connected with it. There was no CCTV 'cause I checked during my initial recce, and we got the holdall back," Lee added.

"Yes, and once they realise that Billy was an ex-informant then the flood gates will open on potential suspects. Like I say, they are going to be busy chasing dead ends."

"Do you think they will make a link with Cabilla and the collapsed trial?" Lee asked.

"I shouldn't think so, they will know about his previous injuries from when he was in hospital, though they obviously didn't make the link then. Billy, no doubt told them nothing, probably not even his name, after such a brutal incentive. That said, they'd know now who he really is, now they can access his DNA. If they write off the original attack to Cabilla—which I'm sure they will—then his killing must be something else by someone else," Burrows answered.

"I see what you mean, If Cabilla was going to kill him, then he would have, at the time of the original attack," Lee said.

"Hopefully they'll see it that way. I'm sure Frank will be keeping his finger on the pulse."

"Anything else from Frank?" Lee asked.

"Just, that the U/C lorry driver still hasn't turned up. His DI from Manchester has travelled down to London to meet up with his counterpart in the Met. There is absolutely no sign of him, and they're all starting to get a bit twitchy."

"Are they linking his disappearance to Cabilla?" Lee asked.

"They seem to see no reason to at the moment. It could be any number of things; he'd apparently only just returned from being off after the lorry park massacre, so probably shouldn't have been put out operational again so soon. They are all crapping themselves thinking he may have had a bit of a wobbler, and just gone off on one."

"What do we do now then? What do you reckon Mr ex-detective?" Lee asked with a playful grin on her face.

"Well, we need to chase up whoever owns that phone. The cockney; he can only be one of Cabilla's men. That's the best lead we've got at the mo, unless you see it different, Miss ex-secret squirrel," Burrows replied, also grinning.

"Nope, let's get back to London Town," Lee finished.

***

Steele was driving a large lorry, with Sickly-2 as his sidekick, into Stour Valley Business Park, which was just off the A26 in Kent a few miles west of Canterbury. It seemed a fairly modern industrial estate, with several units up for rent Steele noted. Having been directed to pull up outside one, Steele waited whilst Sickly-2 got out with a bunch of keys, and disappeared through a small door next to a steel roller shutter door. Moments later, the roller shutter doors were being automatically raised and Sickly-2 was waving for Steele to reverse his wagon into the large space inside. Sickly-2 told him to wait in the wagon, as their cargo would be arriving soon. Steele still had no idea what the cargo was, but he knew that they were not far from Ramsgate, which is an international ferry port, and Kent International Airport was also nearby. He wasn't sure whether the airport handled much, if any freight, as it was only a small airfield, so he guessed Ramsgate was the most likely entry point for anything coming in from overseas.

He was panicking a bit that the cargo might be drugs, but there was nothing he could do about it. Since he had been stuck with Sickly-2, he'd not had the opportunity to ring his boss to let him know he was ok. He was sure by now that his DI from Manchester will have come to London to meet up with the DI there, and they would be actively looking everywhere for him. He just hoped that they kept looking, but without going public on it. He was praying that if they put his picture in the paper, then they did so, as if he was any missing or wanted person, and not as a cop. That way, it wouldn't compromise his position as an undercover officer. But even done like that, it would no doubt still mean more questions to answer, and the last thing he wanted, was for Den Mackey to start getting suspicious again.

The other thing that bothered him was that he'd been forced into what he was now doing, and because he was incommunicado, he was acting without due lawful authority. He could only imagine what would happen if they got stopped by the cops whilst driving this cargo—whatever it was—and end up doing twenty years for importing cocaine or suchlike. His reverie was broken by the sound of the shutter doors being raised again and sunlight flooding back into the unit. Sickly-2 told him to stay put, and jumped out of the wagon to help direct a new lorry as it reversed into the unit. It parked alongside Steele's wagon and he heard muffled noises as its rear doors were opened, as were the rear doors to his trailer.

Steele tried to see in his rear view door mirrors what was being unloaded from one wagon to the other, but the open doors on the other wagon closed off his view down the middle. Then Sickly-2 closed the shutter doors again and most of the light disappeared.

He couldn't see what was being loaded into the back of his wagon, but there were a lot of footsteps to-ing and fro-ing within the rear of his trailer. He couldn't make any sense of it. Twenty minutes later, and Sickly-2 opened the shutter doors again. The other wagon left first, Steele couldn't read the registration number but did see that the plate was blue with yellow digits and numbers on it. The first two characters were KN, he had no idea where the plate related to, but committed it to memory. As soon as the other wagon had cleared, he was beckoned to drive out the unit and then stop, by Sickly-2, who then locked the unit up, and jumped back into the cab, and directed him to head back to London.

"Where to exactly," he'd asked.

"Dulwich," Sickly-2 replied, "the warehouse in Dulwich."

Chapter Seventeen

Cabilla was with Mackey at an outside café bar near to his rented Docklands flat. The sun was shining and Cabilla was enjoying his liquid lunch, watching the world of commuters and tourists go past. He liked London; so many people all around, and yet you remained unseen, everyone going about their business, purposefully keeping their noses out of anyone else's. He received two calls on his mobile phone in quick succession. Mackey was looking at him quizzically, but he made sure his expression gave nothing away. Mackey had just spent the last twenty minutes bringing him up to speed on the interrogation of Larry, and the problem he'd had with the idiot who'd been guarding him. He was happy with Mackey's ultimate assessment of Larry, and barely raised an eyebrow when told what had happened to the idiot. He'd always thought him a liability.

"Did you get rid of the body good?" was all he'd asked, before his phone started to ring again.

Mackey answered with a nod, without interrupting him as he answered his phone. After short conversations, he ended the call and turned to Mackey. "We have good news, and bad news—but with some good attached."

Mackey said nothing, just allowed him to continue.

"The good news is that the second wagon has left Kent no problems. Jim seems to be happy enough with Larry, so it looks like you were right Den."

Mackey noticeably exhaled loudly down his nose, before asking. "What's the bad news Boss?"

"We need to get to a TV inside the pub and put the BBC news on," Cabilla replied, before getting up and heading for the door.

They found a TV switched on in a poolroom, and he turned it over to BBC 1. There were two young men in their twenties, student types, playing pool. One of them complained to him that he was watching the previous channel. Mackey turned and hit him with the back of his huge hand with such force that it knocked him across the pool table. Mackey then told them both to go. They didn't need telling twice, and hurried out leaving Cabilla and Mackey alone in the room. They both looked at the TV and Cabilla could hear the end of a news bulletin about a double killing in Manchester. Both victims shot dead in a cemetery, one of the deceased was in a wheelchair. Neither has been identified as of yet.

Both men ordered another drink and resumed their seats outside before Cabilla spoke again. "The second call was from the Runt. He said the shooting only happened a couple of hours ago. He said the filth had no idea who our man was yet, but had identified Billy pretty quickly. A call had gone out to all police intelligence units for databases checks."

"So that's the other good news then," Mackey offered. "That little grassing bastard obviously had never learnt his lesson. So I'm guessing the shooter getting hit is the bad news, but how the hell did that happen?"

"I don't know how the shooter got taken out Den. But we can only assume that whoever it was asking after Billy wasn't filth after all. And that it was them, who managed to take the shooter out, after he'd done Billy. In which case, not only are we dealing with another firm of villains, and not the filth; but we are dealing with villains who seem to be pretty handy."

"What about our taxi bloke, did he see who Billy was meeting?" Mackey asked.

"No, he turned up early to collect Billy hoping to get a glimpse, then heard the shots and fucked off," Cabilla answered.

"What the fuck do another firm of villains want with Billy the—knob head— Kid?" Mackey said.

"I've no idea, nor do I have a clue what it means. I've told the Runt to find out."

They both finished their drinks and headed off towards Cabilla's car. He told Mackey that a couple of their girls working up west had taken a liberty and needed 'slapping up' to 'send a message'. He wanted to sort it before they headed south of the river to Dulwich, before the wagon arrived from Kent.

***

It was late afternoon, when Burrows and Lee arrived back in the southeast. Lee dropped Burrows off at his home in Thame before heading off towards her flat in central London. They had agreed to meet with Briers at Pimlico the following morning to update him face-to-face. Lee offered to pick Burrows up, but that would mean her fighting all the way out of London through rush hour traffic, only to fight her way all the way back again. Burrows said he would get a train from Oxford to Paddington in London, and then get the tube train to Pimlico and see her at the office. But she insisted on picking him up at Paddington railway station, even if it did mean driving all the way around Hyde Park. He didn't put up much of an argument; he hated using the underground, especially at this time of year when the temperature in the carriages seemed to go off the scale.

He was looking forward to a few hours down time, time to relax, reflect, and chill down a bit. But after a take-away dinner and a couple of drinks, he was glad of an early night. The next morning he was up early feeling refreshed, the weather was overcast but at least it was dry. He repacked his overnight holdall with some fresh clothes and headed off out.

An hour and half later he was outside Paddington railway station, the site of the world's first underground railway. It had first been served by underground trains when it had been the Western terminus of the Metropolitan Railway back in 1863. The underground-station building still had the Metropolitan Railway name carved in the white stone frontage, an echo of a previous era. He mused about how London would have looked back then, as he waited for Lee. He didn't have to wait long, the car's horn broke his thoughts, he looked up and smiled as he realised it was his ride.

"You looked miles away," Lee said, as Burrows got in the car.

"Yeah, sorry, I tend to let my mind wander when I'm treading water. I was just admiring the building and its history, as sad as that sounds."

"You're different John, I'll give that. I don't know how you manage to switch off like that. Especially, when we are in the middle of an operation."

"Don't worry; I'm plugged back in now."

Twenty minutes later, they were at the round oak table in the windowless meeting room underneath the Pimlico Office, waiting for Briers to arrive. Frank Briers landed a few minutes later, and both Lee and Burrows talked him through their trip to Manchester in more detail than they had been able to over the phone. Lee finished by asking if the mobile phone number they'd got from the barman had produced any answers.

"Well first of all, it was not known on any databases, which is no great surprise. It is a pay-as-you go phone with no identity or links. It hasn't been used much over the last twelve months, but I think you are both right in your assumption that it has links to Cabilla. He'd obviously put a safety net in place, so to speak, after the Manchester acquittal; just to keep an eye on Billy," Briers said.

"I'm surprised he didn't kill him when he had the chance," Burrows said.

"I think it's like you said before, having brutalised Billy, he probably wanted to send out a message to other would-be informers; what could happen to them if they strayed onto the straight and narrow," Lee said.

"I agree," Briers said, adding, "but it may prove to be a mistake. We've had a female agent put in a controlled call into the phone, purporting to be after some bloke who supposedly gave her his number when she was drunk."

"How did that go?" Lee asked.

"Well, a male answered with a London accent and seemed to readily accept it was a wrong number. There was a lot of office type chatter in the background; people on other phones, all talking with London accents, and the backdrop overall had the sort of echo to it you tend to get in offices. I've got the Technical Support Unit working on a recording of the call, trying to clean it up, and clarify the ambient background conversations to see if they throw any further light on to it," Briers said.

"So the phone's user is definitely in the Greater London area then," Burrows said.

"Better than that, we've now got a live cell-siting on the phone, and it's currently pinging masts on the M1 north out of the Home Counties. My guess is that it's heading to Manchester," Briers said.

"He's probably heading for Wythenshawe," Lee said. "Do you want us to head back up there?"

"No need, thanks. I've got a triangulation team hot tailing up the M1 behind the signal, and a second team heading south down the M6 from Manchester. Once they are able to pinpoint the phone's exact location, a full surveillance team will take over and follow it, ID the user, and watch what he does."

"That's good news, it's time we had a bit of luck. I assume then you want us to stick to our original brief?" Burrows asked.

"Yes," Briers said. "I want you two to stay after Cabilla, and I'll feed in any Intel updates we get. Once the phone's user is properly identified, we may need you two to have a little 'off the record' sort of chat with him. But I'll let you know."

"Is there anything on the sniper yet?" Lee asked.

"Nothing on him yet, but the weapon he'd used was an old Winchester bolt action rifle, the type NATO used over twenty years ago. It was firing 7.62mm rounds, so was a pretty lethal weapon. The serial number had been filed off, so the weapon has gone to the forensic lab to see if they can bring the number back with an acid treatment. As for the shooter himself, he's unknown; no form we can find at the criminal records bureau, and he's not coming up as ex-military or anything, but it's early days," Briers answered.

"Well, the fact that he took a rifle with him proves he knew the location of the meet we had arranged with Billy. That tends to rule the barman out a bit; I can't imagine Billy rang him back after he spoke to me to tell him the location of the meet. It doesn't make sense," Burrows said.

"My money's on the taxi driver friend, not that we have any idea who the hell he is?" said Lee, adding, "I must admit we didn't ask the barman about the taxi driver, if need be we can pay him another visit."

"True enough, but there is one little job I want you both to squeeze in before you return your main focus back onto Cabilla," Briers said.

Burrows and Lee both looked at each other before Briers spoke again. "It's another Yankee, Yankee."

Chapter Eighteen

Briers opened his briefcase and handed Burrows and Lee a manila binder each, which Burrows could see had the words 'Top Secret' written on the front in large bold type, with the words 'Eyes Only' underneath. It was similar to the Cabilla file they had read, but a lot thinner.

"All the target details and associated personal information are in those files, which I'd like you to memorise, there's not too much to learn," Briers said.

"I'll give you the Intel brief verbally. Suffice to say, the Executive have given this a 'Yankee, Yankee', and the PM has ratified their decision. But let's grab a coffee first."

Five minutes later, they were back around the oak table and Briers launched into his brief. The subject's name was Joe Croston, he told them, a fat obnoxious man in his early forties. He lived alone in a one-bedroomed flat situated off College Road, London SE21. It was close to Dulwich Park, which is a large family-orientated park that had been extensively refurbished since 2006.

"The significance of the park will come later," Briers said. He continued to explain that Croston is a committed paedophile with several convictions for indecent assaults against children. Usually boys, but sometimes girls, all aged between eight and twelve years at the time of the offences. Police had long suspected him of committing worse offences against children but always struggled obtaining enough evidence against him. He is used to working the system, as years ago he'd been an informant, before the local police who ran him realised the level of his criminality, and stopped using him. The previous year he had been arrested for the abduction, rape and murder of aneleven-year boy from Dulwich Park, Briers explained.

"I remember that job, real nasty affair," Burrows said.

"Yeah, me too," said Lee. "But didn't the bastard get off or something," she added.

"Yes, and no," Briers replied, and then went on to explain in detail.

He told them how at last, the police were confident they had enough evidence. They had a witness who saw a man fitting Croston's description dragging a boy into a car registered to Croston. They then underwent a massive search for both Croston and the car but neither turned up. They put out a large press appeal to find the car, and the police had then taken the rare move to name Croston as the person they were looking for. Find Croston quickly, and hopefully find the missing boy. That had been the theory Briers explained.

"Wouldn't publishing his name in that way compromise any future court proceeding?" Lee asked.

"Possibly," Burrows interjected before continuing. "But in abduction cases like these, the greater public interest is served in finding the boy first, and worry about any negative effect on proceedings later."

"Exactly," Briers said. He then explained how the day after the publicity appeal, Croston turned up at a local nick with his brief claiming he had been out of town, and had returned to find his car stolen. However, they put him on a video identity parade and the witness picked him out. Although the car was never found, the boy's body turned up in a shallow grave in Epping Forrest. It hadn't been well covered, but the body had been extensively burned after death, and prior to being taken to the forest.

"He clearly wasn't too worried about the body being found, because as far as he was concerned, all forensic would have been destroyed," Briers added.

"And was it?" Lee asked.

"Unfortunately," Briers answered. "Also, because of the earlier publicity appeal, the defence severely attacked the credibility of the eye witness identification. The trial was always going to be shaky. Croston's defence included an alibi that at the time of the abduction he was in a multiplex cinema in Brighton watching a film. He had no witnesses to support his alibi but had clearly seen the film when he was questioned about it."

"But he could have seen the film at any time, and at any cinema," Lee pointed out.

"I know," Briers said. "But an alibi like that is like a bad back or whiplash."

Burrows and Lee just looked at Briers with questioning expressions on their faces before he explained.

"It's easy to allege, but damn hard to disprove. Anyway the trial was definitely going Croston's way, but then he played his ace, though it didn't pay off right away," Briers added.

They all refilled their coffee cups before Briers continued his briefing. He went on to explain that during the trial an informant came forward in Hove, and told his handlers that he'd been following the trial in the media, and he knew for a fact that Croston couldn't have committed the offence. Claimed to have been next to him at the Brighton Odeon, watching the same film as Croston had claimed in his alibi. He told his handlers this during a routine meeting when he also passed on other criminal intelligence, not related to Croston. This had given the handlers a massive moral dilemma.

"How come?" Lee asked.

Briers explained that once the police sign up an informant, or CHIS, then they face a number of legal requirements to manage: the CHIS's authority to act as an informant and what purpose they can be used for, including any limitations of their use and conduct, dos and don'ts. But they also have a 'duty of care' towards the informant themselves. And part of that duty of care involves never revealing their status as an informant. In rare circumstances, a Judge can order this to be done in the public interest, but invariably if that happened then the police would drop whichever case was involved.

"Why is that? Lee asked.

"Well, no doubt John can tell you more about this than I can, but if the police ever freely allow an informant to be identified, then they will set a precedent which will prevent them getting protection from the courts in future when they wish to protect an informant's identity," Briers said.

"And not only that, it will severely hamper recruitment of new informants. The one thing that helps them come forward is an unswerving belief that their identity will always be protected. Plus, if it was ever revealed, the police would also be liable to be sued by the informant for any mishap that befalls them as a result," Burrows added.

"I never actually handled informants—or agents as the security services call them—when I was working at five, or at six, but thank God. It sounds like a minefield," Lee said.

"You're not kidding," Briers said. "But this is only half the story."

He then went on to explain how under normal circumstances the information this informant provided would be sanitised, and passed on to the prosecution. The prosecution would then be in possession of material that was of use to the defence team, and as it also undermined their own case, they would be duty bound to pass it on to the defence. Everything was aimed at giving the defence the best possible chances of a 'fair' trial. The only way they could avoid doing so, was if the Judge ruled in private, that they did not have to disclose the information.

"The trouble was that the information, without the informant's name attached, was useless to the defence. They would argue that the individual was a potential defence witness whom they must be allowed the opportunity to make enquires of, in order to best defend their case," Briers said.

Lee just shook her head as Briers paused for breath. Burrows realised a lot of this would be new to Lee. He'd had years of stomaching such one-sided situations. He thought he'd left these sorts of frustrations behind him.

Briers continued, explaining, the dilemma the Judge would face; on the one hand, he would wish to protect the identity of the potential witness—as he was an informant—but on the other hand, the prosecution were clearly in possession of the details of a potential critical witness that the defence were entitled to have access to. In all probability, the Judge would have no choice but to order the prosecution to give the full details of the informant to the defence.

"What would that mean?" Lee asked.

"Well, the dilemma would then be back with the prosecution; they either hand over the informant's details to the defence, with all the ramifications that that would entail. Or they pull the prosecution," Briers said.

"What? Drop the case?" Lee asked.

"You've got it in one," Burrows interjected. "And there is no way they would want to drop such a high profile case."

"So what actually did happen?" Lee asked.

"Well, the Hove handlers realised the implications, so they sat on the info; failed to pass it on. But unfortunately, for them, they did record what the informant had said on their contact sheet—a note of what was said during their meeting with the informant—so the trial carried on unaware of all this, and surprisingly, against the odds Croston was convicted and sentenced to life.

Almost immediately, the defence team put in an application for leave to appeal against the conviction, on the grounds that the prosecution had in their possession material that not only undermined the prosecution case, but assisted the defence's case, as it contained details of a potential critical witness," Briers said.

"But how the hell did they know about that?" Lee asked.

"Yeah, good question Jane," Burrows added.

"No idea for sure, but the obvious assumption was that the informant coming forward was a set up from the start. It turns out, that the informant only came forward to act as a covert human intelligence source shortly after Croston's arrest. The trouble is that during the months it took to bring the

106

case to trial, the informant had provided lots of good info, which had all led to good arrests. So he was being regarded by Hove police as a very reliable source," Briers said.

"The devious dirty bastard," Burrows exclaimed.

"So, Croston had set the whole thing up from the start to muddy the waters, and to get off?" Lee added.

"It certainly seems that way," Briers said. "They obviously had a two-pronged strategy; had the handlers reported the info as they should have initially, then the original trial would have been compromised, but as it wasn't, they just put in for an appeal as soon as the jury result went against them."

"So he got off?" Lee said.

"Yes, the Court of Appeal took no time in saying that the conviction was unsafe and ordered the verdict overturned," Briers answered.

"What happened to the Handlers in Hove?" Burrows asked.

"Both of them, together with their detective sergeant, are on bail charged with perverting the course of justice, which would be a very messy trial in itself because of the sensitivities involved," Briers said.

"Bloody hell," Burrows shouted. "That means after the trial of the cops, the scam Croston pulled will be well and truly out of the bag for every scumbag and villain to have a go at."

"That was the initial fear," Briers said. "But the home office has issued new advice, that in similar situations in the future, when an informant claims to be a witness, or indeed have any information about any case that is post charge; whether the actual trial has commenced or not, the handlers must refuse to listen to it, and direct the individual to the relevant defence team."

"I see," Burrows said. "What you haven't heard, you haven't heard."

"Yes exactly," Briers said. "And the details of the individual can then be passed to the defence via the CPS 'as a person of potential interest' to the defence. That way they can make their own enquiries of the individual without his status as an informant becoming known, or an issue.

And, in order to reduce the exposure of the whole sorry affair, I'm told the three cops will be offered a deal. If they resign from the force and sign a confidentiality agreement then the charges against them will be dropped."

"That seems a fair deal," Burrows said.

"Is that it all then, Frank?" Lee asked.

"No, I'm afraid not Jane, it gets worse. A lot worse."

Chapter Nineteen

Burrows and Lee spent thirty minutes looking at their respective files and then fed them into the cross-headed shredder in front of Briers, before they all went for an early lunch. They opted for the pub across the road to have a break from the office and the intensity of their briefing so far. Burrows grasped Croston's scam seemingly a little easier than Lee, which was only to be expected having worked as a CHIS handler in his previous life; but when he explained it to her in detail she got it quickly. He knew there would be many areas where Lee's skills were greater than his, and vice-versa. He guessed that's why they'd been put together in the first place.

They found a quiet corner in the pub and all three of them opted for a ploughman's lunch. Lee was back wearing her close fitting jeans and T-shirt, and they both sat next to each other on a bench seat, whilst Briers sat opposite them on a stool. A mottled-brass topped, round table between them. Burrows had enjoyed going back over what Briers had said in his effort to add clarity, not in a patronising way, but he just enjoyed being of help to Lee; he found himself enjoying it perhaps more than he should. Briers sat back, and seemed happy to let him do the talking for a while. He had to admit, that as insalubrious as Croston clearly was, his swindle had been clever. Playing off the duty of care to protect an informant, against appropriate disclosure of information to the defence.

Lee asked why the defence team hadn't been made to disclose where they had got their information from; about the informant's suppressed material in the first place. He suppressed a grin as he explained, that the defence were under no obligation to disclose anything. It was a one-way street; onus to prove a case always rested with the Crown, innocent until proven guilty and all that. He stifled his smirk as he didn't want to offend Lee, but it always amazed him how the security services didn't always understand the intricacies of cases. They were excellent at intelligence gathering—as they should be—but they were fairly new to presenting evidence in courts of law.

Every time Lee asked a question, she had to turn to her side to address both Burrows and Briers. Each time she did this, Burrows couldn't help but notice the shape of her breasts as they stretched and moved against her T-shirt. She seemed to catch him on one occasion; she raised an eyebrow, as if asking a question.

Burrows answered the unspoken query. "Sorry, my mind wandered as we talked about 'sensitive material.'"

They both laughed and any potential embarrassment was avoided.

"Right you two," Briers said, "let's get back across the road and finish the briefing."

And with that, they made their way out of the pub. They walked around the block first before going back into the office. It wouldn't have been good tradecraft to walk straight back from the pub. Even though their office's true purpose was not obvious, it was still good practice not to link the pub to it.

Back in the briefing room with fresh coffees poured, Briers continued. He explained that since his release from custody, Croston was far from sated; he now wanted to sue the police for malicious prosecution and false imprisonment.

"I guess that's to be expected, as irritating as it is," Burrows said.

"That was, but what he decided to do after that, wasn't," Briers replied.

He further explained that after Croston had been initially convicted there were a number of high profile media interviews with the senior investigating officer, and with family members of the deceased. How, the boy's father had been particularly venomous towards Croston. This, as understandable as it was, only fuelled the media frenzy for more and more coverage. This had gone on over several days before dying down. Then came the upheld appeal, and the media again made straight to the father for his comments, and lapped up his vocal indignation. Now Croston issuing the father and associated media for libel and slander.

"Does this little shit not know when to quit?" Burrows asked.

"Apparently not," Briers said. "That's probably why he didn't try too hard to hide the body."

"What do you mean?" Lee asked.

"He's arrogant Jane, and clearly enjoys not only the publicity, but the pain he causes," Briers said. He continued. "When he walked out of the Court of Appeal he stopped on seeing one of the officers in the case, and said to him, 'You know I'll never stop... being grateful to the British justice system'. He finished the sentence with a cruel grin on of his face as he left the double entendre to sink in."

"Utter scum," Lee said.

Briers nodded, before continuing to explain how current intelligence is tending to show how his sick taunt is turning into reality. He told them that a car, which was of similar age and description to that currently owned by Croston has been seen skulking around parks and schools in south London. The registered number on the licence plate doesn't relate to Croston's car, but to a different car that is the same model, colour, make etc."

"A ghost plate," Lee said.

"He's making sure he doesn't get caught the same way again," Burrows said.

"Exactly," Briers said. "And with his impending civil court cases due, he's pretty much untouchable, unless evidence against him is very, very compelling. The cheeky bastard has even asked the police for protection. He claims because of their actions, vigilantly groups are after him."

"I'm guessing I know where Jane and I now come into it?" Burrows asked.

"Let's just say the PM doesn't want to wait until another child is brutalised and murdered before we get very, very compelling evidence," Briers answered.

Both Lee and Burrows nodded in unison. Briers then gave them their final instructions before shaking both their hands and saying his goodbyes. Neither spoke for a minute or so after Briers left the room. Silence invaded the space, and created a break from all that had been said over the past couple of hours.

Having gathered his thoughts Burrows breached the tranquillity first. "Let's get out of here Jane. Have a couple of hours of downtime, then kit up and go pay slime-ball a visit."

Lee just nodded, as if still in deep contemplation, and then they both stood up and left the room.

***

Cabilla was pleased with the way things were progressing, the lorry had arrived from Kent the previous afternoon with no problems. The cargo had been unloaded, and each woman had been fed and shown to her room on the first floor of the warehouse. Each had been told that this was only temporary accommodation until their new apartments were ready for them. Each of the stupid women had believed all they were told, with the exception of Amber of course. Amber was the one who spoke some English, Amber was the one who translated everything into Swahili. All the women spoke Swahili, as it was their regional language; all spoke French, as it was their national language. Only Amber spoke English as well. Only Amber was working for him.

He'd wanted to meet the lorry as it arrived from Kent, but had been held up with disciplining the two girls up west. It had taken all night to find them, a fact that just made him more irate. A fact that had made their slap a little more severe than he'd first planned. Nevertheless, they had learnt a hard lesson, and Cabilla was sure it wasn't one they would forget in a hurry. Consequently, he didn't get over to Dulwich, so he had left Mackey to deal with the girls' arrival.

He sat down at his favourite café bar, close to his flat; he was meeting Mackey for a face-to-face update. Mackey arrived a few minutes later and joined him at his table outside on the pavement. Outside at such places were always a better place to talk, all the passing traffic noises masked what they said to each other, and kept their conversations private. The Runt had told him that, one piece of good advice he'd had from him. Mackey brought Cabilla up-to- date on the fine details of how things had gone.

"How long before we can get those bitches working?" He asked.

"It's going to take a couple of weeks at least Boss. They need to be properly prepared first," Mackey answered.

"Yeah, I understand Den; I just want to start seeing a return on my investments."

"You will Boss. Amber's done a good job; wait 'till you see them yourself."

"I'm looking forward to it."

Whilst he finished his latte` coffee, Mackey said he needed some cigars and crossed over the road to a small newsagent's to buy some.

A couple of minutes later, Mackey came back out of the shop and crossed back towards Cabilla. Purpose in his step, and a fixed expression on his face. Cabilla sensed trouble, and got up to greet him.

"I think you had better sit down, Boss," he said as he arrived. He then threw a copy of the London Evening Standard onto the table, face up.

"This is last night's edition," Mackey said.

Cabilla looked down, and saw the bold headline first, 'Have you seen this man?' And underneath it, was a head and shoulders picture of Larry, their lorry driver.

Chapter Twenty

That evening after some respite Burrows pulled up outside Lee's flat, he didn't have to pip the horn; she was straight out the door as he arrived. As she got into the front passenger seat, he noticed she had changed into an old pair of cargo pants with a lightweight cagoule on top.

"Dressed for action?" He asked.

"At least I vary things from blue jeans, T-shirts, and that old brown bomber jacket which you seem to cherish so much," she replied.

Lee looked down at her legs, and then back up at Burrows. "You don't really think my cargo pants are a bit over the top do you?"

"Relax; I'm only taking the piss. You know, to lighten the mood before an operation."

They grinned at each other before Burrows pulled away from the kerb and into the early evening traffic.

First stop was Croston's flat off College Road, Southwark. It was a ground floor flat in a three-storey block of six apartments. Facing from the road, Croston's flat was in the bottom left hand corner. It was still daylight and the curtains were open. There was no obvious sign of life and Croston's car, an old red Ford Mondeo was nowhere around.

They spent the next hour or so, driving around local parks and open spaces looking for his car. They even checked out Dulwich Park, not that they really thought Croston was stupid enough to prowl around there again. But all to no avail. They went back to his flat but nothing had changed. Burrows then found a spot to pull up in the adjacent street. There was a grassy mound between the two streets, which gave some natural cover, but also gave a clear view of the front of Croston's flat, and the approaches to it. They both settled down to wait and discussed how they were going to deal with Croston once they found him.

"I quite like the vigilante angle," Lee said. "He's already complained, albeit falsely, about vigilantes, so anything that happens now can be written off to some justice-seeking citizen."

"It's a possible Jane, but the only flaw I can see is that as he has already complained, the Police will get a whole lot of pain for not having protected the slime ball. And we could do without adding to their problems, if we can avoid it."

"Fair point oh wise one. So what do you have in mind?"

Burrows turned to face Lee, and had just finished telling her when he saw the Mondeo pull up outside Croston's flat. Burrows recognised him from his photograph and Lee agreed, as they both watched him carry a brown shopping bag into the flat. It was going dusk now and the front room light was switched on, followed by Croston pulling closed his thin lightly patterned curtains. They looked at each other, both now fully alert. Time to go, Burrows thought, but waited a few minutes more to make sure Croston was staying put before they both left the car, and walked across the grass mound on a direct line to Croston's front door.

Burrows pulled to one side of the front door and ducked down so he could not be seen, leaving Lee to knock on the door. Women always seemed less threatening somehow. When he had been in the police, and they had decided to do a 'knock and enter' rather than a 'rapid entry', villains always seemed more inclined to answer the door if it was a female calling, as opposed to a man. He'd always reckoned it was a subconscious thing, to do with evaluation of risk; most men would see a woman as less of a threat. Most men hadn't met Jane Lee, he mused.

A few moments later, a gruff voice from behind the solid front door spoke. "Who the fuck are you?"

Burrows could see a spyhole in the door and realised Lee was probably being surveyed.

"I'm from the press, but before you stop me, hear me out; I'm on your side. I want to do a story on how the police have mistreated you."

"Is it worth much?" The gruff voice asked.

"Oh, yes Mr Croston it is, but can we not discuss this through your front door?"

There was a grunt followed by the unlocking of the door. As soon as it was ajar, Lee started to step through it. She then threw herself back first against the front of the door forcing it to its widest opening. This cleared the entrance, Burrows was in, and bundling a startled Croston back into his front room in an instant. Lee closed the door and joined him in the lounge.

It was a grubby small one bed roomed flat; the front door gave direct access into the living room. At the rear, he could see a small kitchenette next to a door leading into a small hallway where presumably the bathroom and bedroom were. The carpet was threadbare and there wasn't much in the way of furniture. An old two-seater settee with faded fabric sat at one side of the room, and an armchair that didn't match, made from a leatherette material sat opposite.

"What the fuck do you think you're doing?" Croston demanded.

Lee pushed him backwards and he fell into the armchair as she answered. "Just shut up and sit still."

Burrows quickly moved through the rest of the flat, he re-entered the living room moments later saying that the place was clear.

"Look, if you're here on the rob I've got fuck all, so you'd be wasting your time," Croston said.

Lee remained in front of Croston; whilst Burrows picked up the brown bag, he had seen Croston enter the flat with. He searched through it and pulled out a Nintendo DS. He powered it up to see what game was loaded onto it.

"I might have guessed, a fucking child's game," he said as he turned to face Croston."You really don't learn your lessons do you slime ball?"

"I'm going to so sue your arses, pig. Where is your warrant? I want to see it now," Croston demanded. His voice was rising and sounding more confident.

Burrows knew they had to get Croston back under control and quickly, but as if Lee was reading his mind, she drew her Glock pistol and pointed it at Croston's head. "Now, will you shut the fuck up?"

Croston fell quiet, his look of sureness draining away as quickly as it had appeared. He looked confused, as if he wasn't sure exactly who he was dealing with. Burrows saw him look at both their hands followed by a look of terror. They were both wearing surgical gloves. The anguish on Croston's face appeared to be increasing, as he continued to stare open mouthed at their hands. Burrows realised he had to calm Croston down to keep him compliant. So he told him that they were coppers, and to relax, as coppers always wore gloves when they searched places. Even aggressive out-of-order cops like them. He sought to confirm his theory to Croston by asking, "Where are your dirty mags?"

"You won't find anything illegal in here," Croston answered, appearing to settle a little.

Burrows repeated the question, and Croston pulled one from down the side of his armchair and handed it to him.

"All the boys in there are sixteen and over so it's not illegal. Borrow it if you like," Croston said.

Burrows ignored the remark. He opened the magazine and saw the crudity he had expected to see. The boys in the images were probably twelve or thirteen years old, but near enough to the age of consent to make it impossible to prove that they were under age. Another clinically cynical ploy by Croston, he thought to himself. He laid the gross item open-paged on the floor, and then went and got a chair out of the kitchen.

Burrows stood on it, and using the butt of his own weapon, he punched a hole through the ceiling plasterboard exposing the wooden rafters above. He turned to Lee and nodded. Plan A was a goer. She left Burrows in charge of Croston and disappeared down the corridor. She came back moments later with a bedding sheet.

Croston just looked on agog.

Burrows took the sheet from Lee and stood back up on the chair looking for a space where he could thread the sheet over the top of one of the rafters. He thought the sheet would slide through better than a rope as it would be flatter, not that they had a rope. He was in luck though; he managed to find a gap where some electrical cabling was threaded above the rafter.

As he started to manoeuvre the sheet through the tight space above the rafter, he glanced at Croston and saw an expression of fearful understanding spread across his face.

"Wait a minute. You're not fucking cops are you? What the fuck do you two think you are doing? Look, if this is what it look likes, there's no need; I'll stop my ways. You'll see, just give me a chance," Croston pleaded.

"Relax Croston; we're not going to hang you. Cops don't do that sort of thing. We just want some photos of you in a compromising position in order to control you. You've no doubt heard of auto-erotic asphyxia? You're probably an expert," Lee said.

Croston seemed to relax again, as if the twisted logic made sense to him. Burrows also noted a hint of recognition in his eyes as Lee said the words 'auto-erotic asphyxia'. She continued to reassure Croston whilst he worked away with the sheet.

Before they'd entered the flat, Burrows had explained his plan to Lee. She claimed to have heard of auto-erotic asphyxia, but he wasn't convinced. After all, regardless of all her talents Lee had not been a cop. Most cops come across it at some time or another during their service. He had explained to Lee that when the brain is starved of oxygen the two strongest human urges surface above all others: the will to survive and the will to perpetuate. Consequently, some pervert had discovered that if one reduced the blood supply to the brain, whilst aroused, it supposedly vastly enhanced the sexual experience.

Hanging was a common way of doing this where the individual would stand on a chair, but rather than jump off it, as with a suicide, they would just bend their knees and start to strangle themselves, but were able to stop the procedure at any time by simply standing up again.

"I'd sort of heard about it, but didn't fully understand it," Lee offered. "So they abuse themselves whilst hanging, is that it?"

"Yep, I'm afraid that's about it."

Burrows went on to explain that where these depraved souls got it wrong was when they hang on for too long. Having apologised for the pun, he carried on to clarify that the pleasure is supposedly so intense they wait until the last possible moment before standing back up, and therefore relieving the pressure around their necks.

The greedy ones wait a bit too long, and pass out before actually strangling themselves to death. Or sometimes, they just accidentally knock over the chair that they were standing on.

Lee appeared amazed to learn that it was not an uncommon form of accidental death among some sections of society. But she did agree that it would be a fitting end for Croston, and one that would be written-off as not suspicious. A win-win all round.

Croston had suddenly become quite compliant. Burrows thought he saw a malignant glint in his eyes as he helped him onto the chair. Perhaps the pervert thought they would let him perform the act, to make the supposed photographs even more compromising. He couldn't have got it more wrong Burrows thought.

Ten minutes later, Burrows and Lee let themselves quietly out of Croston's flat and headed back to their car. As unsavoury as their evening's work had been, Burrows felt relieved in the knowledge that the children of south London were a significant lot safer after tonight. He knew he'd crossed a line tonight, they both had, but he also knew natural justice had been served. Not vigilantism, or spiteful reprisal, but plain old justice; the kind that would prevent further atrocities being committed. He now knew he was up to the mark as regards this new job with the SPU. They both were.

"What if you couldn't have got the rafter thing to work with the sheet?" Lee asked, as they climbed back into their car.

"Plan B," Burrows said, "I'd have just shot him like you suggested, and blamed it on the vigilantes."

Chapter Twenty-one

'Have you seen this man?' shouted the headline on the front page of the evening paper. Cabilla read the whole article before passing the paper back to Mackey. He remained silent as he watched Mackey read the story. Mackey put the paper back down on the table.

"What do you reckon Boss?" he asked.

"Says he's wanted by the filth on behalf of the Turks," Cabilla answered.

"That's what Larry told me when I interrogated him," added Mackey. "Sort of backs him up don't it?"

"Yeah, but that ain't the problem Den. It means he's now high risk what with every fucker looking for him. If this story had broken a day ago when he was driving back from Kent and some nosey twat clocked him…" Cabilla left the sentence unfinished.

"Don't tell me you want me to make him disappear, do you? I'm telling you Shonbo, he's sound…" Mackey started to say before Cabilla silenced him with a wave of his hand.

"No, don't panic Den. We can still use him after things die down. Get Jim to take him to his flat and keep him there. Tell Jim to tell him why, and that it's only for a few days. We'll reconsider things then."

As they walked away, Mackey rang Jim on his mobile and explained the situation. Cabilla heard Jim tell Mackey that they were still at Jim's flat, so there was no problem.

On their way to the warehouse Cabilla told Mackey to go via Jim's, he wanted to speak to Larry himself.

They arrived at Jim's rented flat, and Cabilla introduced himself to Larry as Mackey's Boss. He then showed Larry the newspaper, and noted his reaction when he saw his own face on the front page. He went a paler colour than the paper itself. A genuine reaction Cabilla thought. However, there was something about Larry that troubled Cabilla. He had no real reason to be concerned; the fact Larry was wanted by the Turkish authorities for serious crimes should have totally reassured him. And in a large way, it did, there was just something he couldn't grasp hold of, it was instinctive, and Cabilla had learned long ago to trust his innate reflections.

Therefore, when Larry asked for his phone back, and not to be kept locked in his room when he wasn't eating or pissing, Cabilla couldn't fully explain his resistance.

"Jim will give you free reign of the flat unless you give him cause not to," he said, "but we'll keep your phone for now, just 'till things calm down."

Larry seemed to accept this a little too easily for Cabilla's liking. But he hadn't met him before, and he knew what an intimidating presence he could be. Even larger physically than Mackey, perhaps Larry was just daunted by his size, he wondered as they left the flat.

***

When Steele first saw his own image staring back up at him his heart nearly stopped, and his bowels nearly started. He had half expected it; he just prayed the press appeal was done the right way; still keeping his true identity a secret, whilst effectively enhancing his covert identity. He wouldn't know for sure until he had read the whole story. He was half-way through it before he started to relax. They'd done it right, said he was wanted by the Turks.

When Cabilla had asked him what he was wanted for, he knew he had to ramp it up to gain the maximum kudos, but remembering whom it was he was purporting to be, just a bent lorry driver. He'd had plenty of time to contemplate this over the last few days and by Cabilla's reaction, he was happy he had the balance right.

He told them that on one of his earlier jobs he had accidently run over a pedestrian whilst on his way back to the UK. He hadn't stopped, and it was only after he got back that he discovered he'd hit and killed one of Turkey's top judges. What gave his story legs was the fact that such an accident had actually happened around that time, and the driver of the real offending wagon had failed to stop. Steele just hoped they'd not caught the real driver since then. That was the only bit he couldn't know. But he was sure Cabilla wouldn't waste his time trying to check, he'd seemed happy enough when he left the flat, and after all, they'd brought the newspaper story to him, he'd just filled in the blanks.

***

The following morning Burrows collected Lee from her flat and drove towards Pimlico.

After their previous evening's work, they had both gone back to their respective addresses, to go through an agreed decontamination procedure. Burrows, once home, put his gloves and clothes into a bin bag, together with his shoes. The bag was sealed and then placed into a second bag. Then he took a long hot shower cleaning himself with specially provided carbolic soap, which contained phenyl acid, a very effective disinfectant.

They'd both brought their bags with them this morning, and would hand them over to Briers, who would arrange their incineration at a local hospital. Burrows knew a lot of government departments had contracts with hospital incineration units, in order to dispose of confidential or sensitive material. Police forces disposed of seized drugs the same way.

They met Briers in the underground briefing room and handed over their bags. After they had finished the de-brief, Burrows went to refill his coffee cup from the machine.

"Jane, Frank either of you want a top up?"

Lee shook her head slightly as Briers spoke. "No thanks John. Look, I just want to say I think you both did a first class job last night, and the way you left things is both fitting, and good cover, as the cops won't be treating the death as suspicious."

Burrows and Lee both said, "Thanks," before he continued.

"Have either of you got any post-operational trauma issues?"

Each said they were fine, and Lee added. "After all, the dirty bastard had been back out prowling when we paid him a visit."

"Unbelievable," Briers said, adding. "But I'm glad you're both ok."

"How did the triangulation unit get on?" Lee asked.

"Good news, and bad news," Briers replied. "They found the car that the mobile phone was in, and then stood down, handing over to the surveillance team. That's the good news."

"What's the bad news then?" Burrows asked.

"Well, the surveillance team took over just south of Manchester and promptly lost him once he left the motorway."

He explained that as soon the surveillance team lost sight of the target's car, the team leader sent a car ahead to the Workers' Retreat Pub. As the car was arriving, the crew saw the target's car driving away from the pub, but couldn't catch it. They did notice however, that the vehicle now had a front seat passenger.

"The barman," Lee said.

"Quite probably," Briers answered, "'cause the surveillance car then returned to the pub to find that it had been closed early, there was no sign of anyone."

"What happened then?" Burrows asked.

Briers explained that they staked-out the pub and also watched the motorway junction where the target had left, just prior to the surveillance team losing him. He said they were quietly confident that they would've at least picked him up at the motorway junction on his return route. They waited until 2 a.m. before they had to give up, and stand down.

"What about the triangulation team?" Lee asked.

"Both teams were well on their way home by the time the surveillance team lost the target, so they were out of the equation," Briers answered.

"Shit, that *is* bad news," Burrows said.

"Losing the target wasn't the bad news."

Burrows and Lee, both just looked at Briers clearly waiting for him to explain. And when he did, it was not what Burrows expected to hear.

He told them the target's car belonged to Avis car hire, and discreet enquiries that morning had identified it had been hired from the Charing Cross branch in London the day before. It had been returned during the night with the keys posted through the office letterbox. They had obtained the renter's details, and intelligence checks initially brought up negative returns, until a high-level alert had been activated by their checks.

"What was the alert?" Lee asked.

"That *is* the bad news," Briers said, pausing, then adding. "The renter is a man called Geoffrey Chapman, or should I say, Detective Constable Geoffrey Chapman. Who is currently stationed at a Metropolitan Police Intelligence Unit somewhere in central London."

"Oh bollocks," Burrows said.

"Looks like we've found our mole though," Lee added.

Chapter Twenty-two

Cabilla left Jim's flat with Mackey in tow. As they walked towards the motor, parked near-by, Mackey caught up. "Happy Boss, with Larry I mean?"

"Yeah, for now, but..." he cast his doubts aside, then continued. "Anyway, take me over to Dulwich; I want to check the women out."

He hadn't met Amber Kimba before; it had been a contact back home in the Congo who had approached her on his behalf. He knew there were plenty of attractive young women eking out and subsisting on a pittance in the Colton Ore mines, all desperate to get out of their pitiful existence. All desperate to get into the European Union, and to a better life.

His contact had told him there were no shortage of volunteers of women who wanted to become 'models', and that he'd picked Kimba as she spoke English. Cabilla had insisted that the rest of the women should only speak their native tongues, that way it would be easier for Kimba to control them.

"You did tell Kimba not to address me by my surname, didn't you?" He asked Mackey.

"No worry Boss, I've told her."

Cabilla knew his name was well known all across the North Kivu Province of the Congo, and the last thing he wanted was the women to realise who he was. Well, not yet anyway.

During the car journey, Cabilla asked Mackey about the girls. He said, they were all under twenty-five years of age, and all very slim and pretty, apparently.

"How did things go last night, when they arrived from Kent?" He asked.

Mackey explained how each was told that the five rooms on the top floor of the warehouse was just a stopover, whilst their plush new imaginary apartments elsewhere were being finished. They had all accepted this. Though the warehouse rooms were not the fancy ones the women had been told they were getting, Cabilla knew they would be far nicer than what they would have been used to. He would expect gratitude in due course. That said, he hadn't actually seen the upstairs rooms yet, as he'd left Mackey to arrange all that; he was looking forward to seeing what he'd done. He had just told him, he wanted them functional without being too comfortable; after all, they were working rooms. He didn't want the punters to get too comfy. Each room was to have its own toilet and shower, and not much more, other than the bed of course.

Mackey said that his man guarding Kimba had called each woman, in turn into the office at the end of the corridor, on the pretext of being given her new Belgium passport. Once in the office, the guard had grabbed them, whilst Kimba administered ether across their noses and mouths with a cotton wool pad. Each was now chained to their respective beds, and completely out of it.

On arrival at the warehouse, he followed Mackey upstairs and could smell traces of ether as they walked along the corridor to the office at the end. This was next to Kimba's place, which was more of an apartment than the basic rooms the women were in. The smell in the air reminded him of paint stripper, only sweeter and harsher. As he approached the office, he noted the doors to the rooms now each had a number on them, one to five.

Mackey introduced him to Kimba, who seemed a little remote and distant with him, but he just put that down to nerves. She was indeed as pretty as Mackey had claimed; he just hoped the other five were as well.

"Well, let's have a look at them then," Cabilla said.

"Yes sir, follow me," Kimba answered.

She led Cabilla to room number one. "In here is Divine," she said, as she unlocked the door.

Cabilla knew they would have to give the girls different names; working names. Though Divine would have been a good one, he thought. He followed Kimba into the room and could see that it was sparse. A double-sized bed with a table and chair next to it. On the far wall, was a wardrobe next to an internal door that led to the en-suite. The light was on. It was a low-wattage bulb in a coloured glass up lighter shade, which threw an incandescent soft tone around the room. Mackey had done a good job, he thought, it created the right atmosphere.

Laid on the bed was one of the five Congolese women. She was also very pretty Cabilla thought, noting how smooth her skin appeared, like porcelain. She was dressed in tracksuit bottoms with a sleeveless T-shirt. She was on her back with two intravenous drips coming out of her free arm. The other arm was chained to the side of the bed. Her eyes were open, but looked empty, Cabilla noted.

"Is that the heroin?" He asked.

"Yes, together with a saline drip to keep her hydrated," Kimba replied.

"Has she got a clue what the fuck's going on?"

"No, she is not with it. You can speak as you wish."

"How long before we can use them?"

"About two weeks."

"How fucking long?—" Cabilla started.

"Please let me explain," Kimba interjected.

Cabilla closed his mouth and nodded. This had better be good. She told him it would take that long to make sure that all the girls were properly addicted to the drug. But after the first week, she would start to bring them off the drips, and allow them to become conscious again. Only then, would the withdrawal symptoms start to kick in. Then she would re-introduce them to the drug by either burning it on tin foil, so they could inhale the fumes— 'Chasing the dragon'—or they could smoke it.

"Don't let them smoke it. It fucks the teeth. They're no good to me with fucked-up teeth."

"Sorry, I wasn't thinking," Kimba said.

Cabilla couldn't help but think the timescales were too long. Was this Kimba being over-protective? "Are you sure it'll take two weeks? You know I could have got any number of women who spoke English to do your job?"

Kimba said that her way the girls would become raging addicts, who would do exactly as they were told in order to get their next fixes. If Cabilla allowed her to do it her way, this would ensure no problems with the girls once they were put to work.

Cabilla could see some logic in what she'd said, he just hadn't reckoned on such a delay. Nevertheless, he agreed to Kimba's proposal, but telling her, "Not a day longer though. And Mackey will be keeping an eye on things, just to make sure we keep delays to a minimum."

He declined the offer of seeing the other girls, not whilst they were all in this state. He would wait until he could sample the merchandise for himself in a fortnight. He met back up with Mackey in the corridor and Kimba waved them goodbye with a smile, which he thought seemed false.

Mackey drove Cabilla away from the warehouse and back towards central London."See Boss, I told you they were well fit. You should be able to charge a good price for their services."

"Yeah, they are top shelf, that's for sure. But keep an eye on Amber; just until we can fully trust her."

"Will do Boss, but I'm sure she's ok," Mackey said, before changing the subject."Have you heard anything back from the Runt re the Manchester thing? He sure hasn't belled me or nothing."

"I got a text from him earlier saying he'd been up to Manchester but hadn't got anywhere. Said he wanted to meet to discuss. I've haven't answered yet as I can't be arsed if he hasn't got anything to give," Cabilla answered.

"Probably after more cash, the thieving little shite."

"That's what I reckoned. Look Den, do me a favour will you? Arrange to go and see him. See what he's got, and see what he wants?"

"Will do Boss."

"Just bell me after you've set up the meet, but before you go. I need to consider stuff before you actually speak to him."

Chapter Twenty-three

Gordon Chapman hated driving through the night; he had always found great difficulty facing the on-coming headlights of other vehicles, especially the morons who left their main-beams on. Nevertheless, having calmed down from his fright, it gave him time to mull over things.

He knew he had earned good money since he'd worked for Cabilla and Mackey, and they hadn't been the first. He'd sold lots of information to lots of criminals since he joined the intelligence unit. It had proved to be a real earner; just checking someone or their car out on the police national computer (PNC), to see if they were of interest to anyone in law enforcement would take seconds, literally, and net him two and a half grand a time.

Cabilla had been the best payer, but he had also proved to be the biggest pain. The guy was a nutter, and he took too many risks for his liking, risks that could bring him down as well. The last escapade had scared him; when Cabilla had slaughtered all those cops, there was just no need to go that far. The upshot being that it was he who had suppressed the verbally passed intelligence from Manchester naming Cabilla. It would be he who would face the grief, if the provider of the information ever checked up to see what had happened with it.

He knew this wasn't normal when information or intelligence came in from an outside force; after all, the actioning of it was the receiving force's responsibility. If one force gets info on who's done a robbery in Clapham, they would pass it onto the Met, and thereafter lose interest in it. Why should they give a shit, the robbery is on the Met's patch so it's their responsibility to solve it.

What bothered him though, was that the multiple murders of cops were an unheard of event. He knew it was only a matter of time before questions were asked. Especially, if the investigation team hadn't identified Cabilla as a firm suspect themselves. He'd considered putting Cabilla's name into the frame, that way if Cabilla was seen to be arrested for the murders, Manchester would assume the investigating officers were acting on their intelligence. It wouldn't have happened straight away, granted, but that was normal. Once you received intelligence naming someone you have to go out and secure evidence to back it up; intelligence isn't evidence, as his fat DI was too fond of always telling him. But what worried him about that plan was what Cabilla might say about him once his own skin was under threat. Too risky.

No, he always knew he wouldn't do his full term in the police; maybe it was time. All he needed was enough money to disappear and open a bar on some beach somewhere and he'd be off. He nearly had enough, he just needed to milk some more out of Cabilla first. It would give him great pleasure to ring Cabilla from Heathrow Airport and tell him to fuck off.

"Go fuck yourself you daft thick nutter, and get your girlfriend Mackey to help you do it," he shouted aloud as he drove. Practising his imagined phone call from the departures lounge.

He also knew what they really thought about him, that they thought they were using him, when in reality it was the other way round. He also knew they referred to him as the Runt; he'd heard them whisper it to each other when passing the phone between them. 'Here Boss, it's the Runt for you', he'd heard Mackey say many times when he had rung them. He'd show them who was the real runt, sooner rather than later.

His trip to Manchester had been fruitless; the barman at the Workers' Retreat pub claimed to know nothing more. His description of the guy, who'd been asking after Billy the Kid, if anything, had become even vaguer than when he had first telephoned him to say he'd been in the pub asking questions. One thing was obvious though, he seemed very frightened. He had lost all that jovial Irish bonhomie bullshit. He couldn't work out if he knew something, and was hiding it, or if he was just spooked by the shooting of Billy and the other clown that Cabilla had hired to do the job.

There was something else that bothered him about his trip to Manchester; he couldn't be sure but when he left the motorway and headed towards Wythenshawe, he got the feeling he was being followed. He hadn't seen anything as such; it was just that the same car seemed to be behind him for a while. He wasn't surveillance trained himself but he knew some of the basics—he always thought he'd have been good at it—so he'd pulled a few left and right turns in quick succession, and had seemed to lose the car behind him. Or it had certainly changed. Even though it was dark he could tell the shape of the headlights behind him had altered, and then there was nothing behind him until he got back onto the main road into Wythenshawe.

He panicked himself a bit at first, almost convincing himself that professional standards were following or worse the IPCC (Independent Police Complaints Commission). When he reached the pub, he'd parked up for five minutes before approaching. Nothing and nobody was around. He didn't want to take chances, so he made the barman close up, kicking out the couple of customers he had, and then took him for a drive and something to eat so they could talk.

On his return journey, he'd been very careful and aware of every other car around him, and had eventually calmed himself. This was when he started to take stock of things. By the time, he was back in London he knew he'd just overreacted, letting his guilty conscience get the better of him. And even if he had been followed — which he was now sure, he hadn't—they'd have seen nothing. He'd made sure of that.

He decided to text Cabilla in the morning to ask for a meet. He was going to suggest that the barman was hiding more than he had said, and recommend one of Cabilla's goons pay him a visit. That way, it looked as if he had come back with some info, and he could try to get more money out of Cabilla. He knew by saying so, the barman would likely receive some serious grief, and that it was probable he didn't actually know anymore, but why should he care. That was better than saying the barman knew nothing more, and not being paid. After all, he'd had to take a day off work and hire a car at his own expense, not to mention the cost of the petrol.

The following day he was at his desk having just returned from lunch. He still hadn't gone through last night's intelligence entries from the night shift, and as the DI was due back soon he thought he'd better make a start. He hated this task, usually all the morons working nights just put shit onto the system to pass the time and make themselves look good. He knew it was one of the uniform branch's performance indicators how many intelligence entries they entered onto the system. They should measure the quality not the quantity of the entries Chapman always thought. Anyway, he wouldn't waste too much time on it; he would speed read and delete most entries unless anything jumped out at him.

He'd just logged on to the general intelligence database when his mobile phone vibrated in his pocket. He had it set to silent when receiving text messages. He smiled as he read it, Mackey wanted to meet him tonight. He texted back to confirm while still smiling; another payday was looming.

Chapter Twenty-four

Lee sat in silence for a few moments whilst Briers's comments sunk in.

"The dirty bastard," Burrows said before continuing, "I wonder how long he's been on Cabilla's payroll?"

Lee had been wondering the same thing. She turned to face Briers as he answered.

"We're not sure yet John, early covert access to his bank account is under way, but that will take a bit of time to do via the back door."

"I don't suppose Chapman is working against Cabilla officially, or unofficially is he?" Lee asked.

"That's the first thing we checked. He took the day off to travel up to Manchester, claiming a relative was suddenly taken ill. And don't forget he hired a rental, which is a little strange, as he owns a decent nearly new Vauxhall himself. His professional profile is fairly low too; he's never been trained or been involved in any real covert role. He's more of a desk jockey really, though he is a trained CHIS handler. That said, his remit is only street level crime intelligence gathering, it's not as if he's expected to recruit informants into organised crime groups or terrorism, or anything higher up the criminal pecking order," Briers explained.

"What's he look like?" Lee asked.

"He's a white male, thirty-one years, five feet ten inches tall weighing ten stone. He has dark scruffy hair and, is not blessed with much natural beauty. Consequently, he is single," Briers answered, pausing, whilst he turned over his papers before continuing. "He has served with the Met for just over ten years, starting his career in a central London nick he soon decided that uniform work was a bit too hard and rough for him."

"Sounds like a bit of a runt," Lee said.

Briers continued, "He got into Intel via the back door at a time when a lot of the units were being set up, and they couldn't fill all the vacancies with detectives. He has never really shone, but apparently, always done just enough to keep his position."

"Where's he live?" Burrows asked.

"He used to live in a police section house—Trenchard House—in Soho, before moving to another one in central London when it was sold to a developer to turn into flats."

"What is a section house?" Lee asked.

"Section houses are where most junior cops start off, rented rooms, some above certain police stations and some were stand-alone. Most cops move onto better things as soon as they can afford to. Chapman is described as a bit of a loner, and his last accommodation was also sold off, forcing him to rent a small grubby flat above a kebab shop back in Soho. Which is where he is now," Briers finished.

"Anything further on Cabilla or Mackey? Lee asked.

"No, nothing new unfortunately. I'm guessing they're currently still in London but I don't know. It's over to you two I'm afraid."

"Let's spend a day or two on Chapman, see what he does after his trip last night," Lee suggested.

"Good idea Jane," Burrows said.

With that, Briers wrote down the address of the nick that Chapman worked from and told them both that according to the Met's computerised duty systems he had booked on at 9 a.m. that morning. He then filled them in on something else before he said his goodbyes, and left the briefing room.

Burrows suggested they grab something to eat and then make their way over to central London for late afternoon. Lee was starving so readily agreed. Over a sandwich in the pub opposite, they discussed tactics.

Burrows said, there was no point in waiting too early outside the office where Chapman worked; as he could be in and out quite legitimately all afternoon, and they didn't want to draw too much attention to themselves. Therefore, Lee proposed they plot up outside his building from 4.30 p.m. and take it from there. Burrows agreed.

As the days had passed Jane Lee noticed she was getting more and more comfortable working with Burrows. He was good company, funny, not bad looking, and clearly displayed professionalism about himself. But she had started to notice a steely edge to him when he was actually deployed. It was like flipping a switch; good guy/bad guy. It was a trait she'd seen many times when working for the security services, when they brought in Special Forces like the SAS or the SBS to do the hard bit at the end of an operation. You could be having a cup of coffee and joking with a trooper one minute, and the next he could be cutting someone's throat. She expected that in soldiers, but not policemen, or ex-policemen. She wasn't sure whether it bothered her or not—after all it was part of the job spec.—or maybe she just didn't want to see Burrows's darker side she asked herself.

Burrows, reminding Lee it was her turn, interrupted her reverie. They were parked on a side street, with a long distance view of the front entrance to the office block where Chapman worked. It was yet another non-descript office in a long line of offices on a quiet side street in between main roads in central London.

Maintaining a fixed visual on an object soon becomes very tiring, especially when you dare not look away for a second; a second is all it takes for someone to leave a doorway, and walk down the street with their back to you, and you've not noticed it's the subject you're supposed to be watching. Consequently, they had agreed fifteen minutes on and fifteen minutes off. That would also allow for the one who is resting to glance casually around, and look for anything, or anyone, that could be of interest. Especially, to monitor if they themselves were starting to receive unwarranted attention.

It was 5.45 p.m. and Lee took over the visual. Seconds, later Chapman walked out the front door of the office and set off down the street. A weasel of a man who was easily recognisable from his photograph and description she thought. Even though he was wearing a lightweight blue suit, which looked as if it had been made a round the corner in Mayfair's Savile Row, she still thought he appeared rat-like. Having jumped out of the car, she took up position of lead foot unit some twenty metres behind him. As soon as he was lost from sight, Lee ran down the side street to make up ground, and then slowed abruptly, so as to walk calmly around the corner. As she did so, she could see Chapman some ten metres ahead of her on the other side of the road. She crossed over and took up a matching pace behind him. In her peripheral vision, she could see Burrows on the opposite side of the road, slightly ahead of her, forming a triangle between the three of them.

As they approached a 'T' junction, she sensed Burrows quickening his pace so if Chapman turned left— and out of her view— he would be able to reach the adjacent corner before her, and take up the eyeball before they both lost sight on their subject.

Chapman did turn left, and Burrows was at the junction a moment later. Lee heard his voice crackle in the radio earpiece fitted into her right ear. Burrows said he had a visual on Chapman again, and would take the eyeball. By the time she had reached the junction, Burrows had crossed across the front of her, from her right, onto her side of the road, and had carried on behind Chapman who was still on the left hand side of the street. Arriving at the corner, she turned left, and on seeing Burrows in front of her, she crossed over the road to recreate the triangle. She then quickened her pace so that she was slightly ahead of Burrows, but still a covert distance behind Chapman.

They'd both been briefed that Chapman wasn't surveillance trained, but he had certainly shown some knowledge of it the other night on his trip to Manchester, so they'd earlier agreed to use extra caution so not to be seen. Ideally, they would have a foot team of three or even more for a long foot follow, especially in a busy place like central London. They would just have to be careful and hope he was headed straight home to his flat Lee thought, which wasn't too far away.

Ten minutes later, Chapman arrived at his flat, a first floor apartment above a kebab shop, with the entrance via a door at the side of a ginnel, which ran down the flank of the shop. The place looked grubby, and wasn't out of place with the surrounding streets, all full of neon lights outside premises offering all sorts of entertainment.

A seedy flat, for a seedy man, in a seedy neighbourhood, Lee pondered to herself. She had taken up a position across the street from the kebab shop with a forty-five degree angled view on the front door, whilst Burrows sprinted back to collect the car. Once he'd returned, and they were sat in it with a view of the ginnel, Burrows discussed strategy with her. They both agreed to give the ops until 9 or 10 o'clock to see if Chapman was going to go anywhere, or whether he was holed up for the evening. Thinking he would at least be in for the next hour or two, Lee said she would head out to try and find some fast food that looked edible; neither fancied the wares on display from the kebab shop. She returned with a couple of boxes of Macdonald's and two diet cokes.

"Best I could find I'm afraid," she said, "but at least you can recognise it."

"No, this is perfect thanks; it reminds me of those long hours and days spent on surveillance when I was with SOCA."

Lee just raised an eyebrow, this man was obviously, easily pleased. Then they both ate.

When they'd finished she reminded Burrows what Briers had told them at the end of their meeting with him earlier. He had mentioned that the undercover officer who'd gone missing—Steele, the driver of the wagon when Cabilla slaughtered those cops— was still absent. And they couldn't disregard a possible connection with Cabilla. Briers had gone on to explain that he was remotely monitoring all the specialist ops led activity with regard to the cops' efforts to find him. He told them about the press appeal, and the clever way they had written it, so as not to blow Steele's cover. Lee then produced a copy of last night's London Evening Standard from inside her lightweight jacket and threw it on Burrows's lap. "I picked this up from a newsagent on my way back to the car."

There was a half-page photograph on the front cover, which she instinctively glanced at. She noticed Burrows looking too.

"Shit," shouted Burrows.

"What's up?"

"Look."

Lee followed his gaze and could see that by looking at the newspaper, albeit for only a few seconds, they had both missed Chapman leaving his flat. He had walked several metres down the street with his back towards them. She was about to leap out of the car when Burrows put his hand on her arm to stop her.

As he did this, Chapman slowed his gait to a halt. Waited a few seconds, and then abruptly spun around and headed back towards his flat with purpose in his step, as if he'd forgotten something. He re-entered his front door, and then re-emerged again a few seconds later. He looked both ways, and then set off in the opposite direction than before, turning left down a narrow side street, before he reached opposite where Burrows and Lee were parked.

"At first, I thought he might have genuinely forgotten something, but I'm not sure now," Burrows said.

"I think you're right John; I think he was attempting his own counter-surveillance. I think he's been watching too many James Bond movies."

"Nevertheless, let's be careful with him. If he is doing counter-surveillance then he's up to no good. I'll take up the follow on my own and you can shadow me in the motor; that way we keep our options open if he goes mobile," Burrows said.

With that said Burrows jumped out of the car and set off after Chapman. Lee slid across into the driver's seat and started the engine. Her earpiece hissed into life as Burrows took up his commentary.

"Confirming Alpha has the eyeball, subject heading east on unnamed street in the general direction of Regent Street... Radio check?"

"Bravo to Alpha, I'm getting you loud and clear and will take up a parallel route. Back to you," Lee said.

"Yes, yes there's no deviation. Still heading towards Regent Street."

***

During the next ten minutes, Chapman kept Burrows busy. He kept stopping, crossing the street only to cross back again and even stopped to tie his shoelaces. All of which Burrows thought was very passé. Chapman obviously had been watching too many James Bond films as Lee had suggested. Burrows just cut him some slack and made sure there was always someone between him and Chapman, which wasn't hard in this part of London. However, when they reached Piccadilly Circus he knew this was going to get difficult due to the sheer size and complexity of the area. Not to mention the number of people milling around. Lee had gone ahead and was circling the area, and Burrows had got in as close to Chapman as he dared, which wasn't too hard with this many pedestrians about. However, if he was going to lose him, it was going to be here.

That said, after Chapman's initial shenanigans when he first set off, Burrows noticed in the last four or five minutes he'd seemed to calm down. Villains who were conscious of being followed by the police often did this, he recalled. Performing lots of anti-surveillance when they first set off, and then calming down once they were happy they weren't being followed. The key was to cut them as much room as you could until they settled down.

Fortunately, Chapman seemed to be happy now. Their luck then doubled when Chapman turned off Regent Street down a side street, before they reached Piccadilly Circus. Burrows still hung back before turning the corner just in case Chapman had spotted something and was being cautious again.

One of the things about surveillance that used to irritate him the most, was when a team had to back right off, or even stand-down, not because they'd done something, which had alerted the target to their presence, but because the untrained target had seen something completely innocent, that wasn't connected to the surveillance team, but wrongly assumed that it was. And then having convinced themselves that they were being followed—albeit for all the wrong reasons—they would then abort whatever it was they were about to do, and return home.

However, when Burrows turned into the side street Chapman still gave the appearance of being unaware and not suspicious. He followed him onto Sherwood Street, and they were both now heading away from Piccadilly Circus. Lee radioed that she was frantically trying to catch up, having been held in the early evening traffic around Piccadilly Circus itself.

A few minutes later, Chapman arrived at a small crossroads, which formed a junction with Brewer Street. Aptly named, as on the offside corner of Brewer Street and Sherwood Street, was a traditional looking pub painted black with gold lettering. The pub was called The Crown and its entrance was at a forty-five-degree angle, with half of the pub on Brewer Street and the other half on Sherwood Street.

Burrows held back and watched Chapman walk straight into the pub. A couple of minutes later, Lee caught up and parked further down Brewer Street with a rear view on the front door of the pub. Thanks to the door's position, on the corner of both streets, it would be possible to move the car around and still get a good visual on the front door.

Burrows joined Lee in the car, and spoke as he maintained a view via the passenger door-mirror. They agreed that Lee should go in the pub to see if Chapman met anyone, and to try to get in close, to pick up any conversations. It was often easier for a woman to sit in a pub on her own; she could waste an hour looking at her watch as if waiting for someone. And if Lee started to feel exposed, Burrows could always join her. That agreed, Lee got out of the car and headed towards the pub.

Chapter Twenty-five

Steele, and Jim—as Steele had started calling Sickly-2—had just finished a pot noodle dinner and were watching the TV in Jim's flat. Steele didn't know Jim's full name, but didn't want to ask any questions that might seem inappropriate and raise suspicion. He had stopped thinking of him as Sickly-2 for two reasons; one, he didn't want to forget himself and suddenly call him it by mistake. Secondly, he was starting to get along well with Jim who had dropped his tough guy façade and was quite good company. That was something Steele had learnt long ago when he first got into undercover ops; a lot of really nasty villains were often quite good company. When you faced them as a policeman, you naturally only saw their darker side, but when they thought you were one of their own, they often appeared quite different. That said, Steele knew never to drop his guard; the simplest of provocation could awaken the monster within them in an instant.

Shortly before dinner, Jim took a call on his mobile, after which he suggested they eat something quick, so Steele was expecting something to happen. He didn't have long to wait before Mackey let himself in and came bounding up the stairs into the flat. He told them both that he had a little job on, and he needed both of them. He then gave them their wages, which consisted of a large bundle of twenty-pound notes each. Steele didn't want to count his in front of Mackey, so thanked him and put it in his pocket. But by the feel of it, there must have been at least a couple of grand. Steele was smiling to himself; they were finally happy with him, and if they were going out on a job then surely he would get an opportunity to get away unscathed. He didn't want to sound too keen to be getting out the flat, and knew he needed to stay in character for a while longer. "But if I leave the flat, won't that be a risk? What with my ugly mug being across last night's paper, isn't it a bit soon?" Steele asked, hoping he wasn't overplaying the reverse psychology.

"Well, I need Jim to drive and drop me off somewhere, and then pick me up, and I don't think the Boss will be happy if I leave you here on your own Larry. No offence," Mackey said.

"None taken," Steele replied.

"Plus, there have been developments and I might need the extra muscle. I've got the 4 x 4 outside and its windows are blacked out so you should be all right Larry. Borrow one of Jim's baseball caps if you like, that'll help cover your features, and in any event you'll not be getting out the motor," Mackey said.

"Ok, you're the governor."

He did borrow one on Jim's baseball caps, a plain blue one, and then Mackey further briefed them that he wanted taking to a boozer near Piccadilly Circus. They were to drop him off, and then drive around the block and pull up at the front door. If all went to plan, he would be back out in a minute or two.

As they left the flat Steele found himself in-between Mackey and Jim, he was trying to work out whether he should make a run for it straight away or not. He felt a little penned in, though he didn't think it was on purpose. Having made a quick risk assessment in his head, he decided to leave it until after they had dropped Mackey off at the pub; that way there would be just Jim to contend with. He also knew that Piccadilly Circus would be manic with people, so it would give him greater cover to get away amidst the crowds.

Mackey threw the car keys to Jim and got into the back of the black Ranger Rover, Steele therefore, got into the front passenger seat. His brain was going into overtime as to what was going down. It didn't sound like Mackey intended to be in the pub long; was he collecting a package of something? But then he'd said he might need extra muscle; what did that mean? Mackey and Jim weren't exactly lightweights. He knew he couldn't ask; he didn't want to do anything to raise suspicions now, not with freedom so near.

Over the last couple of days, Steele had plenty of time to contemplate getting away. He'd also wondered what kind of shite he would be in, and how deep it might be once he did get free. After all, he had been acting without authority, and therefore had been involved in some pretty serious criminality. It was true he hadn't realised that the cargo they picked up in Kent had been a human one, until after they got back to Dulwich. Though he wasn't too sure the bosses would see it that way. He would need to convince them that he himself was captive, and doing what he had to do, to stay alive. Even with that, out of the way he wasn't sure if anything he had witnessed could ever be used in a court of law. In fact, the more he thought about it the surer he was that a judge would throw out any evidence he could give long before any jury got to hear it. He'd worry about that later, after he was free.

Mackey had sat behind Jim and Steele knew he would have a clear view of him. He wasn't sure whether Mackey was paying him scrutiny on the short journey into Soho, but he certainly got that impression. Every time he turned to face Mackey, to make conversation, Mackey seemed to be staring at him. Steele wasn't sure if he was being paranoid or not, but it reinforced his earlier decision to wait until he was on his own with Jim before making his move.

Twenty minutes later, they turned off from Piccadilly Circus and headed down a side street. Jim pulled over just past a pub called The Crown, which was on a corner. Mackey got out, and walked into the pub main entrance, which was on the apex of the street corner. Jim accelerated quickly away from the kerb narrowly missing a Ford Mondeo parked up on the side of the road, and took the first left followed by two more. Steele noticed the street name they were now on was Sherwood Street and he realised that the pub would be coming up on the left hand side. He had planned to jump out as soon as Jim had been forced to wait at one of the junctions. Wait until he was looking the other way to give himself a few moments head start. However, the lack of traffic at each junction had enabled Jim to keep going needing only to momentarily slow before making each turn. Steele wasn't over concerned; he would wait until Jim pulled up outside the pub and then make his move whilst they were waiting for Mackey.

**

Lee was approaching the pub when a big black 4 x 4 pulled up outside, and dropped someone off before pulling away. The car was between her and the pub, and whoever got out had only walked a couple of feet before reaching the doorway. She just saw the back of a huge man disappearing into the bar. She followed on in a few seconds later, and could see the bar in the centre of the room, and to her left sat by a window table was their subject Chapman. He had just been joined by the huge man whose back was still towards Lee. She looked all around as if she was looking for someone, and then made her way to the bar. There were only a few people in the pub, and all were at tables leaving the bar empty. She ordered a gin and tonic and sat on a stool.

She turned to her left as if she was checking the entrance; waiting for some imaginary friend to walk in. As she did so, she saw the large black 4 x 4 vehicle pass the window where both men were, and pull slightly forward as it

137

stopped by the front door. As soon as the vehicle stopped, the huge man jumped to his feet, and dragged Chapman with him, literally by the scruff of his neck. He then dragged him out the pub, opening the door with his spare hand, whilst hauling a terrified looking Chapman behind him. She then saw the huge man's face for the first time, and recognised him instantly. She reached into her coat pocket and pressed the radio transmit button several times in quick succession to alert Burrows that Chapman was leaving—albeit not by choice.

She heard Burrows's voice in her earpiece respond. "Rapid pips. Stand-by. Stand-by." Confirming he had understood her silent message, that the target was suddenly leaving, and she couldn't speak to tell him so.

By the time she'd done that, the man had Chapman fully out the door, and was bundling him into the back seats of the 4 x 4. As she reached the front door of the pub, she saw the rear car door being shut as the vehicle sped off down Brewer Street, passing Burrows in the Mondeo as it did. Customers in the pub were just looking up agog, presumably trying to make sense of what they'd just seen, all of which had been over in a matter of seconds.

Lee could see that Burrows had the car engine running by the exhaust gases. She ran down the street the few metres towards it, keeping to the building-line on her left hand side as she did so. Trying to get to the car as quickly as she could whilst remaining covert, using the buildings to mask her approach. Though she was sure, the driver of the 4 x 4 would be too busy looking ahead of him rather than behind as he approached a crossroads. Burrows opened the passenger door from within as Lee arrived, and set off whilst she was still only half-way into the car. The 4 x 4 ahead had already made a left turn onto a further side street.

"Good work," Burrows said as Lee straightened herself up, "your heads up gave me the chance to get the car started. And seconds can make all the difference as you well know," he finished, as he accelerated hard away from the kerb.

"You're welcome," she replied before adding. "Did you see who the big guy was?"

"No I couldn't see; their vehicle was in the way both times."

"It was Mackey. And Chapman didn't go with him willingly."

Lee saw the surprise on Burrows's face and she quickly filled him in on what she'd witnessed, as Burrows expertly negotiated a forced turn as the one-way system directed them towards Regent Street. Up ahead the 4 x 4 was waiting at a red traffic signal sat in pole position. The lights went through the sequence as they approached. On green, the 4 x 4 turned left into Regent Street and headed towards Piccadilly Circus.

Burrows put his foot down harder, obviously trying to reach the T-junction ahead before the lights changed back to red. But it seemed to her that no sooner had they turned to green, they changed back to red. She grabbed the door handle as Burrows accelerated even harder, before he stamped on the brakes.

"Shit. Shit, shit," he shouted, as they slid towards a halt.

Not only had the lights changed back to red, but Lee could see that the vast amount of waiting traffic on Regent Street had set off again, and was streaming past the end of their road nose to tail. They were well and truly blocked in until the lights changed to green again. And by which time, the 4 x 4 would have reached Piccadilly Circus, and be long gone.

Chapter Twenty-six

The black 4 x 4 pulled up outside The Crown pub, braking hard to a stop as it did. Steele was getting ready to make his move when Jim distracted him by screaming. "Open the back door... The back door. Do it now."

Steele was stunned into momentary indecision, he saw Mackey dragging someone out of the pub and across the pavement to the car. Whether he then acted on reflex to Jim's shouting, or not, he wasn't quite sure, but he reached behind and opened the rear passenger door just in time for Mackey to haul his prey—a scrawny looking man—into the rear seats before jumping in next to him.

"Go. Go. Go," he shouted as Jim then put his foot down and sped off down Brewer Street. Steele hadn't any idea what was going on, but decided that now was not the time to ask. He faced back towards the front as Jim sped around the side streets and back onto Regent Street.

"I don't know what the fuck this is all about. But you'd better have a good explanation," the scrawny man shouted as he was clearly getting over the initial shock of what had just taken place.

"You're a blood sucking piss-taker, and I'm not sure we need your services anymore," Mackey answered.

"Any professional relationship we have had in the past can't be proved. I've been careful to make sure of that. So the way it stands now, is that you are in a whole heap of shit. You can't just drag a policeman off the street like this, and expect to get away with it," the scrawny man said.

"Shut the fuck up Runt," Mackey shouted as he drove his right elbow into the man's left temple knocking him unconscious.

Steele glanced over his right shoulder to see the man slumped forward, and starting to breathe heavily in short rapid gasps. He then turned back to face the road whilst the man's words sank in. He couldn't believe the man, or the Runt as Mackey had called him, said he was a cop. And now Steele had been involved in his kidnap. How much deeper in the shit could he find himself.

One thing was now sure though, he couldn't just leg it when the opportunity arose, not with a kidnapped copper in the back seat; God knows what Mackey has planned for him. No, he would have to stick around, at least that way he might be able to help the poor man, who was obviously in even deeper trouble than Steele had been when he was lifted a few days ago. And in any event, he'd no idea where they were taking him. He assumed they'd take him to the warehouse, but Steele still didn't know where that was. Even, when he drove the wagon back from Kent Jim had made him pull up on the outskirts of south London, blindfolded him, and took over the last ten minutes of the driving.

As if on cue, Mackey pulled a strip of material out of his coat pocket and wrapped it around the unconscious man's head covering his eyes. Not that he could currently see through them, Steele thought. Then he pulled out a second strip and flung it over Steele's shoulder.

"Put that on Larry, and do it properly. And before you kick off, it's only to keep the Boss happy. Trust me; you won't have to wear it many more times."

Steele looked at Mackey and could almost see the apology in his eyes, so decided it was not the time to argue.

"Ok mate, whatever you say," Steele said in a resigned tone as he did as he'd been asked.

Once they reached the warehouse Steele took his head covering off, and he and Jim carried the unconscious man into the warehouse, and to the cell where Steele had previously been locked up in. Repugnance flooded through him as they opened the cellar door with their feet, and the chair in the centre of the room came into view. By the time they'd secured the unfortunate cop to the chair he was starting to stir, but had yet to open his eyes. They left the room and locked the door. Jim pocketed the key and told Steele to sit guard outside whilst he went off to find Mackey, who'd gone upstairs as soon as they'd arrived. Steele sat outside the locked door with a distinctive feeling of 'poacher turned gamekeeper' or should that be the other way around? He thought to himself.

***

Back at Piccadilly Circus, Burrows had done a standard search pattern of the immediate area, more in hope than expectation, but the 4 x 4 was long gone. Lee had rung Briers to fill him in, and he said he would try to get backdoor access to the CCTV networks and put the car registration number through the PNC, though he didn't expect the latter to be of any use. The plates shown would undoubtedly be ghosted from a similar vehicle.

Burrows and Lee sat in silence as they headed over to the office in Pimlico. Burrows was down-mouthed at being so close to locating Cabilla; all they would have had to do, was stay on Mackey's tail, and eventually they would have found their man. He could see that in Lee's expression she felt as bad as he did. They parked in the underground car park and entered the building. They'd just sat down in the briefing room with a coffee, when Briers walked in with a folder under his arm.

"First of all, you can both take that look of despondency off your faces. Considering you are only a two-person team, you've done remarkably well. You have to remember we are under the radar, and as such only have access to limited resources," Briers said, before sitting down at the table with them.

Burrows nodded, and so did Lee.

Briers opened the folder in front of him. "The car was ghosted, its real home is in Manchester, and as of five minutes ago, it was parked on the drive at the owner's home address. So the one Mackey was using was either a knock-off, or they were just hiding its true identity."

More nods before he continued. "We did manage to get a still from a camera in Regent Street, which gives a good shot of the front of the car," he finished before handing over a blown-up still photograph from his file.

It was a good shot through the vehicle's only clear glass, the windscreen. Chapman and Mackey could be clearly seen in the back of the car, and in the front, there was a forward view of the front seat passenger. He was wearing a blue baseball cap, but at the point when the picture was taken, fortunately for them, he was looking up, so the shot included all his face. The image of the driver wasn't as clear, as he was looking to his right, so all they had was his profile. As Burrows and Lee studied the images, Briers continued."These are literally hot of the press so we haven't had chance to do any work on trying to identify the front seat occupants yet."

"I can save you some trouble on one of them," Burrows said.

"Bloody hell you're right," Lee said as she looked back at the picture.

"You know one of them? That's brilliant," Briers exclaimed.

"Not so brilliant really Frank," Lee said before adding, "the front seat passenger was all over the front page of last night's Evening Standard."

Briers left the room and soon returned with a copy of last night's paper, and placed it on the table next to the photographs. Burrows could see they were both right.

"I can't wait to see the Home Secretary's face when I tell him that we had Mackey in a vehicle, having kidnapped a corrupt policeman, with the aid of a missing undercover officer, together with an unknown driver," Briers said.

"You could tell him over the phone. That way you wouldn't have to see his face," Burrows said, trying to lighten the mood.

"Very funny Burrows," Briers answered, emphasizing Burrows's surname.

"Sorry Frank," he said, whilst raising his hands in mock surrender.

After further discussion with Lee, it was clear to him that neither of them had seen much of the undercover officer, or Larry as he was apparently known. So it was hard to evaluate his presence at the scene. He appeared to have been passive, and was clearly there of his own volition, as he could have jumped from the vehicle at any time.

"Are we sure he's not been deployed undercover back into Mackey? You know, officially I mean," Lee asked.

"Absolutely," Briers said, "he was put back in *just* to make contact with Mackey, when he disappeared. The initial fear being that, he either ran into some other old target of his, or he did in fact find Mackey, and for some reason they've taken him."

"Well, I know we didn't see much of him Frank, but he sure as hell didn't look 'taken,'" Burrows added.

"The only other conclusion then is that he's turned native. He's one of them," Briers said.

"It sure looks that way," Lee said.

They finished their coffees and Briers said he would have the ghosted registration plate number put into the inner London ANPR, and put his pager on twenty-four hour notice for any hits. Burrows knew ANPR stood for Automatic Number Plate Recognition System. It read the number plate of any vehicle coming into central London, as well from other sites as well. Briers said that most of the larger cities and towns now had a number of fixed sites in what the police called, 'rings of steel'. In addition, they also had a number of mobile units operating as well.

On reflection, it appeared to Burrows, that Mackey had no reason to think he was being watched, so hopefully he would be happy to keep the current plates on his car. That way, at least they would know when the vehicle was being used again in and around central London, and that could ultimately lead them to Cabilla. So the evening had been far from a total loss, he consoled himself.

Briers also said as much, and that he planned to use the same spin when he briefed the Home Secretary. And to be fair, it wasn't untrue.

Burrows suggested they call it a night, and resume efforts in the morning. Lee said that he could crash at her flat for the night, to save him going all the way back to Oxfordshire. He willingly accepted, and all three left to try to catch last orders at the pub across the road.

Chapter Twenty-seven

All arrived at the warehouse and, Mackey left Jim and Larry to take the Runt into the cellar room, whilst he went upstairs to check on Kimba and the women. He'd left one of his men with her, so didn't expect any problems. Apparently, all the women were still well out of it, and compliant. Although, Kimba seemed to know what she was doing, she wasn't over friendly towards him; he wasn't sure why, as he hadn't known her long, but there was a definite edge to her. It didn't matter, as long as she did her job properly. His man said there had been no worries, but confirmed that Kimba was a cool one. This trait made her appear even more attractive than she already was in Mackey's mind. He was starting to picture her in the sexy secretary mould, sensual and aloof. He shook her from his mind as he went back down stairs, he'd probably seen too many porn films, he thought to himself.

Once in the main hall he rang Cabilla to bring him up to date. Cabilla told him to continue as arranged, and then added, that he had some business to take care of over the next twenty-four hours, and that Mackey should keep a hold on things in the meantime. Cabilla didn't explain what he was doing, and Mackey thought better than to ask over the phone, though sometimes he still got the impression Cabilla didn't share everything with him on purpose. It was a reminder that Cabilla was number one, and he was number two.

***

Steele sat on the chair contemplating what he should do next. He just seemed to be getting deeper and deeper in the quagmire, and by no fault of his own. Here he was, a police undercover officer, having been involved in a conspiracy to bring abducted women into the country, currently guarding a kidnapped corrupt police officer. This was one scenario they never put him through when he did his level-one undercover course at Hendon. Even if some abstract instructor had dreamt it up, it would surely have been rejected for being too ridiculous.

One option that kept going through his mind was to tell the bloke in the cell his true identity, and therefore reassure him he had help on his side. Then, when the opportunity arose, they could both make a run for it together. After all, that would increase their chances of success two-fold. The only thing that bothered him was why was the bloke here? If he'd been working for Mackey, then he was surely corrupt; but it appeared as if something had gone wrong. It then occurred to Steele that the bloke might not believe him anyway; he might think of it as a trick of some kind.

Then it hit him. What if this copper bloke was actually an undercover officer like he was? Perhaps his legend was that of a corrupt cop; a cop pretending to be a corrupt cop, in order to infiltrate Mackey and his gang? How clever would that be? Steele's head was starting to spin, and he realised he didn't know enough yet; he would keep quiet and monitor things for now. He was then interrupted from his torturous contemplations by the sound of footsteps approaching.

Mackey appeared outside the cell swinging a set of keys. "I've sent Jim to get some grub. So let's you and me have a little chat with the Runt."

Steele just nodded as he stood up, and Mackey unlocked the door. They both went in and Mackey closed the door behind him. He motioned to Larry to stand by it, and then turned his attention to the prisoner. The Runt, as Mackey referred to him as, was slumped in the chair with his ankles fastened to the chair legs, and his wrists handcuffed behind the chair back. He was awake but still looked a little stunned; his eyes weren't fully clear as he looked up at Mackey approaching.

Mackey stood in front of him, and hit him hard across the face with the back of his hand. The Runt's head snapped from one side to the other, and he let out a yelp of pain.

"Wakey, wakey Runty," Mackey mocked.

The Runt recoiled, and then slowly recovered from the blow. He looked up attentively now. "Ok Den, you've had your fun, and no real harm done, so what's this really all about?"

"I'll tell you what it is all about Runt. It's about you always seeming to drip feed us stuff, a bit at a time, whilst ensuring you're well paid. You think we don't know? Cabilla has long had you sussed, and we are getting a bit fed up. You've done it once too often."

"Look, granted in the past I may have done a bit of that. But honest I've never fed you shit or anything, and you know you can trust me."

"Trust," Mackey shouted, "I wouldn't trust you as far as I could shit." He glanced back at Larry before he spoke again. Steele got the impression he was

145

deciding how far he should go in front of him, before realising that he'd earned his trust by now. He turned back to the Runt. "Manchester."

"What about it?" The Runt answered before continuing, "I told you, the barman knew jack shit, but I got the feeling he was holding back a bit."

"You're sure you're not drip-feeding us again? Or perhaps the guy really does know shit, and you're just trying to increase your number of pay days again?"

"Den, I really don't know what you're going on about?"

"We sent someone all the fucking way to Manchester today, to speak to the Irish twat—on your say so—and guess what? Don't answer, I'll tell you. He's fucked off. The bloke in the bar was a relief barman who said that the Irish had done a runner. Belled them up apparently, and said he was fucking off back to Ireland as he was in some shit.

So you tell me Runt. You tell me what really went on; because I reckon he told you who the other firm were, and you told him to fuck off back to the Emerald Isle. That way, you could drip-feed us, and when we paid him a further visit he'd be gone, and only you would know the proper script."

The Runt's face now looked as stunned as when Mackey had slapped it. Steele wasn't sure whether he looked surprised, or just scared.

"Ok, I'll be really honest with you. I was trying to rip you a bit, I'm sorry. The truth is that the Irish guy really didn't know anything, and to be honest I could see no good reason to pay him another visit. I just recommended that so I had something to give you—no matter how little—and I'd get a bung to cover my costs. But you've got to believe me when I tell you the barman knew nothing, just that it was another firm of villains is all."

"Good effort Runt, but not good enough. Both Cabilla and me think the barman gave you the name of the other firm. And you'd better tell me 'cause if you think I'm a mean bastard, wait 'till you see the Boss lose it."

"If, I knew the name of the other firm, don't you think I'd tell you now? It would make no sense not to. But I can't, as I don't know."

"It would, if you were grassing us up to them. Maybe they're paying you more to find out about us than we are paying you?"

"What? This is madness. I'm not working for anyone else—"

The back of Mackey's hand hit the other side of his face before he could finish his sentence. His head cracked in the opposite direction than before.

"I'm going to have something to eat now Runt. You've got half an hour to fess up the other firm's name before the real pain starts. It's up to you," Mackey said, before turning to leave.

Once outside, the door was re-locked, and Mackey pocketed the key once more. Jim was waiting for them with three boxes of Kentucky Fried Chicken; he gave them one each. Mackey told Steele to eat his on the chair whilst he kept an eye on the prisoner. He then wandered off with Jim back towards the main hall.

As Steele ate, he couldn't help the feeling ofdéjà vu with what Mackey had said to the Runt. He was no doubt going to give him the double agent line next. But more than this, he was intrigued as to what they were talking about. He'd seen Mackey glance at him before he mentioned Manchester, and now realised why. But he still didn't know what this other 'firm' thing was all about. What he was sure of though, was that Mackey was starting to trust him fully, and therefore open up in front of him. And the more Steele could learn about this Manchester angle, and whatever else for that matter, could only serve to reduce the level of shite he would end up in with the police bosses at the end of it all.

More pressing though, was what could Steele do if Mackey came back in thirty minutes and started to give the cop some serious grief? What could he do to stop him without bringing the blanket of mistrust back over his own head? He had absolutely no idea.

Chapter Twenty-eight

Steele soon devoured his meal, and his watch told him he had twenty minutes before Mackey's return. He'd twenty minutes to think of a way to stop Mackey from causing serious hurt to the cop in the cell, and to do so in a way that didn't compromise him. What a dilemma. But he knew he had to do something; he couldn't stand by and watch Mackey beat the guy to death. He'd decided to try to reason with the man, who clearly knew Mackey better than he did.

Steele tapped on the cell door. No answer. He tried again, but this time spoke, trying to raise his voice to a level that was audible to the man inside, but not so loud as to alert Mackey or anyone else in the building. "Listen Mate, my name's Larry, I'm the guy who came in the cell with Mackey a few minutes ago. You don't know me, and I don't know you, but let me give you a piece of advice; tell Mackey what he wants to know, and you will save yourself a lot of grief," he whispered. There was a pause, and Steele wondered if the guy had heard him or not.

"Look, you're right we don't know each other, and if Den has put you up to this, forget it. I've told him all I can," the cop replied.

"Mackey's not put me up to this, but I was in a similar position to you a couple of days ago, I'm just trying to help you."

"There is another firm, but I've no idea who? And the barman sure as shit didn't know. I can't tell Den what I don't know. Anyway, why would you want to help me? You obviously know I'm a cop."

There was another pause, as Steele was on the point of reassuring the cop that he was not the only one. But he still wasn't sure. He still hadn't worked out if the guy was properly bent, or undercover. He hoped that by talking to him he might get a better idea, perhaps pick up on something. Ask him something that would appear innocuous to an outsider, but a fellow undercover officer might recognise and respond to. Like a secret handshake, figuratively speaking. Then he heard footsteps approaching once more.

148

Steele looked up to see Mackey reappear, closely followed by Jim. Mackey clearly had a purpose about him as he pulled the door key from his pocket.

"The Runt will have to wait a while longer," Mackey said as he handed the key to Jim. Steele felt himself relax, as Mackey continued, "I've got to do something before I start on the Runt, and it won't do the little shit any harm to sweat a bit more. Jim will wait with you," Mackey finished, before he turned on his heels, and walked off back towards the main room.

Jim just grinned and pulled up a chair. Steele was relieved at the delay, as no doubt the cop would be. Steele reckoned the cop must have heard Mackey's booming voice. At least both he, and Steele had more time to think, but Steele felt frustrated he couldn't ask any more questions, now that Jim was with him.

It hadn't gone unnoticed to Steele that Mackey had handed the key to Jim, and he wondered just how trusted he was. He asked Jim about it who just said it was nothing to do with trust; it was just about rank and status. Jim being obviously held in higher regard.

"Well if it's not about trust Jim, why can't I have my phone back?" Steele asked.

"Why do you keep banging on about your phone? Who the fuck are so desperate to ring? You know Den wants everything kept tight for the next few days," Jim asked with a note of raised suspicion in his voice that Steele quickly picked up on.

"Don't get the wrong idea mate, I've got no fucker particularly I want to ring," Steele said, quickly hoping to quell Jim's increased interest, "I suppose I was just looking for a sign that I was fully trusted, that's all. No big deal."

"Don't sweat mate, Den trusts you, so you've no need to fret if that's all you're bothered about. And in any event, your phone was smashed up and binned when you were lifted, you'll get a new one in due course."

"Oh, well that's cool then," Steele finished, trying to sound pacified, hiding his disappointment.

It was a blow. He knew that even if he had been given his mobile phone back, he would have no doubt been monitored closely, so initially ringing for help would not have been an option. But he had planned to just turn it on, and check for voicemails and text messages. He knew that any left by his DI or cover officer, would have been done covertly, so as not to compromise him; they would have been only too aware of the risks of the wrong person listing to, or reading them. And, as the phone was his official undercover phone for his deployment into finding Mackey, he also knew that only the above two

149

had the number, apart from their London counterparts, and they all play by the same rules.

No, what was in Steele's mind was the fact that as soon as his phone was turned on again, it would have made contact with the nearest phone mast, and continued to 'ping' it at regular intervals. Steele was in no doubt, that the guys looking for him would be conducting live cell-site analysis, but with his phone turned off, they had nothing to study. As soon as his phone went live again, they would at least know within a mile or so, which part of London he was in. In fact sometimes they can narrow things down even further, sometimes, to within a matter of a few hundred metres. But that opportunity was gone, and it was all Steele could do to hide his inner feelings from Jim. He tried to turn his mind back to the cop in the cell, and what the hell he was going to do when Mackey returned.

***

Meanwhile, Mackey was getting more than a little annoyed at being stonewalled; firstly, by Cabilla wandering off on some solo mission without trusting him enough to tell him what he was up to, and secondly by the standoffish attitude of Kimba upstairs. When he'd popped up to check on things earlier, she'd fobbed him off without seeing the girls. This time, he was going to insist checking on them, whether Kimba liked it or not.

Mackey walked down the narrow corridor on the second floor past the five numbered rooms, and into the office at the end. Amber Kimba was just entering the office direct from her apartment. Mackey turned to the guard and told him to go and take a break, he didn't need telling twice.

"Back so soon Den," Kimba said, as she closed the door from her flat.

"I want to see the girls. Properly, and not just a glimpse through the doorways."

"Why, what's to see? They are all still hooked up to the drips, and won't be fully conscious for a couple of days or so."

Kimba answered, with what Mackey thought was an edge of hesitation in her voice.

"I want a proper look, that's all. And don't forget who's in charge here Amber."

Mackey knew his approach was bullish, it was intentional; Kimba needed reminding of the rank structure.

She told him he could only look, that it would be another week before the girls were brought off the intravenous drips, and allowed to regain their senses. After that, she said, the withdrawal symptoms would start to kick in, and they would plead for the heroin to becalm their demons. Once they'd reached that stage, they would be nearly ready to start work; do whatever was asked of them, and be rewarded with more heroin.

Mackey understood this, but couldn't help feeling that Kimba was being over-protective, even stringing out things longer than necessary. He would keep a closer watch on things from here on in. He walked over to the first door, and waited for Kimba to follow and unlock it. He pushed the door fully open, and walked into the room; he'd only had a glimpse before, and was wondering whether he should sample things for himself. He knew that would piss Cabilla off, but he was considering it nonetheless. However, once inside the room he stared down at the young Congolese woman laid on the bed dressed in tracksuit bottoms and a scruffy T-shirt. The woman could only have been about twenty years of age, small, petite, and slim, with long brown hair and big brown eyes, staring opaquely in Mackey's direction. The eyes unnerved him; they had a haunted hollowness to them. Any amorous feelings he'd been harbouring disappeared.

"Will they always looked this fucked up?" He asked before adding, "It gives me the creeps." Mackey turned to leave the room as Kimba answered.

"Once they are off the drips they will look a lot better."

Mackey thought he could see a worried look on her face as she spoke.

"Look, do you really want to see the others up close? They're all pretty much the same. Why don't you come into my flat, and have yourself a drink. Let us have a chat, and get to know each other better. I don't want to get off on the wrong foot with anyone."

Mackey, surprised by Kimba's change of attitude, grunted and nodded in agreement, before he followed her into the apartment. He wasn't sure exactly where this was heading, but relieved that she had started to show him some respect.

Chapter Twenty-nine

Earlier that day, after Cabilla had visited the girls with Mackey, he'd set off up the M1 headed north. He hadn't told Mackey initially that he was going to Manchester, only later in a phone call. He liked to keep something to himself occasionally, not that he didn't trust Mackey, but it didn't do any harm to remind him who was boss from time to time. He had decided to drive, as he would need transport once he got there, and didn't want to leave any 'footprints' by using rentals or taxis. He'd taken the black 4 x 4, but changed the ghost plates first. He was aware that the set currently on the vehicle were ghosted from a similar car registered in the Manchester area. The last thing he wanted was to bump into it. He knew the odds were short, but it was better not to take unnecessary risks; which was why they used the Manchester registered plates when in London. The plates he now had on were registered to a similar vehicle in Glasgow, so there shouldn't be any problems.

He stopped at the motorway services at Hilton Park just north of Birmingham for a break and something to eat. He also rang ahead to give a more accurate time of arrival, the first person he was going to see wasn't the sort who liked to be kept waiting. Status-wise, Cabilla considered himself an equal, but it was he who was after the favour, and in any event, the bloke could be a grumpy bastard if provoked.

It was mid-afternoon when he arrived in south Manchester; he'd left the M6 at junction 19, and driven the short distance on the A556 that led to the M56. From there he had passed near to Manchester Ringway Airport, and onto the Princess Parkway. He then joined the M60 clockwise.

After that, he put a call into his contact as instructed, and was directed to leave the motorway at junction 7. He was also given a postcode to put into his satellite navigation device, which took him into Trafford Park, the huge industrial estate. He ended up on a small side road between various units, where he pulled over, again as instructed.

Trafford Park was vast, the size of a small town in its own right Cabilla had thought many times. He'd absolutely no idea where he was now, but was sure that the man he'd come to see certainly took security seriously. Cabilla didn't mind all the messing about; it showed that the man was a fellow professional, something he appreciated.

He only waited a couple of minutes before a black 5 series BMW saloon pulled up behind him, and two men got out. Both huge, and both reminded him of Mackey; they walked with a strut of arrogance designed to show they meant business. He didn't get out of his car; he would let them come to him, protocol. As they approached, he wound down his driver's window.

Both men stood side-by-side, and the one who'd got out of the driver's seat spoke. "Mr Moon asks that you leave your car here, and come with us. It's only a short drive."

Cabilla just nodded, and closed the window before getting out of his vehicle and locking it remotely.

"I have been instructed by Mr Moon to ask if you are carrying anything? No offence intended," the driver said.

"None taken," he replied. He'd expected this, "I've nothing on me but do have... equipment in the motor," he answered, opening his sports jacket as he spoke.

The driver nodded at the other guy, who cursorily searched Cabilla before standing back.

"Thank you for your understanding Mr Cabilla. We have no need to search your car as it's staying here," said the driver before adding. "If you would like to now come with us please."

He followed them to the BMW, and without being asked, he got into the rear seat. The driver and his mate got into the front. Cabilla didn't attempt conversation with the two men, nor they with him, it would have been pointless, and of no value. He was driven around several side streets and realised that they were still in the confines of Trafford Park. Eventually they approached a single storey, non-descript building, which looked like a large processing plant, or warehouse. It was a modern design with corrugated steel walls, surrounded by a steel perimeter fence. A large steel gate slid open automatically as they approached, as did a steel shutter up-and-over door set in the side of the building. The driver drove straight into the compound, and into a large garage within the building, which had offices partitioned off at one end.

He was escorted from the BMW into an office, which was surprisingly opulent inside. It was carpeted with leather chesterfield couches and chairs at one end, set in a semi-circle around a large oak coffee table. At the other end, near the door, was a huge mahogany desk with a high-backed leather office chair. Cabilla was shown towards the seats, and told to make himself comfortable. Both men left the room closing the door behind them. Cabilla didn't hear them walk away and was in no doubt they were stood either side of the door.

He'd never met Jonny Moon, but they had spoken many times on the phone, and knew each other well enough. They also knew each other's reputation. Cabilla was still admiring the surroundings when the door opened, and in walked a man saying, "Hi, Shonbo, I'm Jonny Moon."

He was not what Cabilla had expected. He was in his late forties, greying-receding hair, but only about five feet six inches tall, with a skinny build. He was wearing jeans with a bulky leather jacket, as if the extra bulk of the jacket was to hide his petite frame. He looked younger than his years, and had almost an angelic countenance about him. Cabilla knew his description, after all, his nickname was, 'the vicar'. But seeing him in the flesh was somehow more surprising than he had expected.

Cabilla also knew that this angelic looking man was capable of intense cruelty, and always surrounded himself with muscle. He knew better than to let appearances deceive him into any form of disrespect.

Moon walked briskly across the room with a smile on his face and his hand extended. "Sorry about all that cloak and dagger stuff, but those twats at SOCA or whatever it's now called, keep wasting the tax payers' money by aimlessly following my staff around, given half the chance. What the thick fucks don't realise is that I have staff I use specifically for them to follow about." Both men laughed as they shook hands and sat down.

"They don't know about this place yet, so that's why I'm protective of it. It's only rented, and I'll move somewhere else in a month or two anyway, but the longer I can leave it, the better; it does get a bit tiresome always moving. That said, you have to stay one-step ahead of the filth. Anyway, enough of that let me get you a drink," Moon finished.

Cabilla asked for a whiskey and ice, and Moon shouted at one of his men behind the door to oblige. They chatted about business for a while, and swopped small talk. Cabilla knew Moon was aware he still did some business in Manchester, as well as in London, but there was a mutual respect between them; as whenever Cabilla was in Manchester on business, he gave Moon a courtesy call, just to ensure he wasn't getting into anything that was Moon's domain—he'd even helped him out with some premises in the past. He could tell Moon liked him for that. Even with his fearful reputation, Cabilla knew that there were always some slags willing to take the piss, by trying to encroach on Moon's criminal empire. Those who did so, probably only did it once.

"Okay Shonbo, I know you couldn't say too much over the phone, what with walls having ears as well as sausages, and all that shit. I think I know what you're after, but spell it out will you, now we're face-to-face."

He went into detail about the hit that went wrong, and briefed him on Billy the Kid, and how that had led him to believe another firm was after him.

"What about your shooter?" asked Moon, "are you sure about him?"

"Pretty much Jonny, he was a total virgin. Ex-sniper with the Congolese Army, brought in on a fake passport for a job that didn't happen. I just used him for this job whilst he was over here. Completely unknown, and unconnected in the UK, that's why I used him."

"Nice move Shonbo, I like your style. Anyway, look when we spoke on the phone I obviously didn't know why you felt some firm was after you, but just that you may have 'upset someone' to use your words," Moon said.

"Yes well, you can see now that whoever the Kid was meeting was someone serious as he took out my sniper. And as cops don't generally do that sort of thing, that led me to thinking it was another villain," he explained.

"Yes, I can see your thinking man, but seriously I've asked around all over the place, and I can safely say that if a firm is after you, I'd have been told by now. I don't suppose the filth have come up with anything have they?"

"No, they are still running round with their fingers up their arses."

"No change there then," Moon said, and they both laughed again.

"Sorry I can't help you more Shonbo, but if I do hear anything..." Moon said letting his words trail off before adding. "What about your taxi driver who was supposed to be watching Billy's back for you?"

"That's where I'm off to next Jonny. Hey, but thanks for your time and effort so far mate."

They both then said their goodbyes, and Moon instructed his men to take Cabilla back to his car.

He left the unit more confused than when he'd arrived. Moon had seemed certain that no northern firm were involved, yet someone had shot his man. It made less and less sense. Perhaps Moon isn't the oracle he likes to think he is. Or maybe he's holding back for some reason; Cabilla found him impossible to read.

Chapter Thirty

Cabilla knew that Jerry Philips drove his minibus working as a sole trader for hire to any number of different private-hire taxi firms in, and around Manchester. He made most of his income running villains and their merchandise around the city for extra generous fares; but what they didn't know was that he would often double his money by passing on information about their activities to the local police intelligence unit. But Cabilla knew. He also knew Philips was careful about what information he passed, and about whom. He realised that Philips didn't want to compromise himself, or his best payers; and Cabilla was one of Philips's best payers. He also knew that Philips would never dare cross him.

He guessed it was generally those that took the piss out of Philips whom he grassed up. He didn't find Jerry Philips a very pleasant individual. He was a small, unkempt man in his thirties, who lived alone in a grotty one-bedroomed flat in Wythenshawe. It was no surprise to Cabilla that the few friends Philips had, had nicknamed him 'Lonely', after the character in the 1960s television series, Callan. He'd been given the nickname because of his physical appearance, and demeanour as a snivelling individual. But Cabilla found the nickname ironic; as he knew Philips was also a grass, just like the character Lonely, except for the fact that Philips grassed both ways. Cabilla knew all this, but tolerated it, whilst he was still of use.

He'd told Philips to keep a low profile after Billy got wasted. Philips had said he'd no idea what was going to happen to Billy when he'd took him to the meeting at Blackley Cemetery. He'd told Cabilla it was Billy who'd rang him, and asked for transport. Phillips said he'd asked Billy several times what the meet was for? And who with? It all sounded a bit special, but Billy had just blanked him. So when Philips rang Cabilla to tell him about it, he'd said that as far as he was aware, Billy could have been meeting another villain as easily as the police. Cabilla told Philips just to make sure he got Billy to the meet on time. He hadn't told Philips what he had planned for Billy, just to make sure he got him there, and to try and spot who he met.

Philips had been grassing on other villains to Cabilla for a long time now. Cabilla knew he liked to think of himself as some sort of double agent, and he played up to that to keep Philips on side. It wasn't hard to inflate his ego, he was an idiot. After the trial in Manchester, and he had taken his retribution on Billy, he told Philips that Billy was squared; things were even. After all, if he'd wanted Billy dead he'd have just done it rather than just put him in a wheelchair. Thereafter, he'd been paying Phillips two hundred quid a month just to keep an eye on Billy. He'd told him all he wanted to know. If Billy looked like he was ever starting to talk to the police again, then he should tell him immediately, which was what Philips had done.

Philips later told Cabilla that Billy was being so cagey about who he was meeting at the cemetery, he reckoned Billy must have been seeing the filth.

Cabilla reckoned he was no different to anyone else of Philips's acquaintance, sneering at him, and looking down on him. He knew Philips thought he was having the last laugh; grassing the villains to the police, whilst taking their money for errands, then grassing villains to villains, and in Billy's case, grassing on another grass. As far as Cabilla was concerned, Philips was as low as you could get, and now Billy was dead it was time to end their relationship. Pay him what he was due and never see him again.

It was about 4 p.m. when Cabilla rang Philips; he could hear the surprise in his voice when he learnt that he was in Manchester. He sounded even more surprised to hear that Cabilla wanted to see him. Cabilla hadn't said why, but had hinted that Philips was in line for a bonus.

Two hours later, Philips pulled onto a quiet side street in the middle of Trafford Park, and as instructed pulled up close to the rear of Cabilla's 4 x 4. He watched through his door mirror as Philips got out of his own vehicle, and joined him in the front passenger seat, again as instructed.

"Nice to see you again Mr Cabilla, have you been back in town long?" Philips asked.

"Cut the love-in crap Jerry, I just want you to tell me again, face-to-face about the day Billy—the-shit-head—got what he was due."

So Philips went through it all again. How he had taken the call from Billy the night before, and after letting Cabilla know, he'd picked Billy up as arranged the following morning. He explained how Billy was very tight-lipped about it, and how he wouldn't let him drive into the car park at the cemetery; how he had to drop him off outside on the road, and Billy watched him drive away, before he started down the driveway to enter the grounds of the place. Philips also explained how he'd come back earlier than Billy had told him to, so he could hopefully; get a glimpse of whoever he'd met. It was

157

then that he heard the gunshots ring out, and 'did one', as quickly as he could. About half an hour later, he tried ringing Billy's mobile phone but it just rang out to voicemail.

"Did the filth pick up on that?" Cabilla asked.

"Yeah, they came to see me, and asked me about it, but I just said I was a mate of his and that's all. Said I'd spoken to him the night before, and he seemed cool and never said nothing about nothing," Philips answered.

"And they were completely happy about that yeah? Ruled you out of their enquiries?"

"Yeah, absolutely Mr Cabilla, they said they knew I was a mate of Billy's and it was just background they were after, 'bout who he'd met that day and stuff. When I told them I didn't know shit, they had it, no problems."

"And you've heard nothing from them since?"

"Fuck all, honest."

"Good Jerry, that's real good man. Look I've got something for your efforts, follow me to the boot," Cabilla said as he got out of the car.

Cabilla could see Philips's lips form a greedy smile as he walked around to the boot, bonus time, he no doubt thought. Cabilla had a good look around to make sure they were alone before he opened the boot and lent into it.

A moment later, he stood back from the boot of his car, and straightened himself up, before turning around to face Philips, who looked down as Cabilla held out his right hand, and said, "This is for you..." his words trailed off.

He could see Philips's eyes widen as he stared at his hand, which was holding a silenced handgun. As if time had slowed to a crawl, Philips, unmoving, just gawped at it with a look of disbelief.

Cabilla saw Philips's mouth start to move, the greedy smile long gone. He squeezed the trigger, and a small flash of fire blipped from the end of the silencer. There was no discernible noise. Then he made the silencer blip again.

"...you grassing bastard. I hate grasses," Cabilla finished saying, after he stopped pulling the trigger. Two small red holes appeared in the centre of Philips's chest followed a moment later, by two large lumps of flesh flying out of his back. They hit the front of Philips's mini-van, closely followed by his body, which had been catapulted backwards by the force of the close range shots. Cabilla watched as he hit the front of the bonnet, and slid down onto the tarmac. Deep red blood was pumping out from under the body, and onto the road. Cabilla calmly looked around, checking that unwanted faces hadn't suddenly emerged, and when satisfied he was still alone, he bent down, retrieved the spent bullet cases, and put them into his pocket. He then put the smouldering handgun back into the boot of the car.

He drove for about a mile, his sat nav guiding him back towards the motorway when he pulled over by a storm drain at the side of the road. He got out, and bent down appearing to inspect his front nearside wheel, then threw the bullet cases down the grid. He got back into his car and headed towards the motorway, and London.

***

Mackey was still trying to understand Amber Kimba, but couldn't work her out. One minute she was all standoffish, and the next she's all happy days. He'd just finished his third beer, and was getting tired of the small talk, so was planning to make a move on her when his phone rang. It was Cabilla, and he sounded tense. He said he'd been to Manchester and was on his way back. When Mackey told him he hadn't got very far with the Runt, he exploded, apparently neither had he with whomever it was he'd been to see. He reassured Cabilla that he was on it, and would have something for him by the time he got back in a couple hours or so.

At the end of the call, Mackey could tell other things had happened up in Manchester, but knew the boss wasn't going to open up over the phone. He also knew when to hold his own noise, especially if the boss was in the sort of mood that Mackey suspected he was. He'd no time for Amber now; he had to start moving things along. He rang Jim and told him to go to the flat to pick up the cattle prod, and to hurry. He then turned to Kimba as he started to drink the next beer she'd put down for him. He said he had enjoyed their little chat, and they would have to get together again when he had more time.

Mackey headed to the cell as Jim said he'd only be ten minutes, tops. Arriving outsider the cellar, he turned to Steele, and told him to stay put, adding, "Cabilla's on his way back, and he's not a happy man. We're going to need some answers out of the Runt, and quickly."

He then told Steele where he'd sent Jim.

159

Chapter Thirty-one

Burrows only had the one drink and even though Lee said he could crash at her place again, he politely declined. Said he would drop her off, but wanted to get back to Thame to get some clean clothes and check on the house. Briers politely chipped in that he'd drop Lee off to save Burrows having to go back on himself. Burrows thanked him, as did Lee, but Burrows wasn't sure whether he saw a line of disappointment appear on her face. He couldn't be certain so he shrugged off the thought. Truth be known, he fancied some time alone; irrespective of Briers's kind words about them only being a two-person team, he was saddened they'd come so close to potentially 'housing' Cabilla when they'd lost the 4 x 4 that Mackey and the others were in. He reckoned Lee felt the same, and some thinking time alone would probably benefit her as well.

He said goodnight to both of them and was the first to leave the pub. Even though the street was quiet, Burrows still walked around the block before entering the underground car park, and jumping into the Mondeo. He'd arranged to pick Lee up in the morning once the traffic had died down, then they could put their heads together to work out what to do next.

Briers was due to see the Home Secretary to brief him on events to date—he didn't envy his boss on that task. Until then Burrows planned to clear his thoughts and get a good night's sleep. Often when faced with a tricky problem, he'd always thought that to empty one's head, and think of anything but the problem is when the best ideas appeared. Sort of default back to factory settings, he mused to himself using a computer analogy.

Once back in Thame, he grabbed a takeaway meal and sorted out his laundry. Eventually, he sat down with a glass of single malt, and started to mull things over; keeping his mind clear wasn't proving that easy tonight. No matter how much he tried, he couldn't get the mission out of his head, so he gave in to it. Where to start? He thought, before realising the clue was in the question; *start*. One always starts at the beginning.

He was tired of going over events at the Crown pub, and the failed follow on the 4 x 4 car. The fact that the absconded bloke was a bent cop, and that Larry-the-lad had gone over to the dark side, were leading him nowhere. Briers had told them over their drink, that the shooter in Manchester, who took Billy out, was a complete unknown. Fingerprints and DNA didn't provide any UK matches, and were currently with INTERPOL, but so far with no results. The chances were, he was ex-military of some description, but from which country? It was hard enough getting access to UK military databases, but outside the UK was always more difficult, and outside Europe just harder still.

The Irish barman had clearly disappeared, though Burrows was of the opinion the only person he knew—other than Billy—was the bent DC Chapman. No, Burrows decided to go back to the very beginning, to the collapsed trial in Manchester well over a year ago.

Then the obvious struck him; when Cabilla's men had first compromised Billy as a CHIS, they'd taken him to a warehouse they were using as a temporary base. Fortunately, for Billy, Burrow's team had already covertly entered the premises—with Billy's help—and put audio and video probes all over the place to collect intelligence/evidence on Cabilla's dealings. It was soon after this when Billy had been exposed—though they never found out how—and taken to the warehouse to be interrogated by Cabilla. It was the bugs that had alerted them to Billy's predicament, and brought about his release. And provided the evidence of his abduction, which became the platform for the charges they brought against Cabilla.

Their investigation into Cabilla's organised crime activities was obviously blown, so they had to go with what they had, and charged him with kidnapping and assaulting Billy.

Burrows didn't think for one minute that Cabilla would be stupid enough to take Chapman to the same premises, but it would be a place to start. He remembered the original enquiries showed that the premises were on a short-term lease, taken out by a wholesale firm that said they had a cash flow problem after taking out the lease, and therefore never moved into the premises. Burrows and Briers knew at the time that this was bollocks, and guessed that the owner of the wholesale firm had simply rented it on Cabilla's behalf. It was Billy himself who'd said another villain loaned the premises to Cabilla. Whether the wholesaler let the premises direct to Cabilla, or to someone else, who allowed Cabilla to use it, hadn't really mattered at the time, and therefore was never pursued.

The proceedings back then were all about what Cabilla had done to Billy at the premises; the premises themselves were immaterial—until now. It was a link to someone who'd been directly connected to Cabilla.

Burrows looked at the clock on the wall above his fireplace, it was past midnight, nevertheless, he rang and roused a sleepy Lee, and said he'd pick her up at 6 a.m. in the morning. He told her they were going to Manchester, and he would fill her in on route. She grumpily replied that he could have left ringing her until the morning when he'd got up, which would have been all the notice she needed. He apologised, he hadn't thought of that, he was just so charged. He had a good feeling about what they would find in Manchester. Lee ended the call with the words 'goodnight', and 'arsehole'.

***

Steele watched Jim walk away, and knew he wouldn't have long to try and get through to the cop in the cellar. He knocked on the door to raise his attention.

"Listen mate, my name is Larry and I'm trying to help you here. Just tell Den what he wants to know."

"No, you listen pal," came the stiff response, "I'm not playing your stupid game; the good cop bad cop shite doesn't work on me. Guess why? 'cause I am a cop, idiot."

"Look, I haven't got time for this. I'm not doing Den's work here. He's not into taking the softly, softly approach. In fact, as we speak he's sent Jim off to get a cattle prod. So you'd better start wising up pretty quickly."

There was a pause, then. "Ok, I don't like the sound of this. Look, I really don't know the name of any firm that are after them, you heard what I said to Den before."

Steele noticed the arrogant edge to the cop's voice had gone on the mention of a cattle prod. "Look, I was under suspicion a couple of days ago, and spent some time sat where you are now. If you're straight with Den then he'll no doubt let you go. He did me."

"Listen mate, it won't be that easy to let me go, will it? After all, I'm a cop," he said, before adding, "I still don't know why you are so bothered about—"

"Shush," Steele interrupted, "someone's coming."

Seconds later Mackey appeared with Jim following on closely behind him. Mackey had the cellar key in his right hand and went straight for the door. Steele swallowed and tried to see if either of them was carrying anything else, but he couldn't tell. He didn't know how big cattle prods were, he'd never seen one, but reckoned it would be something that could fit inside a jacket or trouser pocket. He swallowed again as Mackey unlocked the door.

He told Steele and Jim to wait outside as he went in. They both stood with their backs to the door.

"You got anything to say to me Runt?" Steele heard Mackey say through the partially open door.

"Look Den, honest I don't know the name of any other firm. You can beat me senseless, and I still won't be able to help. Look, why don't we just call this a misunderstanding so I can get to work on the outside for you—" the Runt was starting to say before Mackey cut across him.

"I'll level with you man. I was going to come in here and stick a cattle prod where the sun don't shine, but the bastard thing's broke. It'll be tomorrow before I can get a new one. It'll also be tomorrow before Cabilla is back in here. He was coming later, but has changed his mind as it's getting late. He'll not get here before late tomorrow morning now. Which, trust me, is lucky for you. If you think I'm gonna hurt you with that prod, then that ain't nothing compared to what Cabilla will do.

"So, you've got overnight to sweat it out and level. If you own up to working for this other firm then we won't kill you if that's what you think. No man, we can use you to grass on them, but we would have to proper trust you again first. So start thinking, that's the deal, straight," Mackey said.

Steele didn't hear the Runt reply, just Mackey walking back towards the door.

He would have smiled to himself but for the seriousness of the situation, hearing Mackey come out with the double agent ploy again. He really should change his interview technique, he thought.

Mackey locked the door again and passed the key back to Jim. He then reiterated about the cattle prod being broken, but by tomorrow they'd have a stun gun instead, which Mackey said was much better. Steele wasn't sure what the different was, but when Mackey says better, he knew he means worse, well worse for the recipient.

Mackey went onto explain that Cabilla was on his way back from Manchester so wouldn't bother calling in tonight. But they would need answers from Chapman before he arrived tomorrow—probably midday onwards. Mackey said he wanted them to guard Chapman overnight, he didn't want to take any chances, and he wanted to know straight away if Chapman suddenly had a memory recall after having had time to chew over Mackey's words. With that said, he turned and was gone.

Steele noticed that Mackey had started calling the Runt by the name Chapman, so at least now he knew his surname. Also, when they made their way into the building through the main hall area, he had noticed an old leatherette sofa pushed into one corner. He suggested to Jim that they take turns on it rather than both of them having to stay awake all night. Jim agreed, but said he would keep hold of the key to the cellar—rank and all that. He also pointed out that Mackey would lock the main doors to the building as he left, so there was nowhere either of them could go. He also said that upstairs was also out-of-bounds, but didn't say why. Steele didn't ask.

He was hoping Jim would take the sofa first, but he insisted that Steele did, as he'd done most of the guarding up until now. He couldn't argue with that, and didn't want to raise suspicion, so he gladly agreed. Jim said he would wake him in a couple of hours. Any chance of taking to the cop Chapman again would have to wait until then.

Chapter Thirty-two

On the drive to Manchester, Burrows filled Lee in with his reflections from the previous evening, asking if she had any different thoughts. She said she hadn't come up with anything else, and as she only had brief knowledge of the original enquiry in Manchester, she would cede to Burrows who had the first-hand knowledge.

Whilst he drove, Lee got to work on the internet via her smart phone, identifying clearly, where the wholesaler lived, and worked. She said she would do the basic checks, and once finished, she gave him the run down. The wholesaler's name was John Mathews, and he owned and ran a distribution business local to Manchester and the northwest of England. He had no criminal convictions, but had been long suspected of having an unhealthy relationship with some of Manchester's finest. His home address was in the suburbs, and his business was run from a small unit on Trafford Park.

Having stopped for breakfast Lee took over the driving and he spent the rest of the journey working out a plan of action with her. After which, he gave Lee a potted account of where they were headed. "Trafford Park was the world's first industrial estate, and is still the world's largest. It's a vast area of over a thousand acres of land, which had originally been parkland," he told her.

Burrows was proud of his northern heritage and only too happy to give Lee the history lesson—whether she wanted it or not—as they passed time on the journey north. He explained how Ernest Hooley, in the late 1900s, set about turning the grassland into an industrial estate, which was then, a completely new concept. He risked further boring Lee, as he added that its further growth was dependent on the construction of the Manchester Ship Canal, which turned the city into an inland port, linked via the seaport of Liverpool. The canal itself, running through the centre of Trafford Park—where they were going—brought about the birth of large industrial estates.

"Wow, you're a man of many talents John," Lee said, with what sounded like mocking inflections in her voice, when he'd finished.

"Well, you know how it is with you southerners, you all think the M6 is cobbled, and the north is still full of workhouses."

An hour later, he directed Lee to a quiet side street off Barton Dock Road in Trafford, where they pulled over. As agreed, Lee put a call into the wholesaler to establish if he was at work. The unit was only around the next corner.

"Hello, yes this is Mrs Mathews," Lee started, and then continued, "Is Mr Mathews in?" A pause, followed by, "Good, no don't bother putting me through, just ask him to meet me outside on the car park in five minutes," a further pause, then, "Yes, that's right, the car park. Thanks." Lee ended the call before turning to face Burrows. "Well, that's the first risk over, the receptionist obviously isn't used to speaking to his wife; she kept calling me Mrs Mathews."

Burrows knew it was a strategy with risks; If Mathews believed the call was from his wife, hopefully, he would come outside to see what she wanted—Lee said she got the impression from the receptionist's reaction, that wifely visits to work were not the norm. If Mathews knew, or suspected the caller was not his wife, then, with any luck his interest would be sufficiently piqued, for him to come outside regardless.

On the way up, Lee had managed to obtain a grainy photograph on her smart phone, but it wasn't very clear, they both agreed they needed to see Mathews in the flesh to identify him properly. After Lee had made the call, Burrows directed as she drove around the corner, and parked up opposite the entrance to the car park in front of Mathews's unit. It was a relatively small car park with spaces for about twenty cars. At an earlier recce, he had noticed the offices were at the rear of the property, with no windows over-looking the car park itself. There was just a small entrance door next to a large up-and-over shutter door, which was obviously for vehicular access.

A couple of minutes after they had pulled up Burrows saw the small entrance door open, and a small stocky man in his forties with a bald head walk onto the car park with purpose in his step. Stopping abruptly, he turned around to survey the seven or eight cars that were parked there. All were empty. Burrows suspected Mathews would now be very confused, he'd have no doubt tried ringing his wife after receiving the receptionist's message, and Lee agreed, adding that they should assume Mathews would have spoken to her, and therefore now know the caller wasn't his wife. Burrows was confident though, from seeing the man, that it was indeed Mathews, and even though he would now be on his guard, it had been a necessity .At least when he left for the day they would be confident in following the right person.

166

It was just after midday now, so they would no doubt be in for a bit of a wait. Plenty of time for Mathews to calm down. Once he went back inside the premises Lee said she would find a better place to park up.

Mathews stood for a couple of minutes continually looking around and seemed to relax, as there was obviously no one waiting on the car park. He then turned and walked back towards the door, but instead of going back inside; he pushed the door shut, turned around, and walked over to a silver coloured Jaguar XF, opened it and got into the driving seat.

Burrows hadn't expected this, and realised how vulnerable they now were; having pulled up virtually opposite the entrance to the car park. There was only one way on and off the car park, and if Mathews drove off, they would be right in his line of sight. Whilst Mathews had walked towards the Jag, his back was facing the exit, he'd also given Burrows and Lee some warning by using his remote key fob to unlock the car, making its indicators flash as he did so. Lee used this brief opportunity to reverse slowly up the street, taking care not to rev the engine more than was necessary. She then ducked down out of view, and turned off the engine. Burrows leapt from the vehicle and started to stroll slowly towards the car park. A moment later, the Jag appeared at the entrance junction, it waited momentarily, before turning left away from Burrows and Lee. It drove off at speed towards The Parkway, which Burrows knew was a busy urban dual carriageway that crosses over Barton Dock Road.

He walked back towards the Mondeo and got in. Lee made no attempt to drive after the Jag, and Burrows understood why. They were still directly in his rear view, and if they set off from the kerb to follow straight away, they would potentially blow their cover. They'd previously agreed it would be better to lose him, than spook him, they knew where to find him again. Even so, it felt very unnatural to Burrows to watch their target drive off without going after him.

As Mathews's Jag approached The Parkway, it turned left onto the slip road, which would join the dual carriageway in the direction of the city. The moment it was out of view Burrows shouted, "Go," and Lee set off after him. He knew she didn't need telling, it was instinctive.

Sedately at first, until they were past the unit, Lee explained it was just in case Mathews had someone watching out for him, to see if he was followed away. Burrows was impressed again at Lee's tradecraft. As soon as they were clear of the premises, Lee put her foot down. She joined the dual carriageway, which was busy, but not prohibitively so. Ahead in the distance was a large roundabout but Burrows couldn't see any sign of the Jag. It was clear Lee couldn't see it either, as she caned the Mondeo along The Parkway, and then had to brake hard on the approach to the roundabout. As they neared the roundabout itself, Burrows caught a brief glimpse of the rear of the Jag, leaving at the first exit. He shouted at Lee to take the first. They followed onto Ashburton Road West, the Jag was a few hundred metres ahead of them and there were several cars between them, they had good cover.

"Got it," shouted Lee, confirming she now had the Jag in sight.

Mathews seemed to have settled down, he had slowed markedly. He did a couple of left and right turns, but fortunately each time, at least one of the cars in-between also went with them, ensuring that they were never directly in his rear view mirrors.

After ten minutes, he pulled over, got out of his car, and walked to a telephone box; the blank side of the kiosk was facing back towards his Jag. Lee pulled over, and Burrows noticed that Mathews hadn't locked his car. He told Lee this, and then quickly hatched a plan with her.

A couple of minutes later, Burrows watched Mathews leave the phone box, and return to his car, climbing back into the drivers' seat.

***

Lee watched Mathews as he got back into the car, and as soon as he closed the driver's door, she sat up behind him, and prodded the cold hard end of her pistol into the back of his head.

"What the—" Mathews started to say.

"Don't turn around," Lee interrupted, as she sat up straighter, behind Mathews. She had put on a baseball cap and pulled it down, together with a scarf over her face, before she'd got into the back of the Jag. She was also now wearing sunglasses, but still saw Mathews's eyes flash across the rear view mirror.

"Look at me again, and I'll shoot your ear off. This handgun is low calibre and silenced, so no one will hear anything and coming running to help you. Do you understand Mr Mathews?"

Lee could see the fear in his eyes as she used his name, indicating that she knew him, and this was more than some random robbery taking place. She also saw his gaze quickly move away from the mirror as instructed.

"Look, just calm down whoever you are. I'll do whatever you say, but what is it you want from me? You obviously know me."

"Just shut up and drive where I tell you, we just want a little word with you. Do as we ask and you'll be ok. Fuck us about and…" Lee said, emphasising the 'we' and 'us' just to let Mathews know that she was not operating alone. She wanted to increase the fear in him to ensure his compliance, to prevent things getting messy.

She glanced behind to see Burrows in their car pulling away from the kerb. She knew he was going to follow her even though he knew where they were going. Ten minutes later, they were at the second place they had recced that morning; it was a disused warehouse down near the ship canal. They hadn't wanted to take Mathews too far, as the further they went, the more likely he would regain his confidence, and stop being compliant. The Jag drove into an old wooden building through the open doorway, she glanced behind to see Burrows follow, positioning the Mondeo sideways from within to block the open entrance. She told Mathews what was going to happen next, so he wouldn't try anything daft when she pulled a black ski mask over his head, backwards with the slits facing the wrong way. Burrows joined her and they led Mathews out of his car, and sat him on the concrete floor.

She nodded at Burrows, and he spoke first, as agreed. "We just want to know about a building you let out a while ago. Nothing more," he said.

Mathews's head turned abruptly towards Burrows, which Lee hoped would only add to his terror with the realisation that she indeed wasn't alone. Lee joined in, naming Mathews's wife, and listing their home address.

Then he started talking.

Another ten minutes later, Lee and Burrows were on their way to see a Mr Jonny Moon. Mathews had gladly told them how he'd rented premises over a year ago for Jonny Moon, but he had no idea what he intended to do with them. It was obvious to Lee that Mathews didn't know any more, and Burrows agreed. It was also clear that he'd soiled himself, and the stench had become unbearable. They hadn't actually threatened Mathews; she just told him the name and address of his wife. Lee was a firm believer in that the unsaid, often carries far greater menace. In the same way, she had told Mathews that if he agreed never to mention their little conversation to anyone, she was fairly sure they would never meet again. But to be on the safe side they put Mathews in the boot of his car; Burrows told him they would ring his office to tell them where he was after they had spoken to Jonny Moon. It was at this point Mathews suddenly remembered Jonny had recently taken over new premises.

Chapter Thirty-three

Steele didn't think he'd sleep much; his mind was going full tilt. Yet as soon as he lay down on the old leatherette sofa, he dropped off. He was clearly more tired than he'd realised, emotional stress had plainly taken it out of him. It only seemed a few minutes later, when Jim was rousing him.

"Wake up you greedy twat, it's my turn."

As Steele stirred, he looked at his watch and was shocked to see it was 3 a.m.

"Sorry mate, I had no idea. Anyway, how's our captive?"

"I gave him some water and let him take a piss, and I've not heard a peep from him since," Jim answered.

Steele picked up his jacket, which he'd been using as a blanket, and put it back on. He bade Jim goodnight and left him making himself comfy. Steele sat back on one of the plastic chairs outside the cellar door and waited. As soon as he heard a faint snoring noise coming from Jim's direction, he tapped lightly on the cellar door.

"Hey, wake up, it's me. I can't talk too loud or I'll wake my partner up."

"I'm hardly asleep in this shit hole, am I?" came the response.

"Look man, if you know the name of the other firm whatever you do, don't tell Den. He gave me the same sort of speech; about being a double agent, and when I didn't go for it, I had to take a couple of slaps before he believed me."

"I can't tell him what I don't know. There is no other firm involved, not at least one I know about. And I'm definitely not grassing on them to anyone else. Christ, I wish he would believe me."

"I just didn't want you to buy the double agent line, and make up a name to try and please Den, 'cause after I was spoken to, he later told me if I'd gone for the double agent bait he'd have killed me. I just didn't want you to make that mistake."

"I appreciate your concern mate, but I saw through that crap as soon as he said it. The daft twat seems to forget what my day job is. Anyway, I'm still not sure why you are so concerned?"

This was it, Steele thought, time to put a feeder-line in, to try to establish if the Runt was an undercover officer. It would be quite ironic if he was playing the role of a bent cop; he really would be a double agent, but just not the sort Mackey was suggesting.

"I think we have something in common," Steele said slowly.

A pause, followed by, "What do you mean?"

"Well I know you're a cop, but you seem more than that."

"Well I'm in intelligence, if that's what you mean. And how does that give us something in common? You're not a grass are you?"

"No, for fuck sake don't start thinking that. I've already had all that with Den. No, I've met some people before who were cops, but not cops, so to speak," Steele said.

He was starting to struggle to find the right words, not wanting to hint too heavily, but trying to find a question to ask so that if Chapman was undercover, he would recognise it, but if he was just a bent cop, he would not. The last thing Steele wanted to do was to confess his true identity to him—in order to work together getting out of there—only to discover that he was just a bent cop, and not to be trusted.

**

Chapman wasn't sure who Larry was, but he was sure who he wasn't. His questions and remarks were becoming more and more obscure. 'Cops, but not cops', he had said. Then it hit him. The guy thinks *he's* undercover. Perhaps that's what this is all about, this entire double agent rubbish from Den. They obviously suspect that all the time he has been selling them information; he has been doing so as an undercover officer. That's why the slimy bastard on the other side of the door has been giving him all this 'new best friend shite'. Very clever, Chapman thought to himself. But they were wrong, so wrong. He was just about to tell this creep asking all the questions that he had sussed out his game, and that he was no undercover cop, that he'd always played Mackey and Cabilla fair and square, when he had a sudden flash of genius.

He'd always known he was smarter than those two thugs were, and he was definitely smarter than the idiot at the other side of the door. Instead of denying that he's undercover, working against Mackey and Cabilla, suppose he said that he is. Suppose he said, he had always been working against them and that every time he met them, or talked to either of them, those meetings and conversations had all been recorded. That it was all part of the process of stacking up the evidence against them, until the bosses were happy they had more than enough proof to send them both away for a very long time. In reality, Chapman was sure that no undercover officer would have been allowed to continue for as long as Chapman had been 'engaged' with them. He was no expert, but he knew there was a limit to how much criminality an undercover officer could lawfully get involved in, even if it was for the greater good. But one thing was for sure, he knew a damn sight more than those morons did.

He started to smile to himself as a plan occurred to him .All he had to do was convince the thick twat behind the door that he was an undercover cop, and that he was prepared to cut a deal with Mackey and Cabilla. He'd offer to get hold of all the evidence that had been amassed against them, and to give it to them for one final payday. It would be easy enough to mock up several intelligence reports of all their meetings, on letter headed paper. And he could put some empty cassette tapes together, all sealed up looking official. By the time they played them, he'd be long gone.

But the payoff would have to be serious money, as afterwards he couldn't go back to being a cop, he would obviously have to disappear abroad—which had always been his plan anyway—not that they knew that.

He could hear thicky whispering through the door as he was thinking through his plan, he hadn't answered, but after a long pause, he was ready.

"Hi, I've just been thinking, sorry. I think I know what you're saying but I'm not what you think," Chapman replied. He didn't want to sound too keen at first. He would wait a short while before he admitted he was undercover, and then when Mackey came blustering back in, he would make his play for the deal. He knew they would have to accept, the risks would be too high for them not to, and the potential rewards too great; the thought of getting hold of every bit of evidence the cops have ever had on them. It would be a no-brainer.

"What is it you think I'm suggesting?"Larry said.

Chapman was tiring of this guy, and decided to go for it. "You think I'm an undercover cop, don't you?"

A further pause, then. "Yes mate, I do. But don't worry, there is a very good reason why you should feel free to say so," he replied.

Chapman wasn't quite sure what he had meant by this, but no matter, now was the time to start his play. "Ok. You've obviously already sussed me. Yes, I'm undercover. I'm telling you something you obviously already know. But why do you say I should feel free to confirm it to you?"Chapman asked.

"Because I'm undercover too," Larry said, and paused before continuing. "So we can work together and get out of here."

Chapman could barely believe what he was hearing. He certainly hadn't expected this. Then he smiled to himself, even wider than before. This was just getting better and better he thought.

Chapter Thirty-four

Burrows said he thought that Jonny Moon would need a very different approach to that, which they'd employed against Mathews. Lee agreed, saying he sounded a more difficult prospect. Burrows was driving again, navigating the short distance back into Trafford Park. He asked Lee to dig up what she could about Moon via her smart phone. She told him that Jonny Moon was fairly high up in Manchester's criminal hierarchy. She showed him a full-length photograph of Moon on her phone. On seeing it, Burrows noted the slight, insignificant appearance of Moon, with an almost immature face, and could see the surprise in Lee's eyes as she looked at it."I've come across his kind before," Burrows said, continuing, "don't let the timid appearance fool you. Muscle can be easily hired; it's what's in here that defines them," Burrows said, whilst pointing to his head.

"I know what you mean, but from a slightly different perspective," Lee said.

"What do you mean?"

"When I was with the Intelligence Services we often used special forces such as the SAS to take the executive action required. And they're not all brick built outbuildings as their stereotype suggests. It was often the small quiet and unassuming individuals that were capable of the most explosive violence when it was called for."

"Well, I've heard of this bloke and it's not too nice; we'll have to show him we mean business, and that we are capable of crawling around at his level," Burrows added.

"Agreed," Lee said.

It was only a short drive back to Trafford Park, and using the sat nav, they soon found the industrial unit that Mathews said Moon was currently using. It had been obvious to them both just how terrified of Moon, Mathews had been. So they knew they were going up against a nasty bastard. Lee went over his previous record briefly, and it was obvious that he was not as clever a villain as he probably thought he was, just one whose criminal empire was founded on gratuitous violence. His nickname was the 'Vicar', and although this probably started life due to his choirboy looks, the fact that he could be so violent made the nickname all the more sinister.

Burrows told Lee that he thought Moon was obviously trying to compensate for his lack of stature, but doing so through a psychotic mind. Lee agreed, and said they should call him shorty. They briefly smiled at each other before starting to formulate their engagement tactics.

Thirty minutes later, Burrows was in a public call box on the fringes of a housing estate in Eccles. The suburb was very close to Trafford Park, and had originally been a market town famed for its currant cakes of the same name. That was until Manchester had grown up and enveloped it. Burrows dialled the mobile telephone number that Mathews had given them. It was answered on the second ring, but no one spoke and the line crackled as it remained open.

"I know you are there Moon."

"Who the fuck is this," The recipient abruptly answered.

"Now, now there's no need to be rude, I just want to have a chat—" Burrows started to say, before he was interrupted.

"I don't know who you think you're talking to? And I don't know how you got this number? But if you want a little chat arsehole, get yourself down to Piccadilly railway station in the city centre, and find a nice rent boy to talk to," the line went dead.

"Lovely man," Burrows said aloud to himself before redialling the number. This time it rang and rang and Burrows was sure it was about to go to an answering machine, when it was answered. Burrows quickly spoke first, before the person answering had chance to.

"To answer your last question, I got your mobile phone number from the police and it cost me a lot of money," Burrows lied. The ensuing pause showed that his remarks had had the desired effect; letting the recipient, who he was sure was Moon, know that whoever it was ringing him, was a player, and not just some punk.

"Ok. What do you want? And whoever you are, be fucking careful what you say." The recipient said.

"First, let me apologise for this intrusion, I mean no disrespect," Burrows said, with fake humility. Now that he had the person's attention, he knew he would have to ensure he kept it. "I have urgent business to attend to, and I need to speak to you face-to-face. It will be in both our interests," Burrows said.

"Put the phone down, and I'll ring you back," the recipient replied, before ending the call.

Burrows had expected this, Moon was obviously a cautious man, and as soon as Burrows said he'd got Moon's private mobile number from the police, Moon would consider it compromised. If the police, had in fact got the number, then there would be a chance it was being monitored. But the call box telephone would be clean; Burrows expected Moon to call him back from a different number. He spoke into his jacket lapel to tell Lee what was happening. She was in the car about 100 metres away, keeping a watch on the phone box and any potential approaches to it.

"If he hasn't called back in ten minutes John, then get out of there; it probably means he has the software to identify which public phone box you are in, and is sending a team round to lift you," Lee replied via his earpiece.

"Agreed."

Five minutes later the phone rang and Burrows picked it up. "Hello," he said, straight away so if it was Moon calling, he would know it was still Burrows in the phone box.

"This had better be as important as you claim, or you're a dead man. You might still be a dead man; depending on what it is that you have to say. Still want to meet do you?" said the same voice as before.

Burrows said that he did, and they arranged to meet on some wasteland down by the ship canal in thirty minutes. He was warned to come alone. Burrows put the phone down and spoke to Lee via his lapel mike. "It's game on Jane, come and get me. Now it'll get interesting."

Burrows rehearsed several potential scenarios with Lee, and an open space such as waste ground was one of them. Though he thought they'd have more than thirty minutes to prepare; clearly Moon was not allowing any time for a set-up.

Twenty-five minutes later, Burrows parked the Mondeo in a small lay-by. He locked the unoccupied car, walked across a narrow grassy verge, and onto an embankment that led downhill for about twenty metres. Through sparsely planted silver birch trees, he walked towards the ship canal tow-path. He headed toward a bench on the path as instructed, and could see the back of a middle-aged man sat in the centre of the seat, alone. Two established trees flanked the bench, and when Burrows was about halfway down the embankment, two very large individuals stepped out from behind them.

Burrows read the tacit command and stopped in his tracks, slowly raising his hands in the air in front of him. One of the men approached, and as he neared, Burrows told him that he wasn't armed. The brute ignored him and subjected Burrows to a thorough search. It was obvious due to the intensity of the examination he was looking for more than just weapons. When he was finished, he turned and nodded to the other guy who had been constantly scanning the environment. He in turn spoke to the man on the bench, who had still not turned around.

"He's clean Boss," Burrows heard the sentry say. The man on the bench just nodded once in reply.

The sentry in turn nodded at his mate who was now behind Burrows, who had dropped his hands. He prodded Burrows in the back, and they both started walking towards the bench. As they arrived, the guy behind him stood opposite his partner, so they were either side of the bench. As the man on it had still not turned around, Burrows walked to the front of it, conscious as he did, his back was now only a couple of feet from the canal's edge.

He looked at the middle-aged man on the bench and could see that he had his right hand on his lap, holding a silenced handgun, which he turned to point roughly towards Burrows.

"You're not Jonny Moon," Burrows said, with genuine surprise edged with a rising feeling of dread. He continued. "What the fuck's going on?"

"No, I'm not Mr Moon, but I'm here to represent him. And I'm asking the questions."

At this, the two brutes each took a tight hold of Burrows's arms, and stood in close using their large bulk to secure him in a human sandwich. He made no attempt to resist, as he knew it was pointless.

"It looks like I've underestimated Mr Moon," Burrows said.

"That's for sure, dick spit. And you've got thirty seconds to tell me where you got the phone number from—which only a privileged few have—before I blow you away into the canal with all the other turds," the man said, raising his gun hand as he spoke.

Chapter Thirty-five

Burrows quickly looked around surveying his options. There was no one around, the place was deserted; they'd chosen their rendezvous well. This wasn't exactly going to plan. He knew if he gave up Mathews's name they were both as good as dead. He had to stall for time, by saying enough to keep their interest levels going, to ensure his survival for a little while longer. This bloke wasn't Moon, though he had a similar build to him, but nevertheless he wasn't the boss, and anything Burrows said that was of interest, would surely need the guy on the bench to speak to Moon about it, before they decided to waste him. Or so Burrows was hoping.

"If you kill me now, you'll be sentencing Moon to the same fate. There is a contract out on him, and I've come here to warn him," Burrows lied.

"Why should you give a fuck?—" the guy started to say, when he was interrupted by the ringing of his own mobile phone. He broke off his sentence, and fished his phone out of his pocket. The guy answered it, and listened in silence, but Burrows could see his eyes widening with astonishment.

"Are you sure Boss?" he stuttered, before his shoulders jumped slightly at what must have been a fierce rebuke. He then handed the phone to one of the goons stood next to Burrows. He too, silently listened before replying. "Yes Boss," then in turn, handed the phone to the other brute, and the process was repeated.

Burrows took the opportunity to stand away from his two guards, and now stood at right angles to all three of them, whilst looking on with suspicion. He saw the last guy throw the phone into the canal before he addressed the other two. "You heard the man."

With that, the guy on the bench stood up and threw his gun into the canal. Each of the brutes drew fearsome looking handguns, and also threw them into the canal.

Burrows was utterly confused now, and was drawing on all his undercover experience so as not to show it. The first thought that ran threw his mind was perhaps the cops had been following these guys, and had them

178

all surrounded. But if that was the case why hadn't they showed themselves after making the contact phone call. As Burrows briefly pondered this, things took a more bizarre turn.

All three of Moon's men now turned towards the canal, and the one who had searched Burrows turned briefly towards him.

"If you hurt him in anyway, I'll kill ya. I don't care who you are, I'll find ya, and kill ya."

Then all three jumped into the canal and started to swim towards the other side. The visage would have been farcical but for the seriousness of the situation.

Then, Burrows heard the sound of footsteps approaching. He spun towards the noise only to see Lee walking briskly towards him with Moon stumbling right in front of her. It was clear to him that she had a gun in the middle of his back.

Burrows rolled his head across his shoulders as he felt the relief in seeing Lee.

"My, am I glad to see you. I thought it was going tits up here for a minute," he said.

"It was. So you owe me, yet again," Lee replied.

"Have you two love birds quite finished," Moon said.

"Shut up and sit on the bench, or I'll shoot your other hand," Lee ordered.

Burrows then noticed a bloodied handkerchief wrapped around Moon's right hand, which was being cradled by his left.

"I found him sat in a car round the corner listening to events unfold down here, obviously one of them was wired. So when I first introduced myself, the grubby little man threatened to have me raped, so I shot him through what I took to be his courting hand; as he appeared to be right handed," Lee explained.

Burrows was struggling to hold back the smirk on his face. Then Lee explained how she'd ordered Moon at gunpoint, to make the call, and issue the orders that had unfolded in front of Burrows.

"I must admit, you really had me there," Burrows said, having to make a mental effort not to use Lee's first name.

"Well, we have what we came for, so let's tie him to the bench, and get the hell out of here," she said.

Five minutes later, they were both walking back up the grass bank with a variety of threats being voiced towards them from Moon. Burrows turned to see that the three in canal had now reached the other side, and one of the brutes had dived back in, and was headed back towards his boss. When they'd got back into the Mondeo Burrows said he would drive, and turned to face Lee once she was in the front passenger seat. He leaned across and gave her a kiss on her cheek. He saw her blush momentarily, as he sat back straight in the drivers' seat.

"What was that for Mr Burrows?"

"You proper saved me back there Jane; I was starting to get a real bad feeling. Thanks."

Then to move away from any embarrassment, he started the engine, and began to drive out of the lay-by.

"Do you want to ring Mathews's office and tell them where he is, and I'll get us the hell out of this town," Burrows said.

Lee then filled Burrows in on what Moon had told her. Burrows turned to Lee and suggested she ring Briers with the good news, after all, she was the one who'd obtained it. She smiled, before picking up her smart phone and dialling a number.

"Zulu, this is Bravo," Lee said, when the call was answered. She had her phone turned to loudspeaker, Burrows realised as he could hear Briers's voice in reply.

"Hello Jane," said Briers, "you can speak freely I'm on my own."

"Good news Frank, we are just leaving Manchester on route back to London. John is here and can hear you too. We know where Cabilla will be; we're going after him."

Chapter Thirty-six

Steele could see Chapman was going along with him, and told him his name was Larry. Chapman had started calling him by it, and he started to think of him as Chapman, rather than the Runt, now that he knew his name. He asked Chapman where he'd done his undercover training course, and Chapman answered Hendon.

Hendon, as the Met's main training centre seemed an obvious answer, but he'd replied without hesitation, which placated him. He went on, trying to discuss a joint escape plan, but their discussions were interrupted by the return of Jim, who apparently couldn't sleep properly. His verbal demeanour gave no hint that he'd overheard anything, but Steele was frustrated by the disruption; the more he could have conversed with Chapman, the more he could have tested him.

It was nearly 4 a.m. now, and the pre-dawn summer light was starting to glow; not that it really became too dark during the night at this time of year. Steele accepted Jim's offer of a second go on the sofa, though he knew he wouldn't sleep now; his mind was too active trying to work out when he and Chapman should make their move. He wondered why his bosses had sanctioned his re-deployment in the first place if they already had Chapman deployed as a U/C into Mackey and Cabilla. It could have been to give an objective feedback on Chapman's activities, or it could simply be two different investigations crossing over each other, without either realising. Blue-on-blue, as they liked to call it in the trade. Steele knew that this sort of cock-up was supposed to be impossible with current cross-referencing systems, but there were always cock-ups from time to time, no matter what.

By 9 a.m., Mackey was back, and he told Steele and Jim to go back to the flat and get some downtime for a couple of hours, but to be back by eleven, as he was expecting the stun gun to arrive by then. Steele realised this was his chance to locate where they were, and then give Jim the slip back at the flat—whilst he was in the shower, or similar opportunity. Then he could raise the alarm, and send in the cops to rescue Chapman.

181

That was until Mackey insisted on Steele wearing his blindfold again, and he told Jim to make doubly sure Steele wore it on the way back as Cabilla could well be here by then. Steele tried to complain to Mackey saying it was about time he was fully trusted, but Mackey was having none of it, not with Cabilla coming. He did say though, that after they'd finished with the Runt, he would have a word with Cabilla, and things would be ok after that. Steele knew he had to relent, it was only for another day, and if he over-complained then he would only undo the trust levels he had already achieved. He would have to wait a little longer, and go to plan B; once he had a plan B.

He reassured himself that nothing would happen to Chapman until they returned at eleven; as Mackey said that was when the stun gun would arrive. He had until then to come up with something.

Back at the flat, Steele was grateful on getting something to eat and taking a hot shower. Jim lent him some more clean clothes, which fit pretty well, apart from the denim jeans, which were a bit short in the leg, but Steele didn't mind, it was just great to get some freshly laundered gear on.

***

Mackey unlocked the cellar door, and walked inside closing and locking it behind him. He felt a malevolent grin on his face; he was pleased the stun gun had arrived half an hour early. It was a rubberised hand-held black unit, which looked similar to a conventional flashlight; he was surprised at how light it was. Apparently, it was capable of discharging five million volts between its two metal prongs sticking out the front of it— according to the blurb on the box. Mackey could see Chapman couldn't take his eyes of it.

"It's show time Runty," he said, "if you thought a cattle prod sounded bad? T hen, you have no idea. I've just tested this on the guy upstairs; fuck me you should have seen him jump, and I only touched his arm slightly. Imagine what this'll do to your bollocks?"

Then, before Chapman could reply, he lunged forward and stuck the device into his right leg.

He knew that electrical pain would have flooded through Chapman's entire body in an instant. He watched as Chapman tensed in obvious agony, and fell back onto the mattress on the floor beneath him. Mackey stood back up, he had only used the thing for a second, yet the apparent level of pain and debilitation had obviously taken Chapman's breath away, literally. His breathing was now shallow and ragged, and as he slowly showed signs of regaining his motor responses, Mackey spoke. "That was just for starters. Wait until I get really going; so this is your last chance to spoil my fun. The name? Runt. The name of the firm?"

Chapman sat up, appearing to recover a little, and then he spoke. When he'd finished talking Mackey was just staring at him, he couldn't believe what he'd heard. After a short pause he shouted, "You slimy double-crossing bastard," as he threw the stun gun down, and started to lay into Chapman with his huge fists and feet. It was personal now, and he wanted to feel the blows that inflicted the pain.

"Stop, for God's sake, or you'll never get the evidence," Chapman shouted, as he pulled himself up into a ball trying to cover his face with his arms.

Having unleashed several blows to Chapman's head and body, Mackey did stop. He stepped back and looked down on Chapman. His face was covered in blood, and Mackey was sure he'd broken at least one of Chapman's ribs.

"If this is more bullshit Runt, I'll kill you... very slowly," Mackey said, before turning and picking up the stun gun. He then unlocked the door, and left the room relocking it from the other side.

He marched away towards the large atrium of the building, and saw Jim removing Larry's blindfold. He threw the key at Jim and told him to go and clean Chapman up, as he needed to ring Cabilla. He could see that both men had registered something serious had happened by the expressions on their faces. However, he noticed something else within Larry's look. He wasn't too sure, but it confused Mackey; it looked like fear.

Mackey rang Cabilla, and was careful with his choice of words; they agreed to meet for lunch at the café bar near to Cabilla's docklands apartment. When Mackey arrived, Cabilla was already waiting in the poolroom. By the look of the scattered balls and discarded cues, Cabilla had already persuaded whoever was there that they should abandon their game and leave. Mackey was glad that Cabilla wanted to meet in a public place; it would limit his ability to lash out when Mackey briefed him on what the Runt had said.

He told Cabilla word for word, as best as he could recall exactly what the Runt had told him, and the details of his offer. Cabilla sat, looking stunned, whilst he appeared to absorb the depth of Chapman's betrayal.

"And the scheming little twat wants ten grand for the evidence?" Cabilla said, breaking the silence.

"Yes Boss."

"How do we know this isn't just another one of his scams?"

"I guess we don't, until he delivers the goods. But if it's true…"

"I know Den; we can't afford to take the risk. What of the other firm?" Cabilla said.

"I don't think he knows, it would have been easier to just give us a name, any name, rather than claim to be a fully-fledged undercover cop, don't you think?"

"I just want to kill him Den, So bad I can taste it. But first, we have to get whatever it is he is claiming to have on us."

There was one last bit of news that Mackey hadn't mentioned yet; he wanted to ease Cabilla into the bad news a piece at a time. "He also claims that we have got a mole within us, and if we double his payday to twenty grand, he'll give us the name. Then he says we won't see him again, and neither will the cops, says he is going to disappear."

"He's got the last bit right Den, that's for sure. But for now, play along with him; get the money ready and let him go, but I want Jim shadowing him every step of the way. Tell him to stay in Jim's sight at all times, and if he tries to run out on us, tell him Jim will shoot him down where he stands, and we'll take our chances. Set the exchange up for tonight, and ring me with the time and the place. You got all that?" Cabilla asked.

Mackey nodded, and downed the drink Cabilla had waiting for him. Then they separated, and Mackey headed back to the warehouse.

Thirty minutes later, he was back at the warehouse and briefing Jim and Steele on what Chapman had said, though he kept back the bit about a mole. He told Jim he wanted him right up behind the Runt every bit of the way, and told him what to do if he tried to leg it. He told Steele, he wanted him at his side, as they had work to do setting up the place for the exchange. Then he went into see Chapman, and told him how it was going to play out. Chapman tried to resist his escort until Mackey told him what Jim's final instructions were if he tried to lose him.

"Ok, I can understand that, but I'll have to go into the office to physically get the reports and tapes won't I? I can't take Jim in with me," Chapman said.

"You can, and you will," came the reply, "you're supposed to be in intelligence; no one's going to challenge you entering your nick, not if you do it out-of-hours when all the other Intel pigs have fucked off home. You'll be able to vouch for Jim at the front desk, and he can help you carry the stuff," Mackey reasoned.

"I suppose that would work…" Chapman said, pausing briefly, before continuing, "We can watch the office from the front street, and when all the lights are off, give it half an hour and go in. No one inside the nick will have access to the Intel office."

"That's more like it Runt. But be warned, if you try to double-cross us, Jim will take care of you whether you are in a nick or not. Got it?"

Chapman nodded, before asking, "What about the other matter?" appearing to choose his words carefully as he glanced at Steele, and then back to Mackey.

"If the exchange goes smoothly, we can probably deal on that too," Mackey told him.

Chapter Thirty-seven

Steele wasn't quite sure he understood what Chapman and Mackey were agreeing to. Was Chapman really bent after all? Or was this part of the plan to entrap Mackey and Cabilla? Granted, he wasn't there when Mackey tortured Chapman with the stun gun. He and Jim had just landed after Mackey had finished speaking to him; apparently, the gun arrived earlier than expected. That said he could understand why Chapman had to come up with something believable, and fast. But outing himself as a U/C? That was pretty high risk. All Steele could do was stick with Mackey for the moment and see how things panned out. All least they hadn't killed Chapman, which had always been his initial worry; he just had to hope Chapman knew what he was doing.

As if on cue with Steele's thoughts, Chapman gave him a clandestine wink as he walked away with Jim. Steele breathed a small sigh of relief as he trotted off after Mackey. He could see Mackey was headed towards the main entrance, and as he caught him up, asked, what they were going to do.

"We're going to set things up for tonight's exchange with the Runt," Mackey said.

They were nearing the doorway and Mackey had made no attempt to blindfold Steele. He was a little unsure as to what he was supposed to do. "Am I coming with you Den?"

"Yes, why do you ask?"

"Well, I've got no blindfold on."

"We haven't got time for all that bollocks now Larry, you should be pleased," Mackey said.

"Yeah, cheers for that Den," Steele said, not wishing to over-stress it.

He followed Mackey out of the main door onto a large car park, which was mainly rough ground with some gravel on it near the building. Steele looked around to get a proper look at the place. It looked like an old Victorian, red rough-brick factory, which was probably leftover from the industrial past. There was hard-standing all around the building, with tall conifer trees, and a high steel railing fence securing the perimeter. Steele could see the big black 4 x 4 they had been in several times parked up, but

Mackey headed towards a blue Vauxhall saloon. He flipped the central locking, and then threw the keys at Steele before getting into the front passenger seat. Steele took the hint and got in the driver's seat.

"Where to Den?"He asked.

"Just drive, I'll direct you."

Steele did as he was told, and manoeuvred through a narrow gateway, which had a steel barrier attached that was currently open. Steele thought to himself as to his options. He would take in the environment, and hopefully soon realise exactly where they were. Then he had a dilemma; did he cut and run at the first set of red traffic lights, which up until now would have always been his plan, or not. The problem was he didn't want to do anything to spoil Chapman's plan, whatever it was. Steele presumed that Chapman would try to get a message out whilst at the nick—notwithstanding that he had Jim to contend with—and then detectives would covertly watch the exchange. Perhaps the bosses would let the exchange take place, and simply observe and record it, with a view to making arrests later in a more controlled environment. Or perhaps they would allow the exchange to take place, and then pounce on everyone. He was leaning towards the former, as the cops would still not know about the warehouse, or if they did, not where it was; he was sure Jim would have blindfolded Chapman as they left. No, the last thing Steele wanted to do was to cock anything up, especially with those poor girls kept captive in the upstairs of the warehouse. He decided to sit tight, and go along with whatever Mackey asked of him.

Mackey gave him directions, and by the time they had hit a major road he realised they were south of the river, in Dulwich. He hadn't been able to see the street name that the warehouse was situated off, but he was sure he would be able to direct or describe how to get to it.

***

Chapman had been blindfolded by Jim, and bundled into the back of what seemed like a large utility vehicle. He'd noticed a large step-up, whilst clambering into it and onto the back seat. After ten minutes, or so, the car pulled over, and Jim removed his blindfold. He was then told to climb through the central divide into the front seat where Jim said he'd be able to see him better.

Chapman did as instructed, and once in the front seat, he saw a handgun stuffed down the front of Jim's jeans. Ignoring it as best he could, he took in his surroundings; they were south of the river, heading towards central

London. He then directed Jim to Soho police station. When they arrived, Chapman guided Jim to an adjacent street with a good forward view of the side of the building, including the front entrance. The time was just before 3 p.m. and Chapman pointed out which offices were the Intel ones, on the ground floor, adjacent to the street. They were behind three windows, covered with white fabric blinds. Even though it was broad daylight, Chapman could see the electric lights on in the office through the blinds. He explained that most staff worked an 8 a.m. – 4 p.m. shift, and due to budget cuts, overtime was a rarity unless there was a serious job on. He told Jim that the DI would probably be the last to leave, but because DIs were salaried and didn't get paid for overtime, they didn't hang about longer than they had to.

"So are you saying that once the DI's fucked off, we should be clear?" Jim asked.

"Pretty much, yeah; If both DSs leave as well as the DI then I think we are pretty safe in assuming it has been a quiet day," he replied.

Two hours later, everyone had left the Intel unit and the lights had been turned off. They gave it a further thirty minutes to make sure no one was popping back, and had indeed left for the day. Chapman led, with Jim close behind as they entered the foyer of the building. A civilian counter clerk looked up, and seemed surprised to see Chapman, saying everyone had been looking for him all day. Chapman said, he'd been involved in an accident, and had suffered a mild concussion, but was all right now. The facial injuries Mackey had given him helped back up his story. He tried to look surprised himself, saying he thought the counter clerk would have heard this.

"We're always last to hear anything down on the desk, but glad you're ok," the clerk replied, before adding, "though your face looks a bit sore."

The conversation had kept the focus away from Jim, and Chapman wanted to move before it changed. He muttered a suitable reply before walking on into the building. He could feel Jim literally breathing down his neck as he accessed the Intel unit office by way of a fingerprint recognition system, and a passcode. Once inside, Jim sat down by a desk, and watched, whilst he went into a small inner room to collect the stuff. The inner room had a window looking back into the main office and Chapman wedged the door open so that Jim could see him. There was one computer terminal on a desk next to a cupboard with one chair; it was obvious they both wouldn't fit in there.

Chapman explained that he would have to copy the files from computer onto a disk, as he didn't have sufficient authority to print anything off the system. He told Jim he would then delete all the entries.

"Can any of the deleted files be recovered by someone at a later date?" Jim asked.

Chapman was surprised with Jim's level of knowledge, "No, as it's part of a covert investigation all the information is stored on a closed system on this one terminal, for security reasons. Once I've deleted the files I'll make sure by destroying the hard drive."

Jim pulled out his handgun and started to screw a silencer onto the end of the barrel.

"I'll do it with this, just to be sure," he said.

Chapman flinched on seeing the weapon, and then relaxed when Jim said he would use it on the computer. Its presence reminded him of the consequences of trying anything foolish. Jim kept it out, and on view. Chapman could feel the intensity of Jim's attention as he hurried himself on the key board transferring the files onto disc. When he'd finished, he emptied one of the litterbins and put the CD, together with some cassette tapes, into the plastic liner, to use it as a makeshift carrier bag.

"Give it here," Jim said.

"No way, I'm not letting go of this until I see Cabilla and the money," Chapman replied.

Jim nodded, seemingly conceding the point, and then turned towards the base of the computer and fired four rounds into it, completely destroying it. Five minutes later, they were back at the car and Jim was on the phone updating Mackey.

Chapter Thirty-eight

Mackey received Jim's call updating him, and was pleased they had got in, and out, of Soho nick without any problems. He could hear the relief in Jim's voice; he probably thought he was going to tell him to shoot the Runt at the first opportunity, and simply take the CD and tapes from him. It would obviate the need for an exchange without any money having to change hands. But instead, he'd told Jim to play along with the Runt, and take him straight towards the exchange location. He knew they needed the name of the mole before they could sort the Runt out, but he couldn't tell Jim this, just in case it was him. Jim hadn't questioned Mackey as to why they were going along with the exchange, and he knew Jim was restricted in what he could ask with the Runt sat next to him. He felt obliged to say something to Jim, to quell any worries, so he told him Cabilla and he wanted to sort the Runt out themselves, in their own way, things had become very personal now. He then gave Jim the address of the location in the east end of London, but told him not to tell the Runt where they were going. He also told him to keep the Runt on side, and keep him calm; tell him that if he keeps his side of the deal, there would be no problems. Tell him Cabilla has ordered it so, they just want the info, with no comebacks like a murdered cop investigation. Jim said that he understood, and he would tell him and keep him sweet.

Having ended his call to Jim, Mackey then rang Cabilla to give him the time and place of the proposed meeting; he'd chosen an old building that had been derelict for some years on the outskirts of Hackney. The compound was sealed off with high fencing and a locked gate, but that was no problem, as Mackey had the key for the padlock. He'd picked this spot as both Cabilla and he knew it well; they'd used it from time to time to conduct business from, though not in a while.

Ten minutes later, he and Steele arrived, and after unlocking the gate, Steele parked the car whilst he tried the key in the door. It opened no problems, and he and Steele entered, and searched the place to make sure no unwanted visitors had moved in. He knew the place used to be a school of some kind back in the fifties, and though still owned by Hackney Borough

Council, it had not been used for years. There was a sign outside saying the site was due to be demolished as part of an inner city regeneration initiative, which was another reason why Mackey had chosen the place as the venue for the exchange.

Inside the main door was a large vestibule area measuring roughly fifteen metres by twenty metres from which two corridors led off to what had once been classrooms. The only unwanted guests they found was the odd brown rat scurrying around in the shadows.

Mackey looked at his watch and then rang Jim again, "Cabilla's on his way here so if you can bring the Runt over for about 8p.m. Ring me once you've parked up, but before you bring him in," he then ended the call, and turned towards Steele."Once Jim brings the Runt in here, we'll do the exchange. The money is in two large manila envelopes in the boot of the car, which I'll bring in here in a minute. Jim can stand with the Runt, and Cabilla and me will stand a few yards away from them. I want you to physically do the exchange, after which, you stand on the other side of the Runt so that you and Jim are stood either side of him, got it? Mackey asked.

"Yeah, no probs," replied Steele.

"And when I say grab him, then you each grab an arm and hold him tight, ok?"

Steele nodded. Then there was the sound of a car parking up outside followed by the clatter of a door being slammed. Mackey looked at his watch, it was 7.40 p.m. and then Cabilla walked in with a huge smile on his face.

Chapter Thirty-nine

Steele could see the bulge underneath Cabilla's jacket and knew what it represented. He seemed remarkably relaxed though, and was chatty, and pleasant with Steele. Mackey went to his car, and returned with two manila envelopes, which he stuffed in the inside pockets of his leather jacket. Mackey and Cabilla walked away from Steele, and chatted privately in a huddle for a few minutes. It fleetingly crossed Steele's mind whether he should take the opportunity to cut and run, as he was feeling more and more anxious the closer to 8 p.m. it became. He held his nerve, and looked at his watch to see the time now approaching eight. Then, he jumped slightly as he heard Mackey's mobile phone ringtone. He could hear him obviously talking to Jim, and giving him his final instructions. Mackey ended the call which was closely followed by the sound of a car parking up outside.

The three of them took their positions as Jim and Chapman walked into the large room. Cabilla, Mackey and Steele were stood roughly in the centre, and when Jim and Chapman were about fifteen feet away Jim stopped, and put his hand across Chapman's chest to signal him to do the same. The two groups were facing each other. Chapman broke the silence first.

"Look Shonbo, I know you never really liked me, but let's be fair, I always gave you good info and advice."

"Yeah, at a heavy cost, whilst all along you were betraying me," Cabilla answered.

"I couldn't tell you, could I? But you've got to believe me that I would have given you the heads up, before it all came down on you. Honest."

"We'll never know now, will we Runt. I guess I'll have to take your word for that," Cabilla said.

"I wouldn't have told Den I was an undercover officer otherwise, would I?"

"The only reason you told me that," Mackey interjected, "was because you're soft as shite, and you saw a way to save yourself pain, and make some more dosh. So spare us the best friend bullshit."

"Ok, fair point. But let's not argue now I've got the stuff," Chapman said, as he held the makeshift carrier bag up in the air.

Cabilla nodded at Mackey, who in turn pulled one envelope out of his pocket and handed it to Steele, who took it across to Chapman, as instructed. Then, he returned with the carrier bag, and went to stand next to Chapman, who was busily checking the inside of the envelope. Cabilla did the same with the carrier bag, and then asked Chapman to explain its contents. Chapman told him that the cassettes were all sealed original tapes of all the recordings when he'd worn a wire, at his meetings with either Cabilla or Mackey. He told them that the transcripts were in the form of documents, together with all the resulting intelligence reports, which were all on the CD disc. He then went on to explain, that all the information on Cabilla had been housed in a stand-alone, closed-computer system, operated from a single terminal. He told Cabilla that he deleted all the entries, and that Jim had destroyed the hard drive.

"That's right Boss," Jim said, "I put four rounds into the fucker. Shredded it to bits."

"You sure it's totally destroyed Jim?" Mackey asked.

"Absolutely Den, I left it in a thousand pieces."

"I need to speak to you two in private, re the other matter," Chapman added.

Cabilla and Mackey glanced at each other, and then Cabilla nodded his approval. Mackey told him to walk over to them, and told Steele and Jim to stay where they were.

Both he and Jim just glanced at each; Steele didn't know what was going on, and by Jim's expression, he didn't either. Then he saw Chapman, Cabilla and Mackey walk to the side of the room, and have a whispered conversation. After a short pause, Mackey handed Chapman the second envelope, and in return Chapman handed Cabilla a small sealed white envelope. Chapman then stared to walk away from them on course to pass Steele and Jim, as he headed towards the door. He turned back to Cabilla and Mackey as he walked, "Don't open it until I'm out of here. I don't want to see what happens after that."

As if on cue, Mackey nodded towards Steele and Jim, and Steele followed Jim and flew at Chapman as he was walking past. He grabbed one arm as Jim took hold of the other.

"Hey. What the fuck—" Chapman started to say, but was interrupted by Mackey shouting instructions.

Following the orders, Steele helped Jim drag Chapman backwards to the end of the large room, and into a narrow corridor. At the end of the corridor was a door with the word 'Headmaster' still visible on it. They hauled Chapman who was kicking and screaming into the small room that had once been a headmaster's office. In the centre of the room was an old chair, but nothing else apart from pieces of cut rope laid next to it, which Steele had seen Mackey put there a little earlier. He and Jim quickly tied Chapman's hands behind his back and his feet to the chair's front legs. Once secure, they stood back, and Mackey and Cabilla came into the room proper, shutting the door behind them. The room was about five metres square so they all got inside easily. On one wall, a steel grill covered the space where a window had once been. This allowed some light into the room, it was still bright and sunny outside with at least an hour and a half of daylight left, Steele reckoned.

Cabilla walked between him and Jim, and punched Chapman full on in the face, he howled in pain as his head slammed backwards.

"Make another noise and you'll get more you filthy Runt," Cabilla said.

Chapman fell quiet. Mackey retrieved the two brown envelopes of cash from his jacket pockets. As he did so, Steele was half expecting the charge of the light brigade to come rushing through the door, but he could hear nothing other than Chapman's ragged breaths. He started to edge slowly towards the door, but as if Mackey had read his mind, he backed up past Steele, and stood with his back to the door.

Cabilla then ripped open the white envelope that Chapman had given him, and appeared to read what was on the piece of paper within it, he then started to smile as he turned to face the others. As he twisted to face all three of them, he turned the paper around so that they could all see the words written on it. 'LARRY IS THE UNDERCOVER COP'.

Time seemed to slow to a crawl for Steele as he stared, disbelievingly, at the words written on the paper. As his brain started to assimilate the depth of Chapman's betrayal, he was only too aware of three sets of eyes glaring at him. He glanced at Chapman who was looking down, and avoiding any eye contact. Then time caught up, as Jim and Mackey grabbed hold of him, and forced his hands behind his back. He felt them being tied with rope.

Coming to his senses, he shouted, "This is absolute bollocks. Christ, what do I have to do to prove myself to you? Surely, you are not going to take the word of a shit like Chapman. This is obviously another con," he protested.

"It may well be Larry, but we can't take chances. I only hope for your sake that you're right. I hate nothing more than betrayal," Cabilla said.

He then faced Jim and Mackey, and told them to take him back to Dulwich and lock him up; they would deal with him later. Cabilla said he wanted to have another word with the Runt before joining them.

Jim and Mackey walked Steele through the building. He continued to protest his innocence, and show his indignation at Chapman's allegations, but decided to walk with them without a struggle. He realised he was clearly going nowhere, so to struggle unnecessarily might only serve to fuel further suspicion; as if it would somehow confirm Chapman's allegation. Mackey just told him to shut up and save it until later.

Once outside, Steele desperately looked around, but knew his search was fruitless. There would be no cavalry coming. He realised that Chapman had conned him good and true; he grasped that in Chapman's eyes, he simply represented a second brown envelope. As he was being bundled into the back of Mackey's vehicle, he heard the report of a gunshot ring out from within the school.

"That's the sound of a traitors' fate," Mackey said.

Chapter Forty

Lee and Burrows were clear of the Manchester traffic, and heading down the M6 with all speed. Burrows was driving, and said he hoped the Birmingham rush hour would have eased by the time they got there. Lee had not long come off the phone from briefing Briers, and was about to start researching the address Moon had given them. "Do you think Moon will warn Cabilla?" she asked Burrows.

"He might do, but that would mean coughing to Cabilla, that he'd given us the info."

Lee could see it both ways; if Moon warned Cabilla of their impending approach, then he'd be in trouble with him—even though he had only given it up under extreme duress—she doubted whether Cabilla was the sympathetic sort. On the other hand, Moon could say nothing, and just hope that Cabilla could look after himself.

After further discussion with Burrows, they agreed that Moon would probably keep his own counsel, but they would have to assume that he hadn't. Therefore, they would need to approach the location with added stealth, just to be on the safe side.

She turned back to her research, and started to wonder what their approach tactics would be.

By the time they cleared Birmingham, Lee had finished her research on the address Moon had given them. It was some sort of old, disused building with no intelligence listed against it. Lee wondered if the address was correct, but recalled how frightened Moon had seemed, after she'd shot him. He'd also seemed astonished; men like Moon often underestimated the female gender. That said, once shown the error of their ignorance, Lee was only too aware that men like Moon could then find the female adversary very intimidating. They go from believing a woman is not a threat, to thinking that she is capable of anything.

As if Burrows could see what she was thinking, he turned to her and said, "Don't worry if it's a bum steer. But from the way you described how Moon gave up the address, it sounds right."

"Only time will tell John, but he did spit it out pretty fast; he certainly knew the address off by heart. But thanks anyway."

She found herself enjoying Burrows's company more and more, even if he had that steely harshness when things went tactical, and as much as she found that a little disturbing, she knew it was his professional persona. She didn't know why that bothered her so; after all, he could say the same thing about her after events of the last two days. She knew her shooting of the sniper in Blackley cemetery had been a defensive act, but what she had done to Moon was nothing other than torture, albeit necessary in her mind. 'Pain assisted learning' Burrows had called it, which made her laugh. That was something else she hadn't done too much of lately.

She was pretty sure Burrows was enjoying being with her too. She noticed the sideway glances when he obviously thought she wasn't looking. She knew he was practised in the use of his peripheral vision—all surveillance-trained operatives were—but what he couldn't know, was that she used to specifically train surveillance students in the art of it, whilst she was at MI5. A fact she intended to keep to herself; she didn't want to lose the upper hand, or the attention.

It was mid-evening when they were entering London; most of the rush hour traffic had abated. It was just busy now. It didn't take too long before they were reaching their destination, and Burrows pulled up in a quiet car park at the side of a retail park. They were close to their destination, and this would allow them to make their final preparations, Lee realised. They both checked, and re-loaded their weapons, and each put a dark blue covered Kevlar vest on beneath their lightweight jackets. Wearing a jacket at all, at this time of year can raise attention, especially when wearing bulky ballistic protection underneath. But it didn't matter, as they weren't expecting to be mingling with the general public. People seemed far more aware of anybody with bulky jackets, particularly in summer, during the current political situations.

They agreed to allow themselves one drive past the entrance to the building, in a recce of it. You could always allow yourself that, if any vehicle is seen once, it doesn't matter. It only registers when it's seen more than once.

They drove through a fairly quiet residential area, an estate away from the busy urban thoroughfares, and down the street towards the building. Lee could see the entrance set back with a steel gate at its perimeter. Then they circled the plot, and could see a large set of trees, and fencing around land, which itself encircled the building. Light was fading now, but Lee could still see fairly well. They parked the car in a side street near the back of the target premises, and did a final recce on foot. Having walked around the perimeter, their view had been incomplete; dependant on the thickness of the bushes and trees at any given point. But it was obvious that the place seemed quiet with no electric lights on inside. Having arrived back where they started, they agreed to attack from the rear; it was where the shrubbery was at its weakest. They each pulled on a ski mask.

"You ready Jane?" Burrows asked.

"Come on John, the suspense is driving me mad," she replied.

Burrows smiled back, before he slowly started to pull himself through the undergrowth. It was going dusk now, so they had some cover from the failing light, but enough illumination to direct their paths. Having cleared the bush, Burrows scaled the steel fence, and secured himself on top of it by folding his feet between the upright sections. He helped pull Lee up into a similar position. They both climbed slowly down the other side to avoid making any noise on landing.

Burrows then stayed on all fours and slowly made his way across the twenty or so metres to the back of the building. The perimeter was at its closest to the building here, which was another reason why they picked this point as their entry route. Lee followed, and once they were both at the back of the building, they gave themselves a few seconds to catch their breath and survey their surroundings. Lee suggested they both stay low below the height of any windows, and slowly recce the premises around its building-line, stopping below the windows to listen for any sounds. Burrows whispered his agreement and they moved off.

Twenty minutes later, they'd slowly completed one circuit, and Lee was grateful to stand back up fully, and stretch a moment. She hadn't heard or seen anything that suggested anyone was inside, and Burrows said he hadn't either. In fact, she was certain the place was empty.

"What now? She asked.

"I appreciate we can't hang around here forever, but let's have a look inside. That should tell us whether or not anyone is using the place," Burrows said.

"Agreed," Lee said, "It might also provide some new leads, depending on what we find."

They slowly made their way around to the double front doors, and Lee was surprised when the door appeared unlocked. They entered slowly, and found themselves in a large room with corridors leading off in differing directions. Both drew their weapons.

Burrows whispered in Lee's ear that he would lead; she nodded and turned around so that she was walking backwards. Both of them were semi-crouched with their guns held out at arm's length, in front of them, in a two-handed grip.

At the other end of the large entrance room was a narrow corridor just past a staircase. Burrows whispered he would check the ground floor first for obvious reasons. As they reached the corridor, Lee looked over her shoulder and could see a room at the far end, but first there was one off to the left. The door was open. Burrows nodded at her, and she turned around so they were both addressing the open door. As they reached the corner Burrows dropped down even further to a squat position, as he was obviously preparing to turn the corner into the room. If anyone was there, waiting with a gun in their hand, they would probably instinctively aim any shots at where they expected the central body mass area to be. Lee squatted down right behind Burrows, as they both prepared to enter the room.

Lee watched as Burrows let his gun go around the corner first, she slowly followed, and could see that there was no one in the room. She was on the corner, but could clearly see into the room as Burrows rose to his full height. It looked like an old office of sorts, but was devoid of any furniture. Then she heard a shot ring out.

Chapter Forty-one

Burrows spun round to see Lee firing two shots back down the corridor, in reply to the single incoming gunshot, she then leap back into the office. He realised that the first shot had been fired from within the large room near the entrance. Luckily, it had missed Lee.

"Contact from the foyer area, large white male who has jumped to our left. And he'll know he has us trapped in this room," Lee whispered.

Before Burrows could answer, he heard the faint sound of footfalls heading slowly towards them. He looked at Lee, and could see in her eyes that she'd heard them too.

She whispered quickly in Burrows's ear and he nodded. She then dropped onto her front and crawled up to the edge of the door. The plan was for her to move quietly around the doorjamb at ground level, which would hopefully take the shooter by surprise, and give her the split-second she needed to loose off a shot. Burrows would then reach around the corner, and fire from normal height, to add to the confusion of where the threat was coming from.

A moment later, Lee extended around the corner and fired. Burrows followed an instant later, but as he was pulling his trigger, he knew he would miss. The man in front of him screamed, and was heading for the floor. Lee's shots must have hit his legs. Burrows burst into the corridor, over a horizontal Lee, and ran towards the man who was only fifteen feet away. The assailant hit the floor still holding a small-barrelled revolver. Burrows kicked his hand hard, sending the weapon spinning across the tiled floor. He noticed the huge brute reach behind his waistband, for what Burrows knew, must be a back-up weapon. Burrows didn't give him the chance to use it, as he fired two rounds into the top of the man's head. The exit wounds took out most of the back of his neck.

In the eerie moments that followed, Burrows took in their environment with renewed awareness. His heightened senses scanning for indication of further threats. He heard nothing. "Can't hear anyone else, what about you Jane?" He asked.

"No nothing," she answered.

Burrows felt his legs starting to shake from the overloading of adrenalin flashing through his system. Lee walked past him to get a closer look at the body. Fortunately, due to the angle of Burrows's shots, the rounds had passed through the top of the man's head on a fairly straight trajectory leaving his face untouched. Burrows walked closer, and saw a face he recognised, he knew Lee would realise too.

"How the fuck did he get here? He asked. "The last time I saw him, he was practising his breaststroke in the Manchester ship canal," Burrows said, with his typical, post operational black humour.

Lee didn't reply; she simply put a finger to her lips as she picked up the dead man's revolver. Burrows nodded his understanding. Her unspoken words appeared in his head saying, 'If this is one of Moon's men, then where's his partner?'

Then, he heard a click behind them. As he pivoted about-face, the boom of a gun's report, was followed by the sight of Lee crashing onto the floor, face first. Burrows fired two shots as he crouched down. He could clearly see the other of Moon's men stood square on, in front of him, about twenty feet away at the end of the corridor. The second man was starting to re-aim his next shot, but one of the incoming bullets from Burrows's gun, torn through his throat, dropping him.

Burrows raced to where Lee was lying, but couldn't believe it when she started to stir. He helped her to her feet, realising she had taken the shot in the middle of her bulletproof vest.

"I'm ok, I'm ok…" Lee said, rushing the words out, before pausing and adding, "But I'll have one hell of a bruise there tomorrow."

"Bloody hell, you had me worried there for a sec."

"Glad to see you care," Lee replied, with a smile on her face.

They then went back into defensive mode, first checking that the second brute was dead, and they confirmed to each other that he was the second canal swimmer.

Ten minutes later, they had cleared the rest of the building, and were back where they'd started. Burrows couldn't understand how these two had got down from Manchester so quickly. And why had Moon sent them; why not leave it to Cabilla? Then he worked it out. It could only mean, that Moon didn't warn Cabilla, which is why he'd sent his own men to London to sort them both out.

"But how did Moon know that Cabilla, or his men, wouldn't be here?" asked Lee.

"Perhaps he rang Cabilla after all, and sent him and his men on a wild goose chase, to clear the way for his men," offered Burrows.

They chatted over what it all meant, then Burrows saw Lee glance at the closed door to the room behind the second man's body, and realised they still hadn't searched in there. Had there been anyone in there, they would have been long gone, or had come out fighting by now, Burrows said, and Lee nodded. But they needed to search it nonetheless; there may be some leads in there. Not that Burrows expected to find anything, and he was sure Lee didn't either; by the time they'd finished searching upstairs they were both of the opinion that anyone who'd been using the place, had upped and left before they arrived. Whatever Moon may have said to Cabilla, not only got him out the way, but had ensured he'd fled, taking anything of interest with him.

They both stepped over the second body, and opened the door slightly, Lee then kicked it open, and Burrows stiffened in shock at what he saw.

It was obvious that the body flopped on the chair was dead; a small black, bullet entry wound in the centre of his forehead made that clear. Flies buzzed around the grisly aperture. It was also obvious they were both looking at the cadaver of detective constable Gordon Chapman.

They stared at each other; Lee looked as baffled as Burrows felt. She said she didn't understand what was going on, but suggested they should both make themselves scarce, and pretty quickly. Burrows nodded. The noise the un-silenced weapons had made in the close confines of the building was still ringing in his ears. It was made worse by the emptiness of the building acting like amphitheatre; someone must have heard the shots.

"I know, I'm confused too," Burrows said, before continuing, "but let's work it out later."

"Come on John, it's time to go," Lee said.

They hurriedly picked up their spent shells, and cautiously left the building the way they had come in. By the time they'd reached their car, he could hear the sound of sirens approaching; but that could be for any number of reasons in this part of London. Nevertheless, they wouldn't hang around to find out, and within five minutes, they were well on their way. They headed for Lee's flat so they could change and shower as per, post operation protocol, before Burrows rang Briers to update him, and to decide on what their next move should be.

They'd talked things over as they travelled to Lee's place and although they hadn't worked it all out yet, there were two things they were agreed on. It looked as though Chapman was left there on display for a reason, maybe to scare them off, if Moon had indeed told Cabilla the truth. And secondly, the fact that they had to find Cabilla, and quickly, before he 'displayed' anyone else.

Chapter Forty-two

On the journey through London's mid-evening traffic, Steele could see the light outside failing, along with his mood. He spent the time trying to sound as normal as he could, and pleading with both Mackey, and Jim that Chapman was lying. His entreaties were ignored. Eventually, obviously tiring of him, Mackey simply told him to 'shut up and save it for later'. Steele went quiet, fear racing through him on hearing the words; what exactly did 'later' mean he wondered. What would that entail?

On arrival at the warehouse in Dulwich, Steele was put back into the cellar they used as a cell. This time he wasn't tied to the chair, just thrown into the room, for now anyway, though his hands were still tied behind his back. The room being windowless was always dark, but with the failing daylight, it was even darker. Mackey didn't turn the light on when he left the room, probably on purpose, to add to his fear.

He didn't know how long he had, until Cabilla would arrive from the other place, so he knew he had to collect his thoughts quickly, and try to raise his mental processes above the abject fear that was gripping him. When he was locked up before, they suspected him of being a grass, which Steele thought far worse than being thought of as an undercover cop. In fact, he had always kept open the option of outing himself, believing they would not want the death of a cop on their hands, with all the grief it would bring them.

Well, as of forty or so minutes ago, Steele now knew that to be a false premise; Mackey's boss Cabilla was certainly a nutter. He knew the single gunshot he'd heard when leaving the old school building had not just been for effect. He knew Cabilla had killed Chapman, and although he was as corrupt as they come, he was still a cop.

The one good thing he could see was that Chapman had sounded genuinely surprised, when he stupidly told him who he was. Therefore, if he didn't know about Steele being an undercover cop, then he shouldn't have known about the operation he'd been previously involved in with Mackey—when it had all gone so very wrong—and all those colleagues lost their lives. So assuming that, whatever intelligence reports Chapman had handed over to

Cabilla, should have had no reference to either Steele's op, or indeed any intelligence from it. Steele surmised that it could only relate to what Chapman had done.

This gave Steele a glimmer of hope. He could insist that Chapman was lying, and that Cabilla and Mackey should look closely at what they'd been given by him, before making any rash judgements on Steele. His breathing was returning to something like normal now. He was even starting to feel a little less fearful, having a plan always helped in pressure situations, especially, if there was some obvious merit to it. Having no plan at all was what tore you apart, and made you appear guilty.

Ten minutes later, the cellar door swung open, and in walked Cabilla and Mackey. Steele swallowed, and tried to control his anxiety.

"So, you're an undercover pig as well are you?" Cabilla said, pausing before carrying on, "I bet you and the Runt had a pretty good laugh behind our backs, eh?"

Steele, who was on the mattress by the wall, started shuffling up it back-first to his feet, whilst squinting at the sudden illumination from the room's light.

Mackey stood forward, and kicked Steele hard between the legs, sending him crashing to the floor, as he cried out in pain. "Stay on the mattress until we tell you," he added.

Steele took a second or two to let the worst of the pain subside before speaking. "I'm not a cop, honest. This is just a scam by that lying bastard to increase his pay-off. I can prove it."

"I hope you can, because if not, you've made Den here look pretty stupid, and he gets real mad when people take advantage of his otherwise good nature," Cabilla said.

"Look Mr Cabilla, if I was undercover like Chapman, then surely it'll be all over the stuff that he gave you. Please, please give me the benefit of the doubt, at least until you've seen it?" Steele pleaded.

Mackey and Cabilla glanced at each other. Steele knew Mackey desperately wanted to believe Steele to be innocent, as it would make him look such a twat in front of Cabilla if he wasn't, especially after he was the one who'd vouched for him.

"Don't forget the newspaper either; I'm wanted by the Turks for fucks sake. That can't be right if I'm a cop," Steele added.

"He makes a good point Shonbo," Mackey said.

It was the first time he'd heard Cabilla's first name being used.

"I don't know who the fuck to believe Den, but he actually makes two good points, granted. Look Larry," Cabilla said, turning to face Steele, "I'd forgotten about the newspaper thing, and I can't see how that can be so, if you're a cop—even a bent one like the Runt—'cause if the cop bosses knew you were bent, and wanted by the Turks, then they wouldn't be using you. I can see that."

Turning back to Mackey, Cabilla added. "Let's go and look at the stuff the Runt gave us, like Larry suggests, then we'll re-think this."

Mackey nodded, as Cabilla turned once more to face Steele, "But if you're lying, you are going to suffer real bad." And with that, both Mackey and Cabilla left the room, locking the door, but leaving the light on this time.

Steele saw the malignant glint in Cabilla's eyes as he said his final words, leaving him in no doubt as to the man's capacity for evil. He shook it off though, as he was feeling more confident now, they had even used his first name, which had to be good sign. It seemed that the newspaper article, and more importantly, the way it had been written, might have done the trick—written in a way that still protected his legend. As and when he ever got out of this mess, whatever consequences awaited him, he was going to buy the author of that article a whole host of drinks. The London cover officer Bill Jones, or even Johnny back in Manchester, had probably written it; but whoever had, might have just saved his life.

***

Mackey and Cabilla locked the cellar door behind them, but left the electric light on in the cell. Mackey suggested using the computer upstairs to view the CD the Runt had given them. Cabilla said he would rather do it in private at his apartment. Mackey looked around to see where Jim was, and as if reading his mind Cabilla told him that he had sent Jim on an errand.

"Do you want me to get the bloke upstairs to guard Larry, whilst we are away?" Mackey asked.

"No need Den, he's not going anywhere, and this shouldn't take too long," Cabilla answered.

They drove the short distance to Cabilla's plush apartment, it had been a while since Mackey had been there, but it always struck him as very exclusive. Certainly a lot nicer than the grotty flat he had the use of in Fulham. As soon as they walked in through the entrance, Mackey noticed a new white leather suite in the lounge. He made himself comfortable in one of two recliners that were side by side opposite the fireplace. Cabilla poured them each a scotch, before disappearing into the bedroom; he emerged moments later with a laptop under his arm. He sat down next to Mackey, and put the computer on the ornate hand-etched glass coffee table in front of them. He placed the disc into the machine's CD drive, and took a sip of his drink whilst the hard drive whirled and loaded.

Seconds later, a list of word documents appeared in front them as thumbnail icons.

"Right Den, let's see what that little shite had on us."

Both men lent forward, and Mackey could see about twenty documents, but only the first one had a title; 'Read this first'. Cabilla doubled clicked on the icon, and the whole document opened up as a plain page of A4, with three words written on it in bold large font; 'You've been had'.

"What the fuck…" Cabilla said. His words trailing off as he hurriedly opened the second file. This one was entitled Operational Intelligence Report – Street Robberies. Mackey looked at Cabilla, and shrugged his shoulders, he'd no idea what the title meant. They both leaned forward again, and Mackey read the report, then the next, and continued until he had read them all. None of them had anything to do with either Mackey or Cabilla; they just appeared to be random reports saved to the disc. None of the reports even appeared to relate to each other. Mackey thought they just appeared to be a haphazard compilation.

"The slimy little twat," Cabilla roared, as he threw the laptop crashing across the room into the far wall. "And I don't need to listen to those tapes to know there'll be fuck all on them either," he added.

"Well, look on the bright side Boss," Mackey said, continuing, "it means that the filth have nothing on us. Surely, that's all that matters now. And anyway, the Runt got what he deserved, you saw to that," he said, trying to calm Cabilla down. He knew only too well how difficult he could become when he was in this sort of mood.

"Yeah, I suppose you're right Den," Cabilla said, sitting back down, and draining his whiskey glass.

"Well, it tells us something else as well Den," Cabilla added.

"What's that Boss?"

"It means we owe Larry an apology,"

"Yeah," Mackey agreed, feeling more than a little relieved, again.

"That little shite must have took a dislike to Larry, and decided to throw him in to cause him grief, and cause us maximum confusion," Cabilla concluded.

They each had a further glass of scotch before getting up to leave, and go give Larry the good news. Cabilla's phone rang so Mackey took the cue to go and use the bathroom, whilst Cabilla answered his call. When he came back out into the hallway, he could see that Cabilla's face was fit to burst, again. Obviously, he had been given some more bad news. Christ, what now, Mackey thought before saying, "What's up Boss?"

"It's Jim," he answered, continuing, "he's about to be fucking nicked."

Chapter Forty-three

By the time they arrived at her flat in Milbank, Lee had started to tire as she came down from the operational high. It was going dark outside, and the adrenalin buzz was clearly wearing off. Burrows looked as if he was also starting to flag.

"You're looking how I feel," Burrows said, before quickly adding, "It has been a long day."

"You say all the nicest things to a girl, no wonder you're on your own."

Burrows just smiled and glanced away, but as soon as Lee had spoken, she regretted the 'on your own' bit, but it didn't look as if he taken too much offence.

Eventually, Lee found a parking space just round the corner from her flat, and they both trudged inside. Lee poured them both a vodka and coke, whilst Burrows went first in the shower. Half an hour later, they were both showered and changed, Lee sat in her armchair, and Burrows on the two-seater settee opposite. She poured them both a second drink, whilst the microwave oven hummed with two cottage pies from the freezer in it.

"Where do we go from here?" Lee asked, after they had finished eating.

"Well, I brought Frank up to speed, whilst you were in the kitchen, and he is going to have the Met's airwaves remotely monitored, and let us know when the bodies at the school are found. But for now, I suggest we get a good night's sleep and then start again tomorrow with clear heads."

Lee nodded in agreement, and then poured them each a large nightcap, before sitting down on the settee next to Burrows, swigging half her drink in one gulp, before putting her glass down on the occasional table in front of them. She was wearing a three-quarter length, white towelling robe, and as she turned to face Burrows, she was only too aware that the fall of her robe was displaying her amble cleavage. She caught Burrows glancing, but made no effort to adjust her gown. She felt a heady mix of fatigue, the remnants of the adrenalin rush, and the warming effects of the alcohol. She looked Burrows straight in the eyes and held his gaze, noting he made no attempt to look away. That was all the encouragement she needed, on top of the obvious chemistry she'd felt building between them over the last few days.

"I'm going to turn in now, John," she said, noting what looked like a hint of disappointment in his eyes, continuing, "but as you know, this is only a one-bedroomed flat, and that small two-seater sofa is hardly big enough for you, so I suggest we…"

Having left her sentence unfinished, she rose to her feet, finished her drink in a second gulp, and walked slowly towards the lounge door. Burrows didn't answer her, but she could hear him rising from the sofa, and then following her into the bedroom.

"Are you sure about this?" Burrows asked, as they each reached a different side of her king sized bed. Lee turned to face Burrows, and before answering, noticed his obvious arousal through the thin tracksuit bottoms he had put on after his shower.

"Well, you're little friend seems up for it," she said. And with that, they both burst into laughter, which removed any embarrassment.

The lovemaking that followed was passionate, fast, and desperate. Her pent-up affections exploded in a primeval outburst of emotion. His urgency matching her needs.

After the second time, she fell back onto the bed, sated and spent.

"What happens now?" Lee grinned, as Burrows lay next to her, catching his breath.

"Sleep," he exhaled. Adding, as his breathing slowed, "We'll make sense of everything in the morning."

And with that, she snuggled up towards him, and fell straight into a deep sleep.

Chapter Forty-four

"Nicked, what do you mean Shonbo?" Mackey asked.

"Well, I sent Jim back to the disused school to get rid of the Runt's body, before it was found by kids fucking about, or whatever," Cabilla said.

"Fair enough," Mackey muttered.

"Well, he's just rang and said that he'd only just arrived, and then the filth had poured into the car park. He smashed his way out through a rear window, and had got himself to the hedge at the back, when he rang."

"Did the cops see him?"

"He didn't know, but he was ditching his phone anyway, he asked can we get to the rear to pick him up, just in case he does get away," Cabilla added.

"What about his motor?"

"I asked him about that, said he had parked it away, whilst he checked the place out, but didn't want to go back to it with all the cops everywhere," Cabilla said.

"At least he had the brains to do that," Mackey added, as they left the flat and headed for the car.

Cabilla threw the car keys at Mackey, they had both had a drink, but if anyone was going to be stopped for drink driving, then better it be Mackey than him he thought. As they made their way over to East London, Cabilla told Mackey not to get too close, but just get to the estate at the back of the school, and let Jim find them; that was if he hadn't been lifted already.

It was about 10.30 p.m. and traffic was light; it only took twenty minutes to get to the back of the school in Hackney. Mackey suggested they drive once past the front entrance to the school, but Cabilla didn't want to take any chances. Five minutes later, they parked up in a quiet street about a quarter of a mile behind the school in a housing estate. Mackey killed the engine, and the lights, and they waited.

Cabilla noted that they were parked about 100 metres in from a major road that passed the outskirts of the large housing estate at the back of the school. It seemed to be the most obvious route from the back of the school to the major road, probably the one all the kids had trooped up and down years ago, when the school had been a school. A police patrol car slowly passed the end of the road, but didn't seem to react to their presence. Cabilla hoped they would just look like a parked up vehicle. Nonetheless, he was just about to tell Mackey to move when someone banged on the front passenger window.

"Fuck me Jim," Cabilla said, as he opened his door, "you nearly gave me a heart attack."

"Yeah, I know how that feels Boss," Jim said, as he jumped into the back seat. Cabilla closed his door, and Mackey had already started the engine and was driving them away.

Jim went on to explain that he'd parked his car in a side street near the entrance to the school as a precaution, whilst he checked it out. Once happy, he was going to go back and move his car to the front door, and then shift the Runt's body straight into the boot of the motor.

"How the fuck did the cops get there so fast?" asked Mackey.

"That's no doubt because of all the gunfire," Jim added.

"What gunfire?" Cabilla asked, before continuing, "I only shot the Runt once, and that was hours ago.

"Not you Boss. The others," Jim said.

"What are you banging on about?" Mackey asked.

"The gunfire relating to the other two bodies," Jim answered.

Cabilla just looked at Mackey who looked as bewildered as he was, before Jim continued.

He went on to explain how he had found two other dead bodies, one in the corridor, and one by the door to the room where the Runt was; the headmaster's office. He said they had both been shot, and were still oozing gore from their wounds, so he reckoned they hadn't been there too long. That's when the cops started to arrive, and he smashed his way out through the headmaster's office shuttered window.

Cabilla couldn't make any sense of this, and told Mackey to head back to Dulwich. Mackey told Jim about the stuff that the Runt had given them, and how Larry could now be trusted. Jim said he was glad, as he thought he was an all right bloke. When they arrived back at Dulwich, they all walked into the main room as Cabilla's mobile phone rang again. He looked down at the display on the screen and saw the caller ID.

"What the fuck does he want?" Cabilla muttered, before answering the call.

Cabilla mainly listened to the caller, threw in a few threats, but at the end thanked him, though added that the caller owed him. He then turned to Mackey and Jim who he could see had been looking on intently.

"That was Jonny Moon in Manchester. And I think we have some trouble coming our way."

He went on to explain how Jonny had received a visit by two bastards he referred to as 'Bonny and Clyde'. What they had done to him, and the fact that he'd given up Cabilla's address. He'd said he wasn't sure if the school was still the place used by them, but rather than admit to Cabilla what had happened, he'd dispatched two of his men to London to go to the school, and deal with Bonny and Clyde. He said that if Cabilla, or any of his men, had been at the school when they arrived, then his men would have told him so straight away, and he would have immediately warned Cabilla. It was at this point in the conversation Cabilla said he'd threatened Moon, as he didn't believe a word. As far as he was concerned, Moon had sold him out, and left him to fate.

He said, he'd eventually agreed to differ, to keep Moon on the line, and let him continue. Moon went on to explain that he'd received two calls from his men saying firstly, they were at the school and the place was deserted, and then secondly, shortly after, to say that Bonny and Clyde had arrived and they were about to deal with them. Then nothing; Moon had waited an hour before trying both men's phones, neither were answered.

Then he explained, how ten minutes ago one of his men's phones rang in, and when Moon had answered and asked, 'was it sorted?' an unknown voice asked what he meant. Seconds later, he ended the call, and the phone is now at the bottom of the Manchester ship canal. He also explained that before he ended the call, the stranger had identified himself as some detective or other, and started asking who he was in relation to the owner of the phone. When Moon had asked why, he'd been told the owner of the phone was dead. That was when he had put the phone down, and could only assume the same fate had happened to his other man.

Cabilla said he had taken some pleasure in being able to confirm to Moon that both his men were dead, and then laid it on thick how because of Moon not warning him, he had almost lost Jim to the filth. Moon kept apologising until Cabilla had heard enough, and he just ended the call.

"When this is all over, I'm going to sort Moon out; I don't care how big he thinks he is. We need to send a message," Cabilla said.

But what does this all mean?" Mackey asked.

"It means we are in the shit Den. It means that we've some serious grief after us. It means we need to prepare ourselves," Cabilla said, before adding, "but whoever the fuck they are? They're going to pay."

Chapter Forty-five

It was still dark when Burrows started to stir. He hadn't slept too well; it had been a long time since he had shared a bed with anyone, and it felt a little uncomfortable and hot. It made him realise just how long he had been sleeping alone, and reminded him how awkward it always felt when you first slept with someone new. He glanced at Lee and saw that she was fast asleep with her back to him. As the sleep-haze cleared, he saw the bedroom properly for the first time. The large bed took up most of the room, and to its left was a dressing table and chair, with a wardrobe between them and the Victorian style sash window. He then realised his mobile phone was ringing, and the ascending ringtone was becoming louder. He heard Lee mumble as he got up and grabbed his phone before it rang off. He looked at the screen noticing the time was only 3 a.m., he saw the caller ID was Zulu.

"Hello Frank, to what do I owe this early morning pleasure?" he asked.

"Sorry about this John, but are you still at Jane's flat?" Briers asked.

"Yes," Burrows answered, before adding a little too hurriedly, "I'm on the couch, she's in the other room." As soon as he spoke the words, he realised how unnecessarily defensive they must have sounded.

Briers, paused a second before continuing, "Good news and bad news; the good news is that the black 4 x 4 that Mackey used to lift Chapman, has pinged an ANPR camera in east London."

Burrows knew that Automatic Number Plate Recognition cameras were on fixed sites around the capital, and that Frank had the ghost-plated number put onto the system, with instructions to flag up any sightings.

"What's the bad news Frank?"

"It happened over three hours ago, it's taken that long for the lines of communication to reach me."

Burrows finished his call with Briers, and then turned to Lee, who was now sat up in bed fully awake with the quilt pulled up to cover her modesty.

Having relayed the details of the phone call to her, she said, "So unless the real owner of that registration number is in London, that's our subject's vehicle?"

"It's our subject's all right. Frank has had a night detective do a drive past at the real owner's address in Manchester, and the vehicle legally showing that registration number is parked on the drive," Burrows added.

He went on to explain that the site of the camera that had been activated was in Hackney, and the vehicle had been heading towards central London. It was too dark to get a good photograph of the occupants, but from the image recorded, it looked as if there were several shadows on-board. The best they could do, he suggested, was to get out whilst it was still dark, and do an area search near the site of the activation on the off chance the vehicle was near the end of its journey when it pinged the camera, and was now parked up nearby in some side street. It was a long shot, but it was all he could suggest.

One shower, and two cups of coffee later, they were each about to leave Lee's flat, when Burrows's phone rang again. On seeing who was calling, he answered quickly.

"The lines of communication are quickening John, fifteen minutes after the subject vehicle pinged the first camera, it activated a second one, this time south of the river entering Dulwich," Briers said.

"Thanks for that Frank, give us the exact location and we'll be in Dulwich in ten minutes."

Ten minutes later, they were in Dulwich. Burrows had brought Lee up-to-date, and they were both fully awake and in operational mode. He thought that the rude awakening by Briers's call had helped save any embarrassment, that might have otherwise been present, had they both just woken up naturally in the morning. He guessed Lee felt the same way, as she appeared to be almost overdoing her business-like persona.

Having found the ANPR site, they started to work in ever increasing circles away from it; cruising the side streets. The camera itself was located on the A205, which is the south circular road, near to Dulwich Park. Croston country, Burrows thought. After about an hour and a half of weaving in and out of the residential streets off the A205, Burrows pulled over. They hadn't found the 4 x 4. By now, they were getting ever farther away from the camera site, and agreed that the chances of just happening on the vehicle parked up now were becoming increasingly remote.

"It's almost five now," Lee said, "why don't we head back and get a couple of hours sleep, and then come back here and sit near the camera site, see if we can't pick it up in the morning rush hour traffic?"

"Yeah, good idea Jane, at least that way if the vehicle gets pinged again, anywhere, in the morning traffic, we will be out and about, and in a position to try and get on it."

Whilst they had been driving about, Lee had broken the ice first with regard to what had happened earlier. "That was great before John, but I'm not sure if I want a full blown relationship? Can we just park things until after this job is over, and see where things go from there-on?"

On hearing Lee say this, it took an awful lot of pressure off Burrows. He'd been thinking the same thing. As passionate, and impromptu as the previous evening had been, they needed to stay focused now. What became of things later, only later would tell.

"I'm really glad to hear you say that Jane. Let's get this job done and then see what we see," he said.

Lee smiled back at him, and he felt the atmosphere return to how it had been over the last few days. However, he knew he couldn't kid himself, he really did like Lee, and not just for the obvious reasons. When they arrived back at her flat, he told her he would kip on the two-seater in the lounge, and she hurried off to find him a blanket.

Chapter Forty-six

It was after midnight by the time Cabilla arrived back at Dulwich with Mackey and Jim, and he felt in a foul mood. Trying to understand, whom the hell they had pissed off so much, as to send a couple of guns after them. "It's not those fucking Turks is it Den?" he asked, before adding. "They don't think we ripped them, do they?"

After the shootings on the retail park, he knew he had to leave without getting the drugs from the lorry. And even though he had paid the Turks £100,000 in advance, through Mackey, it had only been half the money. The agreement they had with them, was to pay half the money up front, and the other half on completion of the deal.

"Nah Boss, they were a bit sus when I rang them, but after they saw all the press coverage, they knew it was legit."

"Well, fucking think will you, the sooner we work out who it is, the sooner we can sort it. And get Larry out of that fucking cell, we need all the hands we can get," Cabilla said.

Inside the warehouse, Cabilla sent Jim off to the storeroom at the back to grab some camp beds stored there, whilst he followed Mackey towards the cell.

"On second thoughts Den, leave Larry until the morning, he'll be asleep now, and I want people fully alert by then. We'll get our heads down on those camp beds in the main hall, and then we'll look at this pile of shite through fresh eyes after some sleep."

He had already discussed the threat on the way back to the warehouse, and was of the opinion, that Bonny and Clyde, as he had started to refer to the hired guns as, clearly didn't know about Dulwich, so they should be secure there for the time being. Mackey and Jim had both agreed with him. Now, he just wanted to consolidate his resources in one place, until they dealt with these bastards properly.

"It's obviously the same people who met Billy the Kid in that cemetery, I wonder if he could have given them anything useful before our man popped him?" Mackey asked, as they headed back into the main hall.

"Billy never knew about this place, and he didn't even know about the school. They got that bit, off that shite Moon," Cabilla answered.

"Suppose," Mackey said.

Jim had pulled two camp beds from the store, and set them up next to the old settee, all three of them then settled down to get some rest.

Cabilla slept fitfully, until he was awoken by Jim, offering him a cup of coffee, which he gratefully took. He hadn't slept well, even though he'd taken the old sofa over the camp beds. Mackey was already sat up, sipping his brew.

"Any ideas yet Den? You know, 'bout who these guns are? Or who has sent them?" Cabilla asked.

Mackey just shook his head.

Cabilla waited until Jim had moved away before continuing. "Well as soon as we get it sorted, the sooner we can get those sluts upstairs earning their keep." He then went onto explain to Mackey that if everything went according to plan, and their trial brothel worked, he intended to bring more women into the country the same way, a lot more. He could see the surprise in Mackey's face. He continued, "I've got a good contact at the Colton ore mines back in the Congo, and he says they can provide as many women as we want, and they will all be top quality."

Cabilla carried on, saying he envisioned opening as many warehouse brothels as he could, all over the UK. He intended to open one in Manchester next, and then move to every major city.

"And I want you to run the organisation throughout, with local managers reporting to you. Of course, I'll be able to pay you serious money if it all comes off. So you see why we need to get rid of Bonny and Clyde, so things can start moving," Cabilla finished.

"Fucking hell Shonbo, you kept all that quiet," Mackey said.

Cabilla enjoyed the look of astonishment on Mackey's face. "I know I keep you in the dark sometimes Den, but it's all done for good reason. I don't like to say too much, until I'm sure about things."

Mackey was full of it now, and Cabilla was enjoying see him fawn all over him. Cabilla went on to explain that his contact in the Congo could bring in hundreds of women; as they would only have a limited amount of usage, before they were too fucked up, drugged up, or just too used. So they could ensure regular replacements.

"What do we do with those who have passed their sell-by dates?" Mackey asked.

"What do you think Den? You know we don't like witnesses," Cabilla said, with a vile smirk on his face. What he didn't tell Mackey, was once everything was up and running, he intended to base himself abroad, whilst Mackey took all the risks; that way he would remain fool proof, and could enjoy the rewards of his endeavours without any further interference by the British police.

Cabilla noticed Jim returning with a further cup of coffee, so changed the subject.

"Once you've had that drink Jim, I want you to go with Den to get your motor, and collect some tools," he said, adding, "I'll speak to Larry whilst you're gone."

Cabilla turned to Mackey, "Den, one last thing; I'm pretty sure that Bonny and Clyde don't know about this place, or we'd have had visitors by now, but can you check the three apartments. It's far more likely that they have those addresses, if they have any others, which is another reason why I wanted us all together here last night."

As they headed off, Cabilla went through the inner door and down the steps to the basement cellar. He unlocked the cellar door, and switched the light on as he entered. Steele, squinting against the light was trying to get to his feet, visibly tense.

"Relax Larry, you were right all along. That scumbag Runt was just trying to mix it for you. There was fuck all on that disc, and Den tried one of the tapes at random in the car stereo, and it was blank," Cabilla said.

"I told you Boss, I told you it was all rubbish," Steele replied.

"You must have really pissed him off, which means you did a good job. Look, I'll double your wages this month, Ok. But right now, I need you with me by my side, until we've sorted out a little problem," he added, whilst extending his hand.

Steele shook his hand, "No probs Boss, but will that be the end of raised eyebrows in my direction?"

"You have my word. Now let me fill you in on our little problem. I also hope you know how to fire a gun."

Chapter Forty-seven

Burrows didn't think he'd sleep much on Lee's two-seater settee, but he had fallen into a deep slumber as soon as he'd closed his eyes. He awoke to the gentle rocking of his shoulder, and it took a couple of seconds to remember where he was.

"Good morning John, there's a brew on the table for you," Lee said.

Burrows opened his eyes to see Lee stood over him already dressed; he jumped up with a start, "What time is it?"

"Relax; it's only just gone seven. I've always been an early riser, but I reckon we should be on plot for eight-ish if we can," Lee said.

Ten minutes later, Burrows was in the shower, and by seven twenty-five, they were both walking out the door towards the motor. Lee drove, whilst Burrows put a contact call into Briers to update him from the previous evening. Burrows ended the call, and turned to Lee.

"Apparently, all hell's broken loose within the Met after the situation at the school. Not only, have they got one of their own executed, but they can't work out the connection with the two dead Manchester villains. The poor Murder Investigation Team is in for a tough one, especially now the press have got hold of it due to all the activity at the school."

"I take it there is nothing to connect us?" Lee asked.

"No, don't worry, Frank is covertly monitoring things remotely, and he's sending someone over to your flat to pick up and dispose of our post op bin bags, so there'll be nothing that can link us forensically to the scene," Burrows reassured.

Lee wended her way through the rush hour traffic, but fortunately, the worst of it was going the other way Burrows noticed as they headed over Vauxhall Bridge, and away from central London and the City. By 8.30, Lee had found a side street off the end of the south circular road, with a good view of the approach to the where the ANPR fixed camera site was. She had positioned them on the east side of the A205, saying, that way they could join the traffic heading in the direction of Dulwich.

Burrows took a further call from Briers, and shouted, "Fuck," as he ended it.

"What's up?"

"The 4 x 4 pinged this site twenty minutes ago, just before we arrived, it was heading towards London."

"Double fuck," Lee said.

Burrows suggested they sit tight, and not to react for the sake of it; the car may head back the same way, and then they would have it. Lee agreed.

Over the next hour and a half, Burrows received a number of updates from Briers; the 4 x 4 was pinging sites all over London. The last one was in Fulham around ten o'clock. On the assumption the vehicle may be on its way back, Lee put her body radio on, and got out on foot, walking up and down the main road near the junction in order to try and spot the vehicle a little sooner, and before it pinged their site. Briers now had a live real-time feed from the ANPR analysts, but that would still put Burrows and Lee valuable seconds behind it, and they didn't want another loss like they'd had with it last time. Lee would hopefully see the vehicle approaching, and be able to give him a few critical seconds notice. They'd agreed, if or when the vehicle came their way, he would only pick Lee up if he had time. More important to follow, and house the vehicle first, and then come back for Lee afterwards. Once they had an address that the vehicle was going to, and coming from, it would only be a matter of time thereafter before they saw Cabilla.

Burrows looked at his watch and it was 10.45 a.m. Even though it was dry outside, if not a little cloudy, he was thinking of arranging a swop with Lee. Not just to give her a break, but to change the profile of someone who was just hanging about. For all they knew, the 4 x 4 might live at an address near to where they currently were. He was reaching for his transmit button, but before he could press it, his earpiece erupted into life.

"Contact, contact, contact, Bravo confirming long distant eyeball on the subject vehicle. It's currently in slow moving traffic heading our way. Alpha received?" Lee shouted.

"Yes, Yes Bravo, Alpha received. I'll make to the junction," Burrows responded, whilst firing up the Mondeo engine.

As Burrows drew level with the main road, Lee appeared at the corner, and jumped back in the car. Moments later the 4 x 4 slowly passed them doing about 15-20 mph in a steady queue of vehicles. Two cars passed, and then a space allowed Burrows to join the traffic behind them.

"Perfect, we've got two cars for cover," Burrows said out loud, but as much to himself.

"And we've got Mackey driving it, alone at the moment," Lee added.

For the next ten minutes, Burrows and Lee snaked along the A205, always two or three cars behind the 4 x 4, then it turned off the main road onto a side street that looked more like an access road, than a residential side road. Burrows only had a glimpse of the turning as he approached it on his left. If it was a dead end, or an access road, then they would be mightily exposed if he blindly followed the 4 x 4. He decided to overshoot the junction, and pulled up on the pavement as soon as he was past the corner; thereby, out of sight of the 4 x 4's rear view mirrors. Lee was out on foot before the car had stopped. She walked back to the corner and then hurried back to the Mondeo and got back in.

"You were right to pull past John; the road is only 100 metres long, and leads straight to a gated entrance, to what looks like a small industrial estate. I could see the edge of a large brick built warehouse with a gravel path going around the side. Large conifer trees and a high steel fence form the perimeter. I just saw the 4 x 4's brake lights as it disappeared through the gateway," Lee said.

"It sounds a lot like the disused school in Hackney," Burrows observed.

"Very much so; I think we've found their new base."

"In that case Jane, it's looking like it might be game on."

Burrows moved the car to a less exposed position in a side road opposite, with a view to the turning into the access road. After a brief chat with Lee, he agreed they should stay put for a while in case they were wrong, and Mackey was just making a call on someone before continuing his journey. After about forty-five minutes, they were both fairly happy that they had found Cabilla's base, and were just about to pull back onto the main road, when a further vehicle drove into the compound.

"I only got a glimpse, but I'm pretty sure the driver was the bloke who drove the4 x 4 the night Chapman got lifted," Burrows said.

"I was thinking the same thing," Lee agreed.

Burrows drove to a safer location, another side road, but 100 metres further down the road towards Dulwich. Then he discussed with Lee what they should do next; normally they would wait until darkness before conducting a close target reconnaissance of the place, they both knew that was standard procedure, but Burrows said he couldn't wait that long, and Lee agreed. They also agreed they couldn't make a move on the premises until they were sure of the odds they were facing, and more importantly, confirming that Cabilla was there. But it was summer, and it wouldn't be dark for a long time, but given the apparent thickness of the conifer trees, they decided to do a cautious recce.

Having worked out all the egress and access points to the compound, they slowly moved around it from beyond the trees. As they approached from the outer side, Burrows heard the sound of a car leaving the compound, but knew that the foliage was far too thick for anyone to see through. He looked at his watch and it was just after midday. He glanced at Lee who just nodded back, so they pressed on.

After finishing another circuit, they squatted down and Burrows said, "I'll recap what I've seen, but jump in if you note anything different."

Lee nodded, and Burrows carried on, pointing out that the premises were very similar to the school, in that there was only the one building in the compound, with good security all around. The property was about the same size as the school, and made out of red brick. It appeared to have been industrial premises of some kind, as it had no windows on the ground floor, but rear facing windows at the back, on the first floor.

"Probably once admin offices of some sort," Lee offered.

Burrows continued, noting that the building had only two-stories. Also, there were wooden, drayman-style, floor access doors at one end, which he said, suggested a basement of some kind. This was at the opposite end from the gateway; there was also an old rusty fire escape at the same end. The main access to the place was through two large wooden doors in the centre of the front aspect of the property. There were no obvious signs of alarms systems or CCTV cameras, which he said was a major bonus. "Unless you saw any?" he asked Lee.

"No, none."

"In that case, let's head back to the Mondeo, and discuss what to do next."

Lee nodded, and they carefully made their way out of the grounds.

Back in the car Burrows said, "We can't really do anything until we know Cabilla's home, and even then we'll have to wait until nightfall. Also, I'm sure you noticed too, but when we did the recce the bloody 4 x 4 had gone as well; it must have left whilst we were doing out peripheral research for the best ways to approach."

"Yeah I noticed, though it could also have gone when we were parking up initially. Though, if that's the case, he must have been in and out pretty sharpish, and has been gone well over an hour, do you still think we've got the right place?"

"We'll have to see how things pan out during the day to be sure, but if we have, then there should be plenty of comings and goings, and if not, then we'll just have to wait until the ANPR goes off again," Burrows said. Before adding, "I'm pretty sure though, that this is the right place. It just looks and feels right."

"I fully agree, which only confirms that we can't do anything yet, so why don't we do shifts keeping an eye on the entrance approach, to prepare ourselves for the night shift? After all, it's only quarter to one now."

Burrows agreed, and then rang Frank Briers to bring him up to speed. After which, Briers said he would turn out and pick one of them up, and run them back to Lee's flat for a few hours rest, and then he would bring them back and switch things around. Burrows thanked him as that obviously made things easier, and with less risk of missing any more comings or goings. Burrows told Lee to go first but she refused, saying, Burrows looked the more tired of the two. He relented, and agreed to go first when Briers arrived thirty minutes later. Briers said he would bring him back around four o'clock. He told them both that Intel checks on the warehouse were negative; it wasn't known to them. Burrows glanced back at Lee as he walked away, and saw her hunkering down in the drivers' seat, presumably to get her head as comfortable as she could against the backrest, whilst still facing the entrance to the access road. It was going to be a long wait until nightfall.

After Briers dropped Burrows off at Lee's flat, he thought he would be too charged to sleep, and he was. He was too preoccupied running various attack scenarios around in his mind, but at least he managed to sort of daydream, whilst he mused the differing options. That in itself was a lot less tiring than it would be for Lee, maintaining a fixed visual on the entrance to that access road.

At three-thirty, Briers arrived at the flat and Burrows was ready for him. Apparently, there were no further updates, either from Lee or elsewhere. Burrows asked Briers to drop him off a couple of hundred metres prior to the plot, so he could approach on foot, less obtrusively.

"Have you heard from Jane at all?" he asked.

"Oh yes, I had a contact call from her about three, just to say that there was no change at the plot, and that she was dying for a wee," Briers grinned in reply.

"Well she won't have to hang on for much longer," Burrows said.

"How are you two shaping up as a team?" Briers probed, as they drove through the traffic onto Vauxhall Bridge.

"Always the manager eh Frank," Burrows said, before continuing, "Yes we are gelling together excellently. I don't know how you found her Frank, but she's a top operative with a good sense of humour, and balance... bit like me."

"Thankfully, without your modesty," Briers added, mockingly.

Ten minutes later, Briers took an opportunity in a break in the traffic, to do a U-turn in the road, and pull over to the kerb to let Burrows out.

"Good luck John, and remember, I'll be on standby all night if you should need anything."

Burrows thanked him, and got out of the car, and watched it head back towards central London as he started to walk the few hundred metres to the RV.

A few minutes later, he reached the junction opposite the access road, and turned into the side street he had left earlier. Then he came to an abrupt standstill; both Lee and the Mondeo were gone.

Chapter Forty-eight

Steele listened, as Cabilla finished filling him in on what had been happening, and he said that as soon as Mackey or Jim got back with the toys, they would re-arm themselves. Steele flinched at the mention of arms.

"What's up Larry? I'm giving you a gun; doesn't that show how much I trust you?" Cabilla asked.

"No Boss, it's not that, it's just that I've never held a gun before, after all, I just drive wagons really."

"Don't worry; it's just for your own defence until we sort out Bonny and Clyde. In all reality, me and Den will have to go out, and put our arses up in the air for those two twats to come at us. So any messy stuff will be well away from here. It's just for your defence like I say, just in case."

"Ok Boss, fair enough."

"When this is all sorted I've got really big plans, and I want you to be part of it. I can't tell you yet what they are, but I need to know you're in for the long haul?" Cabilla said.

"You can count on me," Steele replied, straight away with a hint of a smile on his face. He wanted Cabilla to realise he had his support.

Cabilla spend the next few hours working the phones. Obviously trying to get an angle on who Bonny and Clyde were, or whom they were working for. He'd based himself on the settee, and sent Steele out to do regular circuits of the compound. There was no doubt in Steele's mind that he was now fully trusted. He reflected on what Cabilla had just told him; he'd got the surprise of his life when he heard what Cabilla had to say. He hadn't expected the intelligence that Chapman gave Cabilla to involve him—as Chapman had seemed genuinely surprised when he'd told him he was an undercover officer. But he hadn't considered that the whole thing was one big rip; that Chapman had made it all up.

He hadn't got an apology, but had accepted Cabilla's hand as such. Then Cabilla said he wanted him to have a gun; he couldn't believe it, but he knew there wouldn't be many rules left unbroken if he accepted one. He just didn't know how to get out of it. Perhaps he should accept the gun to maintain his cover, so he could take it with him when he made his run for it. That way, he could tell his bosses he took the gun to remove at least one weapon from Cabilla's arsenal.

Then Cabilla had started talking about some big plans, and how he wanted Steele to be a part of it. Another moral dilemma; does he simply get away as soon as he can, as he had always aspired towards, or does he hang on to find out more about the big plans.

The trouble with being an undercover officer, he knew, was that it made you naturally very inquisitive, which is not always a good thing. Steele mulled over his predicament, and decided to stay put, at least a while longer. He figured that he was in so much shit already, a layer more wouldn't really matter. He also rationalised that now he was totally free, and totally trusted, it seemed mad to give up his position when he could learn so much more about the bigger plans, not to mention finding out as much as he could about the hired guns Cabilla called Bonny and Clyde. If all else failed, he could easily get away now, which was a significant difference to before.

Cabilla had asked him to walk around the perimeter of the building every ten or fifteen minutes or so, to keep an eye on things. After all that had gone on, Steele almost laughed out loud at the perverseness of the request; he really could easily leg it now if he wanted.

He was glad of the fresh air as he did his first circuit, and took in his environment. The building looked as he had expected it to, an old brick built warehouse of some kind, probably constructed in the forties or fifties. It had a wide gravel perimeter around it, bordered by a steel fence and trees. There was a gateway with a single barrier that was currently in the up position. After several circuits, he reconsidered his decision; the more he walked around the place, the more tempting it was just to get out of there, he could hear the traffic from the main road, and realised he could be there in minutes. Then, he heard a car approaching, and looked up to see Mackey arriving back alone in the 4 x 4. Steele saw the time was eleven, and Mackey just nodded as he drove past him and parked up. He went inside, was back out again a couple of minutes later, and then drove off.

Steele carried on his circuits, and having reassured himself that he could now leg it at any time he chose, he decided to hold his nerve a while longer. About an hour later, Jim arrived back, and he watched as he carried a heavy blue coloured plumber's holdall into the building. It looked heavy with pointed shapes pushing the thin material from within it.

"Do you want a hand with that?" Steele shouted, across the gravel parking area at the front of the building.

"No, I'm ok thanks Larry," Jim said adding, "I glad they sorted you out, I told them I thought you were a sound guy."

"Thanks mate, I appreciate that," Steele replied. He was tempted to follow Jim inside to have a peek at what was in the bag, but fought the temptation; he didn't want to appear too nosey, especially now he had Cabilla's trust. A couple of minutes later, and Jim was off again too, he told Steele as he left the building that he was off to meet with Mackey, to check the flats and would see him later. He added that Cabilla wanted to see him.

Steele went inside to see Cabilla poring over the contents of the holdall, it was as he'd expected. There were at least four handguns, and two bigger guns that Steele guessed were some kind of machine pistols, they had magazines sticking out underneath them, which looked too long for the weapons. Cabilla handed him a small gun, and said it was a semi-automatic, small calibre weapon. He showed him where the safety catch was, and showed him how to fire it. He told him to keep it always pointed at the floor when it was in his hand, unless he intended to use it. He also told him it was only effective at close range.

Steele had never held a gun before, and was amazed at how heavy it felt, he made sure the safety was on, and then pushed it into the front waistband of his jeans. Cabilla said he would be better with it down the back of his denims, and he soon realised why as it started to push up into his stomach. He switched it around, and tried not to look nervous.

Jim had also brought back some pre-packed sandwiches from a local garage, and Cabilla told Steele to take a break and grab some lunch, an invitation he gratefully accepted. After eating, he went back outside at around twelve forty-five, and after that, he was in and out of the building during his laps of the place. He slowly became more accustomed to the feel of the gun in the centre of his back, and every time he popped inside, Cabilla was continually on the phone.

It was three-twenty, before anyone returned. Steele heard a car approaching, but when he looked up, it was a car he hadn't seen before. It took him a couple of seconds to realise what he was seeing. Jim was in the back seat behind the driver, and as soon as the car was past the gate, he saw Jim raise his hand; he had a gun in it, and he was pointing it at the back of the driver's head. The driver was an attractive woman in her forties, her face surprisingly expressionless.

Jim wound down his door window, and shouted at Steele as the car came to a halt. "Go and get the Boss. I think I've found Bonny."

Chapter Forty-nine

Burrows just stood and stared, trying to make sense of Lee's absence. Perhaps Cabilla had left the target premises, and she had to make a split-second decision to go after him. But if that was the case, he couldn't image Lee wouldn't have rung him or Briers to let them know. He reached for his phone and then hesitated; what if she had literally only just gone, she may not have had time to use her phone yet. Burrows decided not to knee-jerk, but to give it a short while. He saw a phone box about twenty metres further down the main road and headed for it. It was an ideal place to keep observations from, without drawing attention.

Twenty minutes later and there was still no sign of Lee. Burrows resisted the urge to ring her; if she was in a position to ring him, then she would have by now he figured. Ringing her, could possibly compromise her, depending on what situation she was in. Considering the options, the obvious one was the unthinkable one; that she had been compromised and taken by Cabilla, or his goons. Whether he wanted to think it or not, Burrows knew it was the first option, and he had to contemplate it if only to rule it out, before he considered anything else. He clearly couldn't wait until dark now, but would have to recce the warehouse with added stealth, assuming those inside were on high alert. He decided to approach from the rear as he'd done before.

He was glad when they'd initially plotted up, in the side road that they had tooled up, and put their ballistic vests on, just in case. He was also glad he had taken his kit with him when he had stood down to Lee's flat. He might be going in blind, but at least he was armed.

Thirty-five minutes later, Burrows had circumnavigated the entire perimeter, and eventually arrived at a point with a view of the front. There were two cars, and the 4 x 4 parked outside the front aspect, all in a row. However, parked side-on, across the approach to the building's front doors, was the Mondeo.

"Shit," Burrows whispered, on seeing it.

He then saw one of the front doors to the building open, and he remained very still as he looked on. Two men walked out and stood still. He recognised both of them; one was the guy who had driven the 4 x 4 when Chapman had been snatched—the guy they'd seen earlier, arriving in a car—, and the other was Steele the undercover officer, who'd obviously joined up with the bad guys. The two men spoke to each other for a moment or two, but Burrows couldn't hear their words from where he was. Then they started to slowly patrol around the building, each going in the opposite direction to the other.

"Shit," Burrows whispered again; he had been eyeing up the old drayman-style ground level doors, at the other end of the premises, as a possible way in. But that was now a trickier option with dumber and dumber on foot patrol.

He spent the next ten to fifteen minutes timing the patrol, each man took approx. two minutes to walk around the premises, which meant that from any direction Burrows chose to approach, he would have approx. sixty seconds before one, or other, of the patrols would be able to see him. It was enough. Burrows picked his moment, and scaled the fence dropping down as lightly as he could. Without hesitation, he ran for cover at the rear of the parked vehicles, counting to himself under his breath all the way.

"One thousand, two thousand, three thousand..."

By the time he had reached fifteen thousand, he was safely behind the end vehicle—the one nearest the drayman's doors at the end of the building—although he had plenty of time left, he decided to do things in stages. He'd hide and wait for another rotation. By the time thirty seconds had passed, he had got himself underneath the end vehicle, plenty of time to catch his breath before the patrol passed in another thirty seconds. Then he heard a noise from the direction of the doors, and could see that two feet and shins had appeared at the front, obviously having come from inside.

"Jim, Larry. Where the fuck are you two?" said the unfamiliar voice, from above the legs. It was spoken in fluent English, but Burrows could discern a twang and accent from elsewhere. A few seconds later, the original 4 x 4 driver appeared from the other end of the building, and Steele appeared from Burrows's end a moment later. Burrows watched as Steele walked past the vehicle he was under, and then he saw three sets of legs forming a huddle. He couldn't hear what was said, but moments later the original legs, and what Burrows was guessing were Steele's, walked back inside the building. Burrows waited out another rotation, just to confirm what he thought had taken place; Steele had gone inside with his foreign sounding master, and the 4 x 4 driver was now circling the place alone.

Burrows slipped out from under the car, and realised he had the best part of two minutes, before the patrol reappeared. He didn't know how long Steele would be inside, so he knew he had to act quickly. He checked the car he was next to, a family sized Vauxhall saloon, of some model or other; it was unlocked. He quickly found the boot release lever, and popped the lid, which opened a couple of inches.

Burrows then ran to the wall by the drayman doors, and crouched down by the corner of it, at the end of the building line. He heard the 4 x 4 man before he saw him.

As 4 x 4 man turned the corner, Burrows grabbed both his legs as he passed, he then dashed backwards taking the man's legs completely from under him. A split-second later the man hit the ground facedown with a grunt, and Burrows knelt on him in the centre of his back. He drew his silenced sig sauer, and as he pointed the end into the man's right ear, he whispered into the left.

"You can probably guess what's in my right hand... so unless you want to test your theory, behave, Ok?"

The man nodded.

"Right, first thing first; if I'd wanted you dead, then you'd already be dead. So behave, and answer a few simple questions, and you'll live. Understand?"

The man nodded again.

"What's your name?"

"Jim," he answered.

Two minutes later, Burrows knew that Lee was inside the building, probably locked in a cellar, but still alive. He also knew who else was in the building, and what sort of hardware they had. He then used the butt of his weapon to hit Jim heavily on the lower back of his head. It made a dull noise, but he heard no crunching, so hopefully he'd only knocked him out, and not fractured his skull as well. Burrows knew how vulnerable the back of the head was at the top of the neck; he'd dealt with many homicides, whilst in the police where a single punch resulted in death, when the recipient had fallen backwards, and cracked the rear of the skull on a kerbstone or such like. Happy he'd done no permanent damage, he dragged, the now sleeping Jim, to the rear of the Vauxhall. Gagged him for good measure using a handkerchief from Jim's pocket, and then bundled him into the boot. Before shutting the lid, he searched Jim, and relieved him of his snub-nosed revolver, which he'd been carrying in his jacket inside pocket. Burrows was glad that Jim was no longer a threat, and had played the game straight when he'd had asked him to. He knew his compliance had probably saved his life.

Burrows had to move fast now, and turned his attention to the drayman's doors. They were old, wooden, and rotten around the edges, with a rusty chain and padlock holding them together. He used the butt of Jim's gun to break the chain, it snapped on the second strike, and Burrows lifted one of the old doors hoping that its hinges didn't make too much noise. They did squeak, but only a little, moments later, he was inside, and stood three or four steps down a concrete staircase. He closed the door shutting out most of the light as he did so, and then headed down into the darkness.

Chapter Fifty

It was about twenty past three when Larry came running into the warehouse. Cabilla was still on the sofa in the main hall making calls. He looked up as Larry came in.

"Jim's outside Boss, and he says he's got Bonny."

"What?" Cabilla said, as he sprang to his feet.

The front doors then opened again, and in walked a brown haired woman with Jim walking behind her with his gun pointed at her head.

"Found her sat in a motor watching the entrance road," Jim said, proudly, before continuing, "and she had this in a shoulder holster," he finished saying, as he lifted his free hand to reveal a small semi-automatic handgun.

"You've done well, very well," Cabilla said, before turning to face Larry. "Search her thoroughly, and get the handcuffs," he ordered.

Larry searched her, and produced two loaded magazines, but nothing else; no ID or anything personal. He then headed back towards the cellar, reappearing a minute or two later with the handcuffs.

As soon as Cabilla had spoken to Jim, and whilst Larry was searching her, Bonny turned her head sideways towards Jim, saying, "Yes, you have done well haven't you, you're a good boy," she sang, in a childlike mantra.

"Take the piss bitch, and you'll only suffer more," Cabilla said, then continued, "Where's your little buddy then?"

"I work alone," she replied.

"Don't fuck with me whore, I know what you and Clyde got up to at the school. The two things I need to know, and you *are* going to tell me, is who the fuck you two are? And who you're working for?" Cabilla said, before adding. "And why you're coming after me?"

"That's three things, not two," she said, the sarcasm obvious in her voice.

Cabilla walked across the room to her just as Larry arrived back with the handcuffs. He waited until Larry had cuffed her hands behind her back, before stepping forward again and slapping her hard across the face with the back of his giant hand. She cried out, as blood and mucus flew from her face, and Cabilla smiled, enjoying hearing her scream.

"I will ask you as many questions as I like, and you will answer me or I will defile you in ways you cannot begin to imagine. Then I will kill you. If you behave, and answer what I ask, I may just kill you. The only reason you are still alive is because I need you as bait to draw your partner here," Cabilla said, with absolute coldness in his voice. He could see by the look in her eyes that the swagger was being replaced with fear. He liked to see fear in people's eyes.

He told Jim to lock her in the cellar, and Larry to carry on outside on guard. He then rang Mackey and told him to get his arse back as soon as he could, briefly telling him what had happened, but still choosing his words carefully on the phone. Mackey told him he would be there in fifteen minutes. When Jim returned, Cabilla sent him out to bring his car back, which he'd said he'd abandoned near to where he found Bonny.

Twenty-five minutes, later Mackey came rushing in apologising for the delay, saying the traffic was starting to build up. Cabilla waved away his excuses with his hand, before bringing him up to date with what had happened.

"That's fucking brilliant Shonbo," Mackey said, when Cabilla had finished.

"Well, we are only half-way there Den, we still need to contend with the other twat."

He then summoned Larry and Jim back inside, and sent Mackey upstairs to get the hired help. When Mackey returned with the guy, Cabilla gave him a large wedge of money, and told him to disappear. Mackey would ring him when they needed to use him again.

Cabilla waited until he had left before he spoke.

"What I say here is for staff only. We don't need the hired help; if four of us, all armed, can't sort out one idiot, then we are in the wrong business."

All three men nodded back. Cabilla looked at his watch before continuing. "It's past four o'clock now, so it shouldn't be too long before Clyde realises that Bonny's missing. I don't expect Clyde to try his hand until after dark, which will give Den and me plenty of time with Bonny. You two, both outside and patrol the building."

Both Larry and Jim nodded, before Cabilla added. "And I want you each walking around separately, not together holding each other's fucking hands. You understand?"

Both men turned and headed for the door, whilst Cabilla turned to Mackey. "Come on Den, let's go and speak to that bitch."

"Ok Shonbo, then I'll go and get some food; it looks as if we are in for a long night."

***

Lee couldn't believe she'd let her guard slip so easily. Had she suspected for an instant, that she was feeling drowsy, she'd have done something about it. But she hadn't; she must have dropped off like a narcoleptic, if only for a couple of minutes. Though it had been a tiring few days, and there hadn't been much sleep around. She was as embarrassed, as she was shocked, when the 4 x 4 driver had appeared at her driver's window, facing in towards it to obscure the handgun he was using to tap on the glass to shatter her reverie. She'd glanced at her watch, and cursed under her breath when she realised the time was only twenty past three; nowhere near to four o'clock when Burrows would be returning.

She had no option but to follow 4 x 4 driver's instructions as he climbed into the rear of the car with gun still in hand. He'd told her to drive into the compound where she saw the bent undercover officer Steele stood outside near the doors. She wondered to herself if the bad guys knew he had been working undercover against Mackey, before he'd crossed over to the dark side. If not, her knowledge of him might prove useful. She'd tried to muster up as much gusto as possible, as she was paraded and handcuffed in front of the man she immediately realised was their target, Cabilla.

She thought she was holding her own until he threatened to defile her; there was something very dark about the way he said it. A twisted glee in his voice, not helped by her sudden recall of the historical intelligence briefing that Burrows and she had received about him, at the beginning of the operation. Nevertheless, she tried to hide any reaction, so as not to feed his mania, before being carted off to a small windowless cellar, which was obviously, to be her cell. They were waiting for Burrows, they'd said as much, but she knew Cabilla would come to interrogate her, sooner rather than later, for what she knew of Burrows—or Clyde, as Cabilla kept referring to him as—would be of great tactical advantage to them, and they would want that information quickly.

Lee shrugged off her self-recrimination at being caught, and started to think about what she was going to say about Burrows; she intended to use the threat he posed to Cabilla, as she could see he had limited resources. She reckoned, if he had more men available to him, then he would have them here already; that meant just the 4 x 4 man, Steele—or Larry as they were calling him—, and Mackey, wherever he was. She had been placed on a chair fixed to the ground in the centre of the room, and had noticed a mattress on the floor, before the lights had been turned off. It gave her the distinct impression that the room had already been used as a cell or interrogation room, and probably recently.

Lee heard multiple footsteps approaching, and tried to compose herself as best she could. The door was unlocked and the light switched back on. She

234

squinted against the light, but saw straight away that it was Cabilla, now joined by Mackey; they stood side-by-side in front of her.

"Well bitch, it's time to ask those questions, first of all, who the fuck are you?" Cabilla snapped.

"My name is irrelevant Mr Cabilla. I'm just a hired gun," Lee answered, almost formally, trying to give a little order to appease the situation some.

"Who sent you?" Cabilla asked, as Mackey moved to her left hand side, and stood in close. Lee could smell his rancid breath and body odour. She paused, before replying, she knew she had to stretch things out as long as she could. "We never get told who the client is. Safer that way," she said.

"Bollocks," Mackey breathed at her, followed by a punch to the side of her head.

Lee rocked to her right hand side with such force she nearly fell off the chair. The blow had re-opened a wound in her nose from Cabilla's earlier slap. She spat out blooded saliva, before saying, "I'm not stupid, I know I'm in the shit, I'm telling you the truth. Why wouldn't I? I've no personal beef with you guys. The client is just a client, I don't get told who, or why, so that I can't say anything I don't know if I get caught, like now."

She saw Cabilla and Mackey glance at each other, as if her words had some resonance of plausibility with them both.

"Well, even if that was true, you must have dealt with some fucker who was hiring you on behalf of whoever?" Cabilla asked.

"That's true, but Clyde dealt with him. Only Clyde has that information," Lee answered. She felt a twinge of guilt at trying to shift responsibility for answers onto Burrows; she wasn't trying to make things worse for him, should he be unlucky enough to be caught as well, but she had to buy herself some time.

She was then surprised to see that her answers had brought about a reprieve, as Cabilla turned to Mackey and told him to keep an eye her whilst he had a quick word with the other two. He then turned and left the room.

"When we catch your boyfriend, if we get him alive, he can watch what I'm going to do to you. Just to make sure he tells us everything. And just to make sure you've not been feeding us shit just now," Mackey seethed though his teeth, the words as foul as the halitosis wrapped around them.

Lee shuddered, as Mackey left the room locking the door behind him. It was obvious to her that both of them had crawled from the same infected pond.

Chapter Fifty-one

Burrows had only just pulled the trap door shut, when he heard the sound of footsteps on gravel. The noise grew louder, and then stopped outside the trap door, it wouldn't be long before whoever was outside—probably Steele—realised that Jim was missing. Burrows gingerly made his way down about ten steps before his progress was halted. In front of him, where there clearly had once been a door, was now a wall. Light was sparse here, but there was enough for Burrows to see a rough breezeblock wall across the bottom step. He kicked it in frustration and muttered, "Shit."

"Good God, is that you John?" came muffled words from the other side of the wall.

"Jane, yes it's me. I'm at the bottom of some stairs by a breeze block wall," Burrows replied, as loud as he dare through cupped hands against the wall. Elation flowed through him on realising Lee was still alive.

"Listen carefully John, we haven't got long."

Burrows listened intently, straining to hear and interpret each word Lee said, conscious of the fact; she too would be trying not to be overheard.

After they had briefed each other, Lee said she was going to sit back on her chair, and moments later, Burrows heard the sound of a door being unlocked and kicked open. He heard a raised voice clearly, which he recognised as the man he had seen at the front—the one with the accent; the one he took to be Cabilla.

"Right bitch, I'll buy what you said, for now, but I need to know what resources Clyde has? Is he alone? And what firepower has he?"

But before Lee had chance to answer, Burrows heard another voice.

"Boss, Boss, Jim's fucked off,"

"What?" A third voice said.

Burrows didn't listen to anymore of the conversation amongst the three, debating what had happened to Jim, the 4 x 4 driver man; he knew that the three voices could only represent Cabilla, Mackey and Steele. This was his window of opportunity to get inside the building unseen. As quickly, but as quietly as he could, Burrows got back into the car park and ran to the front doors. He opened them a crack, and peered through. The large room was just as Lee had described it, and it was deserted. He ran in, and darted across the space to jump behind the old settee in the corner. It was set at an angle where two walls met, creating a triangle of dead space at its rear. No sooner had Burrows got behind it; he heard footfalls, and voices, approaching from the other end of the building.

The accented voice, was shouting at the other two.

"Larry, get back to that front door and stand guard outside, and have your gun ready."

"Yeah," Burrows heard Steele answer, with more than a hint of nerves in his voice.

"And you Den, stay here and keep trying Jim's mobile, whilst I go back and get the woman, we can use her as a shield, and a bargaining ploy if need be," the accented voice said.

"Will do Shonbo," Den replied.

At least Burrows knew whose voice was whose now. Steele—or Larry as they were calling him—was by the front door, the accented voice, who was obviously Cabilla, had gone to get Lee, and Mackey, had suddenly sat on the settee inches away from him.

Burrows couldn't believe his luck. He drew his handgun slowly, and was about to stand up and challenge Mackey, when he heard him get up and start to walk away. Burrows was about to stand up anyway—as he figured he could be over the settee and behind Mackey before he knew what was happening—when he heard someone else enter the room, through the door that led from the cellar. Cabilla, he could hear him swearing at Lee whose protestations were muffled. It sounded as if Cabilla was dragging her with him, and was possibly covering her mouth as he did so, or perhaps he'd gagged her.

Burrows absorbed this new information, and noticed that Cabilla had stopped talking mid-sentence. He realised he hadn't heard Mackey speak since Cabilla had entered the room, and Mackey's footsteps had stopped. An unnatural silence ensued. Then, Burrows heard the sound of feet swivelling around on themselves. Then he heard the click.

In the instant that followed, Burrows hit the floor behind the sofa, making himself as flat to it, as he could. He heard Lee's muffled voice shout, "John."

Two rounds tore through the back of the sofa, dragging stuffing with them. Burrows had started to move a fraction of a second before he'd heard the click, and the bullets came through the back of the sofa roughly where he had been crouched a moment earlier. Almost instantly, they ricocheted off the brick wall behind, and disappeared at odd angles.

Burrows knew he had been lucky, if the next shots didn't get him, then the ricochets surely would. He'd obviously been discovered, so he screamed out in mock pain. The shooting stopped. In the millisecond of confusion his yell had caused, he jumped up to his full height, bringing his gun to bear in a two-handed pose. Mackey was walking back towards the settee, no doubt to look at his handiwork, and appeared startled on seeing Burrows standing up.

His expression deepened, as Burrows let fly with two double-taps in quick succession. All four rounds found their target in Mackey's central body mass. Two rounds must have ricocheted off bone within his body, as Burrows only saw two exit through his back, to continue their blood-encircled trajectory. Dragging pulped flesh in their wake.

He knew Mackey would be dead before he hit the ground. The ringing of gunfire was echoing around the vacuous space. He could see Cabilla stood facing him, with Lee held in front. His right forearm, tightly across her throat. Lee was clearly struggling to breathe, let alone speak. In his left hand, he held a machine pistol with an extended magazine. He was slowly raising it towards Burrows.

"You're gonna pay for that Clyde," Cabilla spat, as he turned the gun towards Lee's head.

Then, the front doors burst open, and in walked Steele, he had a gun in his outstretched hand, and he appeared to Burrows, as if he was uncomfortable with it.

Cabilla turned towards him, and shouted, "Larry, shoot the fucker."

Burrows realised Cabilla was referring to him, and turned to face the new threat. He was taking aim when Steele spoke. "Let go of her," he said, calmly, now turning his aim towards Cabilla.

"What?" Cabilla shouted, and then. "You're not working for these two fuckers are you?"

Steele had walked four or five metres into the room and was now stood firm with the doors to his rear, both hands holding the gun that was squarely pointed at Cabilla, who was only another ten metres away. Cabilla still had Lee pulled firmly in front of him.

Burrows wasn't sure what was happening now, and by the look of shock on Cabilla's face, neither was he. Burrows took the opportunity to climb slowly over the settee, avoiding sudden movements that might provoke the situation; Steele might be pointing his gun at Cabilla, but that didn't mean the threat to him or Lee was over. This could easily be a 'winner takes all' scam on behalf of Steele, who obviously had more sides than the football league, he thought.

During this impasse, Lee lurched backwards violently, and Burrows watched as she reverse-head butted Cabilla across the bridge of his nose. He grunted in pain, and Lee broke free from him. Cabilla also dropped his weapon.

Steele appeared rooted to the spot, his gun still pointed generally towards Cabilla, who by now was reaching down to try to retrieve his own weapon.

Then Burrows heard the front doors burst open again.

Chapter Fifty-two

Burrows looked towards the noise of the doors swinging open, and saw Jim running in with a tyre lever in his hand. He realised his earlier mistake; he should have searched the boot before leaving Jim.

"Get Larry," Cabilla ordered, as he picked up his gun, and pointed it at the back of Lee.

Steele was starting to turn around, but Burrows could tell he wasn't quick enough; a sickening blow from Jim's tyre lever across the side of Steele's head dropped him where he stood. He fell to the floor, and lay motionless as blood pumped out of a scalp wound. His gun scurried across the hard floor surface towards the foot of the stairs, opposite the front doors.

As Burrows turned his attentions back towards Cabilla, Lee was moving towards him, but he saw fire spit from the barrel of Cabilla's weapon. He realised Cabilla had shot over Lee's shoulder, as several bullets torn into the settee and floor all around him. He cried out for real, as one found their intended target. It felt like a hot lance scything through his outer right bicep. The force of the round spun him in a half-pirouette, and he landed on his side, on the sofa. His gun bounced onto the floor as he fell.

Lee screamed, as she arrived next to Burrows.

"I'm Ok, Jane get the gun," Burrows wheezed, as he fought to swallow the searing pain coming from his arm.

He saw the flash of understanding in her eyes, as she diverted towards the floor, where the gun now lay. Burrows looked up, to see Jim run from the door; he was going to get to Burrows's gun first. But arriving, he wouldn't have time to pick it up, before Lee would've been on him; but he did get his foot to it before Lee's hand, and kicked it across the floor, out of reach of both of them, towards the side of the sofa.

"It's ok Jim, these two fuckers are mine," Cabilla shouted, as he approached, "don't you fucking move a muscle. Both of you just stay exactly where you are."

Burrows had recovered a little now, as he tightly held the wound with his left hand to stem the bleeding. He knew he still had Jim's revolver stuffed down the back of his waistband; he just needed an opportunity to get at it.

"Even with a machine pistol you couldn't do it properly," Burrows said.

"John, I don't think now is the time to enrage this pond life more than we have to," Lee added.

"Go on, enjoy your clever remarks you pair of twats, but I'm going to make you both pay dearly. Instant death is too good for you, so if you are trying to provoke me into finishing you here and now, it won't work. But if either of you move a muscle, I'll start shooting little bits off you, a bit at a time," Cabilla said, before turning to Jim. "Good work Jim, I knew you hadn't legged it, and that twat Larry was sus after all."

"Yeah Boss, and that bastard got the jump on me, and stuck me in the boot of one of the motors," Jim said, aiming his remarks at Burrows.

"Schoolboy error Clyde," Cabilla said, and then added. "You should have finished Jim when you had the chance. Some assassin you are."

"Unlike you Cabilla, I don't kill unless I have to," Burrows said, noting Cabilla's reaction on hearing him say his name.

"I'm going to cut you both a deal," Cabilla said," you must both know you're going to die, and I won't lie, it will be unpleasant. But it will be a lot less unpleasant if you tell me who sent you."

"You wouldn't understand if I told you," Burrows said.

"Try me,"

"Ok, then…" Burrows started to say, before Lee interrupted him.

"John, what are you doing?"

"It's Ok," he replied, before turning back towards Cabilla."H.M.G."

"What the fuck does that mean?"

"See, I told you that you wouldn't understand."

"Oh, I will understand clever boy, 'cause you'll tell me later, when I'm raping it out of your girlfriend here."

Then Burrows heard gunfire ring out from the direction of the front doors.

Chapter Fifty-three

Burrows turned to see that Steele was still prostrate on the floor, unmoving. But stood near him, at the foot of the stairs, opposite the doorway was a young African woman. Probably no more than thirty years old, slim, petite and extremely attractive with her black hair tied back behind her. She was holding Steele's gun in her hand, and then she fired a second shot.

The first one had missed, but the second hit Cabilla squarely in the chest. He went down as he was starting to run at her, bringing his gun arm up as he did. The woman's second shot sent Cabilla to the floor, and both Burrows and Lee dived for cover as Cabilla's weapon burst into automatic fire.

The weapon was firing wildly as Cabilla fell, and then it clattered out of his hand as he landed. It became silent as it spun away from him.

"You Ok?" Burrows asked Lee quickly, as he sat back up.

"Yeah I'm fine, but I'm not sure about good old Jim."

Burrows looked around, and saw that Jim was inert, with several rivulets of blood oozing from him. Cabilla's weapon must have dropped him, he realised. He and Lee both turned back to face the African woman, as she approached Cabilla lain in the centre of the floor.

Burrows watched Cabilla sit up on one hand to face the woman, as she approached him. A look of sheer confusion carved on his face, interspaced with twinges of obvious pain.

"Amber, what the fuck are you doing?" Cabilla asked.

"What does it look like," she answered, in a similar accent to Cabilla's, but hers was thicker and more guttural.

Burrows and Lee just looked on in silence. Burrows could see Lee was as bemused as he was.

"You don't remember me do you?" Amber asked Cabilla.

He dragged himself the few feet to the front wall, and laid his back against it, before he answered. "I know who you are; you're Amber Kimba, who I pay very well. And whatever these two fucks are paying you, I'll double it," Cabilla answered, through his rapid breaths.

"It's always about money with you isn't it. You know, when I first saw you again, I thought you might recognise me, but no. Men like you wouldn't recognise people like me, because we are nothing to you. Even, if I looked the same as I did then, you probably wouldn't know me," Amber said, as she kicked him savagely, as if to accentuate her words.

"Look, I really don't know who—" Cabilla started to say, before Amber cut across him. "I was eleven years old you bastard, eleven years old. But that doesn't matter now. I'm here, and very much alive, unlike my parents you hideous monster."

Burrows looked at Lee, he could see she too had realised who Amber really was.

"She's the girl in the historical intelligence brief Frank gave us, isn't she?" Lee whispered.

"Yes, I've just realised that too, but what the hell is she doing here?" Burrows said, before adding. "When I interrogated Jim outside, he claimed he didn't know what went on upstairs. Said, 'It was out-of-bounds.'"

They both turned back to look at Cabilla, and Burrows thought he saw a flash of recognition in the man's expression.

"Look Amber, back in the Congo life was different. I was in the Hutu; and I had to do what I was told."

"The one thing I have got that you can never take from me is my dignity, and my self-respect. Unlike you, I can show compassion, even to a monster like you," Amber said.

Burrows could see a sly smile spread across Cabilla's face.

Then Amber Kimba pulled the trigger. She shot Cabilla a further three times, all headshots; he was no doubt dead after the first. Then she threw the gun on the floor.

Burrows realised that Amber had showed Cabilla all the compassion he deserved.

Epilogue

One week later, Burrows was nursing his arm in a sling, whilst with Lee at the circular table in the Pimlico briefing room, waiting for Briers to arrive. This was the final debrief before closure on the whole operation. Fortunately for Burrows the injury wasn't too serious, a little loss of muscle, but nothing significant, he had only spent two days in hospital before being allowed home. Briers had arranged for Burrows to go to a military hospital, so that the doctors and nurses wouldn't ask any awkward questions. He'd spent the rest of the week at Lee's place, but could tell he had just about overplayed the sympathy vote.

After Cabilla's death, Lee rang Briers who had arranged for a specialist cleaning team from MI5 to come into the warehouse, clean up the mess, and remove the bodies. Burrows asked Lee who they were, and how secure they would be.

"Don't worry, our secrets are safe. You would be surprised how often we used to use the services of a 'cleaner' after some foreign intelligence service had exacted some revenge on our soil. They are paid not to ask questions, just clear up any mess."

"And we are happy just to go along with that, are we?" Burrows asked.

"Absolutely, it's an unwritten agreement in the intelligence communities; we each cover up each other's messes when operating abroad. Whoever Frank used would just think they were clearing up yet another fallout from a foreign service."

Burrows was amazed, but relieved. He then told Lee how Briers had been monitoring the police airwaves as soon as he had briefed him on finding the Mondeo at the premises, and that nothing had been heard or seen by the public, or if it had, no reports had been made. Apparently, helped by the fact that the building was constructed of solid Accrington brick, and as she already knew, set in its own grounds near a busy main road full of passing rush-hour traffic. They were all happy that any noises had been contained; notwithstanding how loud they had sounded inside the place.

What they hadn't expected, was the appearance of Amber Kimba. Nor had they expected to find a further five Congolese women upstairs, in varying states of diamorphine-induced stupors. Amber had explained, she knew if she hadn't come with the women, then someone else would. This way, she could protect them for as long as possible before, and even after, Cabilla had put them to work. Ultimately, she intended to break free, and take the women with her to a new life in the UK. What she hadn't reckoned on, was Cabilla having her permanently guarded.

Apparently, she'd told Briers that she had been upstairs when the shooting had started in the warehouse, and had crept downstairs to see what the commotion was all about. That was when she had seen the gun at the bottom of the stairs.

It was also then when she heard Cabilla threatening to do things to Lee, and that had given her inner strength she didn't know she had. She knew very well what he was capable of; she couldn't sit back and let that happen again.

Steele, as it turned out was alive, and had been taken to the same military hospital as Burrows, though neither Burrows nor Lee knew what happened after that.

The door opened and in walked Frank Briers, who said his hellos before pouring himself a coffee and joining them. Neither Burrows nor Lee had spoken to Briers since Burrows had come out of hospital.

"Ok, you two, first up, how's the arm John?" Briers asked.

"Oh, it's fine Frank," Lee answered for Burrows, with a grin.

"Well, I'll get down to business then; Kimba has been thoroughly investigated by Five, and she is who she purports to be. She and the other five women will be given indefinite leave to remain in the UK, but in their own identities. All have been required to sign the Official Secrets Act, even though only Kimba really knows anything. All have been provided housing, and counsellors to help them settle, and the five of them with the blossoming addiction have been found places on a drug rehab course," Briers said, stopping to take a sip of his coffee.

"I'm glad about that. They deserve the break. And there's no doubt Amber saved us," Lee said.

"Hold up," Burrows said, before adding, "I was on the brink of operationalizing plan B when she came in."

Both Lee and Briers just raised their eyebrows.

"Anyway, what happened to Steele?" Lee asked.

"Well, we spent a couple of days debriefing him, before we were happy with him. It turns out he hadn't gone over to the dark side, as you would put it

John. But he just kept getting more and more embroiled—albeit for the greater good. Cabilla's mob had suspected him previously, and he'd had a pretty rough time before he earned their trust."

"How are his police bosses viewing his actions?" Burrows asked, knowing just how uncompromising his old firm could be.

"Well, we couldn't tell them the truth. Therefore, we came up with a cover story of how he'd been seconded to Five, for a security service operation. Only the commissioner of the Met knows more, and even that, is way off the truth. Just enough to make him think he knows more than the others, thinks he knows the whole story," Briers added.

"To stop them digging into things we would rather they didn't dig into?" Lee asked.

"Exactly," said Briers.

"What will happen to him now?" asked Burrows.

"That's a good question John. He couldn't really go back to his normal undercover duties, not after what he'd been through, if you include the cop massacre at the start of all this; he'd never get past the police undercover officers' psychological evaluations for one thing. And as he couldn't face going back to normal duties either, he's resigned, put his ticket in, so to speak."

"That's a shame," Lee said.

"Not really Jane, it meant I was able to offer him a job. You're now a three-person team," Briers finished.

Burrows hadn't seen that coming, and by the look on Lee's face, she hadn't either.

"We'll have to give him some extra training, a bit more than you two had, but he has shown his ability to problem solve under extreme pressure, so I think he will be an excellent addition to the team," Briers said.

Both Burrows and Lee said they had no problem with Steele coming on board, though Burrows added that he would need some weapons training. Briers reassured them he would get all the training he needed over the next month, during which time they were both ordered to take a holiday, and come down from the operation mentally.

Briers added that he wouldn't contact them again until the month was out. He stood up to leave, and say his goodbyes, before addressing them a last time.

"Oh yes, the PM sends his congratulations to 'Our secret heroes' as he puts it. The Prime Minister also adds that HMG would be very proud of you both, but for the fact that Her Majesty's Government will never know you exist."

The End.